I0761225

WE HAD A HUNCH

Also by Tom Ryan

The Treasure Hunters Club

WE HAD A HUNCH

A Mystery

TOM RYAN

Atlantic Crime
New York

FIRST EDITION

Printed in the United States of America

First Grove Atlantic hardcover edition: October 2025

Library of Congress Cataloging-in-Publication data is available for this title.

ISBN 978-0-8021-6588-6
eISBN 978-0-8021-6589-3

Atlantic Crime
an imprint of Grove Atlantic
154 West 14th Street
New York, NY 10011

Distributed by Publishers Group West

groveatlantic.com

25 26 27 28 29 10 9 8 7 6 5 4 3 2 1

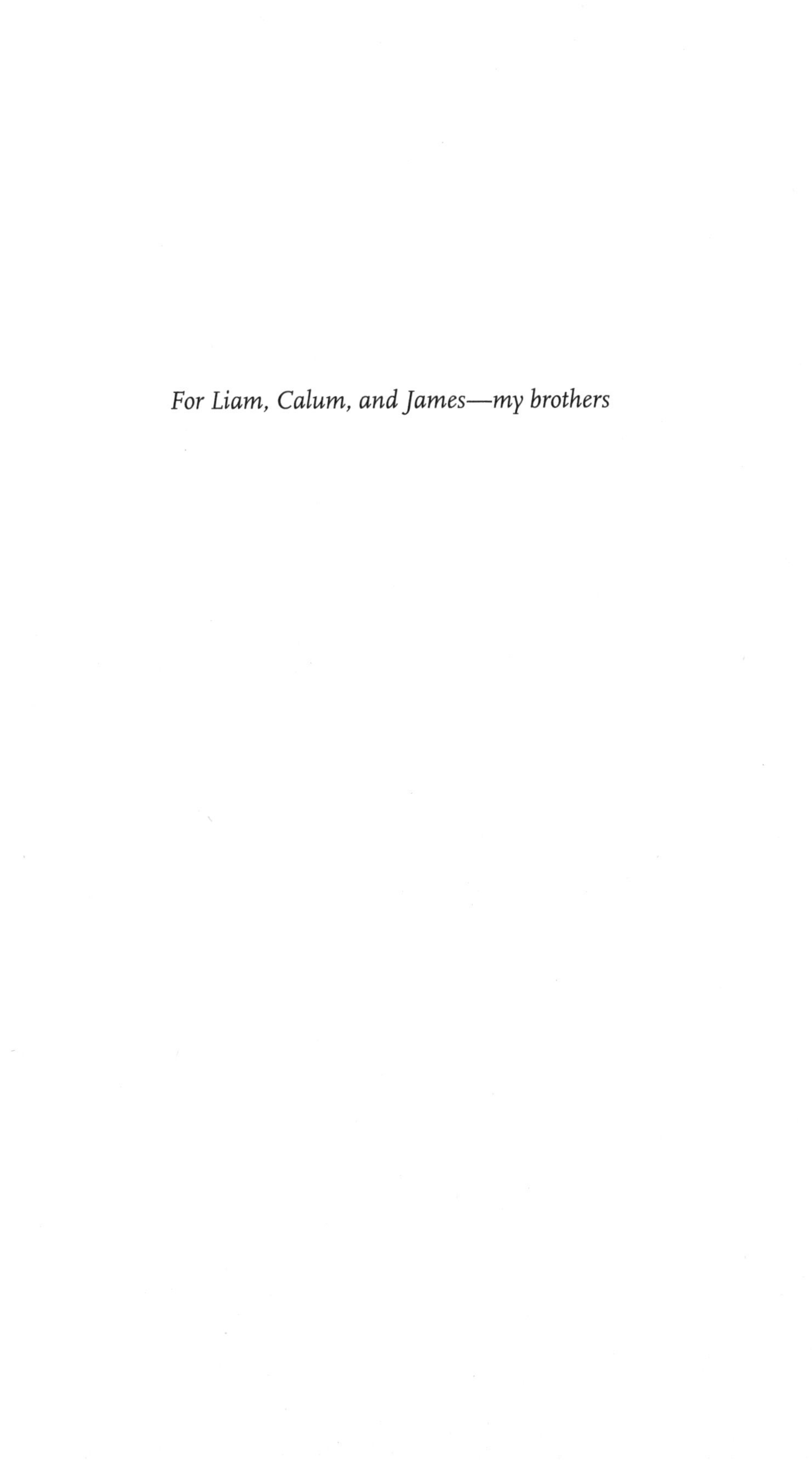

For Liam, Calum, and James—my brothers

Although she was glad it was over, she could not help but look forward to another mystery to solve.

Carolyn Keene, *The Hidden Staircase*

PROLOGUE:
THE YEAR 2000

SAM

The sisters crept up to the edge of the tree line and stared down the hill at Birch Crest Elementary.

To Sam, the building looked like it had been abandoned for much longer than just a few months. Perhaps it was the plywood nailed over the windows or the trash and leaves piled up against the walls and settled into doorways; whatever the case, slumped in the moonlight, the empty school looked like a carcass in the early stages of decomposition.

It looked dead.

"Do you really think he'll show up?" asked Alice. She'd been the one to set this plan in motion, but the closer they had come—parking their car on a quiet road on the back side of the treed municipal property, pulling supplies from the trunk, making their way through the wooded patch that backed the old schoolyard—the more she seemed to be second-guessing the whole thing.

Sam stepped out from the trees and crouched, unslinging her small backpack and dropping it on the ground in front of her. "He'll be here," she said as Alice moved to join her. "He doesn't have any other options."

"He could run for it," said Alice. "Maybe he already has. Maybe he's a hundred miles away by now."

They had talked this through already, but Sam knew her twin sister better than anyone, and it was clear that Alice needed positive reinforcement.

"He's not going to run," she said. "Where would he go? If he doesn't show up, we'll go straight home and tell Dad everything, and he'll be picked up within the hour. But he'll be here. He wants to know what *we* know, and when he shows up, we'll have him cornered like a rat."

"Cornered rats fight back," said Alice.

"Let him try," said Sam. "We've got the boys, and we have this." She unzipped her backpack and pulled out a handgun.

Alice's eyes widened. "What the hell, Sam? Is that Dad's?"

Alice had never shown any interest in joining her sister and their father at the shooting range almost every Saturday afternoon for the past couple of years. But Sam knew her way around a gun, especially *this* gun, the Colt 1911 that had belonged to her grandfather, now her father, and would someday, she assumed, belong to her.

She nodded, taking a moment to register the gun's familiar, reassuring heft. "I grabbed it before we left the house, just in case."

"Is that smart?" asked Alice. "What if Dad needs it?"

"He won't," said Sam. "It's just an insurance policy. Between us and the boys, we'll be able to handle him without it. But we need to be real here: if Kershaw shows up, he's going to try to kill us."

The name floated in the air between them, shimmering with a toxic energy. It was the first time either of them had spoken it aloud since they'd left their house, and Alice seemed to shrink back at the sound of it.

"Maybe this is a mistake."

Sam frowned. "Alice, this was your idea. *You* convinced *me*."

"I know. It's just . . . maybe this is too big for us."

"It's not too late to change our minds," said Sam. "We could still shut this down, call off the boys, and tell Dad everything. Let him handle it."

Alice sucked in her lower lip, thinking, and then pushed back her shoulders as her resolve seemed to harden.

"We are going to tell Dad," she said, "just as soon as we bring this asshole down."

"Okay," said Sam, checking the safety and tucking the pistol into the waistband of her jeans. "Then let's get moving before he turns up."

Alice reached into her own bag and pulled out a flashlight. Pointing it toward another wooded embankment on the far side of the school, facing the main entrance, she flashed it on and off twice. A moment later a light echoed the signal back at them.

"Okay," she said. "They're in place. You ready?"

Sam nodded and stood. She was about to begin her descent when she felt Alice's hand grab hers. She turned to look at her sister, and the two of them smiled, both thinking the same thing: they were made for this, and after tonight the whole world would know it.

"You good?" she asked.

Alice squeezed her hand and nodded. "Let's go."

They descended the slope, breaking into a tight, silent jog when they reached the playground. In tandem, they slipped between the slides and swings, staying in the shadows until they reached the eastern wall of the school. A few dozen yards to their right was the small side entrance that led to the maintenance area of the building. The door appeared locked, but they knew it was breachable. They'd figured that out yesterday when they'd found their way inside and discovered Kershaw's hiding spot. But there was no way they were going to access the building through his entrance and open themselves up to the risk of ambush. Nothing indicated he was already there, but they weren't about to take any chances.

They skirted the edge of the school in the opposite direction, rounding a corner until they came to their destination. Six feet up was a small window covered in plywood. The girls moved to a patch of thick brush where they'd hidden an aluminum extension ladder earlier that day. Together they moved it into place, propping it up in the window.

Sam was about to climb but Alice motioned for her to wait.

"We should go over the plan one more time," she said.

"He'll use the side entrance," said Sam. "It's the easiest way in and it gives him direct access to the maintenance closet. We'll wait across the hallway in the gym, and when we hear him enter the building, we'll call out for him to join us."

Alice nodded and picked up the thread. "Levi and Levon are on the rise across from the entrance, waiting for him to arrive. Once they've seen him enter the building, they'll follow him and wait outside the gym. They'll wait for him to confess, then they'll slip inside and overpower him."

It sounded simple. Too simple. Which was why Sam had brought the gun. If she was being honest with herself, deep down she was as nervous as her sister. But didn't the world expect this from them? Wasn't the entire town of Edgar Mills desperate for an end to the fear, and hadn't they already proven themselves up to the challenge?

But as much as they were aware of the outside pressures, that wasn't why they were here. They were here for the thrill of the hunt and the promise of the big break. This was a once-in-a-lifetime chance to become legends.

Sam climbed first, with Alice holding the ladder in place. At the top, she tore off the plywood and dropped it to the ground, then pushed the window inward, pulling the flashlight from her pocket and shining it inside.

"We're good," she said to her sister. She hoisted herself into the narrow gap, pulling herself through and taking care to land lightly on the long sink counter that ran the length of the room before hopping down to the floor.

A moment later Alice appeared in the window, and Sam watched as she pulled herself through.

"Hopefully that's the last time we have to come in that way," she said as Alice hopped down from the counter and brushed herself off.

"Hopefully we never have to come back here again," said Alice.

Sam turned to the open doorway and pointed the flashlight's beam out into the pitch-black corridor beyond.

"We're not out of the woods yet."

JOEY

Joey O'Day drove straight through Edgar Mills, cursing Levi Brakes under his breath. If only Levi hadn't accosted him this afternoon, he'd be at his buddy Doug's house watching *Event Horizon* and eating pizza in blissful ignorance. Instead, thanks to Levi, he'd canceled on Doug and gone directly home from school and straight down the rabbit hole. Now he was driving through town in a stolen car, somehow tangled up in a serial killer investigation.

Joey hated this teen detective stuff. He'd never in a million years wanted to be a detective. He was just an introverted nerd with a head for computers. If he hadn't given in to his mother's appeal and helped an old lady at church track down the guy who had cleaned out her savings in an email scam, he wouldn't have become associated with the Van Dyne twins. They were the ones with the profile; he was just a convenient addition to the story, a collateral figure who'd somehow found himself dragged along for the ride.

He'd never counted on anything like *this*.

He hadn't even known what Levi was talking about. He'd been on his way out of school when the younger Brakes brother, not quite as tall, fit, or handsome as the good-natured Levon, but ten times the bully, had come striding up to him out of nowhere.

"The twins are onto something major, O'Day," he'd said, his voice low and ominous, "and I want you to tell me you aren't going to screw it up for them."

Joey had just stood there, his eyes wide and his mouth hanging open, a minnow facing a shark.

"Tell me," Levi had said again, jabbing a finger into Joey's chest. "Tell me you'll stay the hell out of it."

"I'll stay out of it," Joey had managed to stammer, even though he'd had no idea what the other boy was talking about.

Levi had stalked off, apparently satisfied. But the intensity in Levi's voice triggered an alarm inside Joey, a feeling that things were about to take a dangerous turn.

Was it a hunch?

Whatever it was that fueled him, he'd ignored Levi's threat and gone straight home to his computer, where he proceeded to break into the Van Dyne family email server. It was laughably straightforward, thanks to their internet provider's lax security, and what he found there in the twins' email account was a back-and-forth exchange that made his blood run cold.

For three weeks, Edgar Mills had been reeling from a series of shocking crimes. Two people had been murdered, a twenty-year-old video store clerk and an elderly widow. A thirteen-year-old girl only narrowly escaped the same fate while walking alone on the Edgar Mills River Trail after dark, slipping out of the would-be killer's grasp. The police were working overtime to figure out who was responsible, but so far there were no significant leads and the community was growing more anxious with every passing day.

If the emails Joey had just hacked were to be believed, the Van Dyne twins had figured out the identity of the killer. Bruce Kershaw. The name was vaguely familiar, but it had taken Joey a few moments to place it. He was the school janitor, a quiet, awkward man who'd spent years in the background of Joey's school life, shuffling through the hallways with his custodial cart. The emails were short and to the point: the twins' declaration that they'd discovered evidence of his crimes, Kershaw's terse denial, their invitation to discuss things at Birch Crest Elementary, his reluctant acceptance.

Suddenly, Levi's vague threats made sense. The Van Dyne twins were indeed onto something major. Could the twins, media darlings who'd become marginally famous for helping their father solve a few low-level crimes, really be planning something this dangerous? This *stupid*?

But it was the last email in the twins' folder that really threw him for a loop. A final message from Kershaw to the twins, sent less than an hour ago. It was still unopened, which meant they hadn't seen it yet, and Joey hesitated for a long moment before opening it, knowing it would bust his cover.

But, of course, he had opened it in the end, and he expected to remember it for the rest of his life.

This is crazy. I'm not going to meet you at the school. I'm going to talk to your father.

The shit was about to hit the fan, and Joey's involvement all boiled down to this: if it wasn't for Levi, he wouldn't have had the hunch. If it wasn't for the hunch, he wouldn't have canceled on Doug. If he hadn't canceled on Doug, he wouldn't have gone straight home and jumped online. And if he hadn't been online, poking his nose where it didn't belong, he wouldn't have opened Pandora's box.

Frigging Levi Brakes.

He gripped the steering wheel tighter, holding his hands at ten and two, keeping just under the speed limit, and carefully scanning the road as he drove down Main Street. By now, his parents had probably discovered that he and their car were gone, but they'd have no way of knowing where he was. Besides, he thought grimly, they'd soon have bigger things to worry about.

It was only seven thirty, but Edgar Mills was as empty as midnight. A thin mist floated through the town, diffusing the glare of the streetlights and dulling the colors that were starting to appear on the trees. Other than a few cars and a middle-aged man hurrying down the sidewalk with his dog, Joey didn't pass a single person. The police hadn't instituted an official curfew, but they might as well have. People were keeping to their houses, blinds drawn, doors locked. There were even a few kids in his class whose parents had pulled them from school and headed out of town to stay with relatives until things blew over.

He passed Cordova's Diner, the only business still lit up from within, and caught a quick glimpse of a couple of old men drinking coffee at the counter, chatting with Mr. Cordova as he wiped down glassware.

A siren picked up in the distance, quickly getting louder, and sure enough, when Joey glanced in the rearview mirror, he spotted flashing lights quickly gaining on him.

He swore out loud, then signaled and pulled to the curb. He expected the cruiser to pull in behind him and demand a confession, but it only sped past, slowing just slightly at the next main intersection before taking a hard right and disappearing in the opposite direction from where Joey was headed.

The Van Dyne house lay in that direction, Joey thought, his stomach sinking.

He checked his mirror and over his shoulder and then cautiously pulled back out onto the street. At the same intersection where the cop had turned right, he turned left, in the direction of Birch Crest Elementary, and pressed on the gas.

The building was dark and the parking lot was empty as he peeled in. For a moment he allowed himself to think that he had the whole thing wrong. A misunderstanding or even a prank at his expense. But he'd seen what he'd seen and he had to at least check on whether the twins were here. He parked and got out of the car.

The evening mist curled through the parking lot and around his feet and ankles as he slowly approached the main door of the school. It was creepy and unsettling and very, very quiet. The door was locked tight, and he briefly considered turning back and heading for his car. But he knew there were other entrances, and so he continued around to the far side of the building.

He had just turned the corner when a hand grabbed his shoulder. Joey screamed and threw himself sideways, landing on his ass in a pile of leaves and skittering backwards until he looked up and saw who had grabbed him.

Levi Brakes glared down at him, his face a mask of rage, his hands clenched into fists at his sides.

"What the hell are you doing here?" He turned and looked back around the side of the building, an anxious expression on his face. "I told you to keep your nose out of things, didn't I? You are going to fuck everything up! You need to move your car now."

Joey pulled himself to his feet. "Kershaw isn't coming, Levi."

Levi's jaw dropped. "How do you know about Kershaw?" he asked finally.

Joey considered how to explain himself, then decided to just rip off the Band-Aid. "I hacked into the twins' email account. I know everything."

"You broke into their email?"

Levi sounded too surprised to be angry.

"Levi," said Joey, "you need to listen to me. Kershaw is on his way to the Van Dyne house right now. I think he is going to confront the chief. I've called the police and left an anonymous tip."

"You called the cops?"

"Levi!" Joey stepped forward, surprising himself with his own assertiveness. "This is serious. Where are the girls?"

"They went into the school a few minutes ago," said Levi, his defiance quickly being replaced by worry. "My brother's in there too."

"We need to tell them what's happening. How do we get in?"

"The side door is unlocked," said Levi, already moving. "Come on."

ALICE

The girls moved quickly and silently through the empty school. The hallways were dark and dank and smelled of mildewed paper and something else that floated just beneath the funk, a scent that Alice recognized but couldn't quite place.

"Do you smell that?" she asked.

Sam paused, sniffed the air. "Maybe?" she said uncertainly.

"It smells like cleaning fluid," said Alice, and the realization caused them to exchange a nervous glance.

They rounded a corner and stopped in front of the janitor's closet, where they'd first discovered the clue—clues, really—that got this ball rolling. Sam reached for the door and pulled it open, and Alice shone the flashlight into the small space. It looked exactly like it had the last two times they'd visited. A well-stocked, neatly organized shelving unit, full of cleaning supplies. A large broom. A mop and bucket.

The heavy odor of pine-scented floor cleaner wafted out from the closet.

"Does it smell stronger than when we were here yesterday?" asked Alice.

Sam considered this. "I don't think so. It's probably just the power of suggestion."

Alice moved the flashlight's beam across the floor, and fear suddenly grabbed at the back of her neck.

"It's gone."

"Shit," said Sam.

For the hundredth time since they'd left their house, Alice wondered if they were making a terrible mistake, if they should have gone to their father as soon as they'd made their discovery. It had been his lead that had brought them here after all, his block letters spelling out BIRCH CREST ELEMENTARY over and over again on the margins around his newspaper's half-finished crossword. It was a regular thing for their father to take to his easy chair after dinner, paper and pen in hand, and spend the evening scribbling and doodling and jotting down ideas and fragments of theories as he mulled over a case.

Usually, he tossed the paper in the recycling bin at the end of every evening. But for the past couple of weeks, he'd been extra distracted, working all hours of the day, trying to figure out who was responsible for the chaos and fear that had gripped Edgar Mills since the body of DJ Cartwright had been found behind the counter at the Hollywood Nites video store just over two weeks earlier. Whatever the reason, two nights ago he'd left the newspaper sitting on the arm of his chair, where Alice had spotted it and recognized the name of their recently closed old elementary school.

She knew it must have something to do with the case, but what? Was it a thread from the investigation? A tip from an anonymous caller? A random hunch he'd landed on himself? There was no way of knowing, but the building had been vacant and boarded up since the end of the last school year in June, and now it was halfway through November. Wouldn't that make it an excellent hiding place for a body or other evidence? She'd been unable to stop thinking about it all evening, and finally she'd convinced Sam that they should follow up on it and explore the school.

That had led them here, to this custodial closet. To the battered backpack they found shoved into a corner behind an old shelf. It held a couple of skeins of rope, some latex gloves, and an empty jug of cleaning fluid. And in a small, zippered pocket they discovered a long-expired credit card with a name punched on it in letters that had been rubbed clean of their silver coating.

Bruce Philip Kershaw.

It had been a perfect clue, pointing them directly at the killer nobody else—not the Massachusetts State Police, the FBI, or even their own father—had been able to identify. But *they'd* identified him, and now they were going to confront him, record his confession, and—with the help of Alice's boyfriend, Levon, and his brother Levi—they were going to subdue him, restrain him, and finally, bring in the authorities to lock him up.

It was crazy. It was bold. It was going to make them famous. Not just local news famous, or puff piece famous. Genuinely, legitimately, notoriously famous.

But now the backpack was gone, along with the credit card and all the rest of the evidence.

Alice looked at Sam. "What do we do?"

Her sister looked as uncertain as she felt. "I'm not sure."

"He's been here already," she said. Another thought crossed her mind, turning her blood to ice. "What if he's still here?"

They turned as a sound caught their ears at the same time. A vehicle approaching quickly. It came squealing to a stop nearby.

"That's got to be him," said Sam. "We need to get into position."

With Alice's flashlight beam leading the way along the floor, they hurried through the double doors into the gymnasium and to its far end, where set pieces from last year's spring production of *Once Upon a Mattress* still sat, gathering dust. They moved to crouch behind the large false front of a fairy-tale castle. Alice shut off the flashlight, and they were plunged into darkness. The only way into the gym was via the unlocked double doors they'd just come through. When Kershaw arrived, they'd have a full view of him and they'd be ready to interrogate.

The thought of confronting him scared Alice more than anything had ever scared her before. Now that they were here and everything was real, she was grateful that Sam had taken the gun, grateful they could rely on the boys. Levon and Levi were strong and athletic. They wouldn't let anything get out of hand.

She found herself suppressing a pang of guilt. Alice loved Levon Brakes, she really did. He was the perfect high school boyfriend, sweet and kind and funny and attentive, but she couldn't imagine their relationship continuing a whole lot longer. Levon's life was already planned. He would go to college and get a business degree, and then he'd begin working at his father's company, training to someday take over, and he'd settle into a nice comfortable life in Edgar Mills and raise a family. She didn't want that. She had other plans.

Of course she hadn't told Levon any of this yet. He still thought they'd be together forever. He'd be fine; girls would line up when he hit the market, but she wasn't looking forward to the conversation. She knew it had to happen soon, just not quite yet.

Tonight, she really needed him.

Next to her, she sensed Sam pulling her gun from her waistband.

The silence was thick and oppressive, and then it was broken as footsteps echoed in the corridor outside the gym.

"That sounds like more than one person," said Sam, and Alice felt a cold tendril of fear tickle the back of her neck.

"Shit, Sam," she said. "Do you think he brought an accomplice?"

Her sister didn't have time to answer. The footsteps came to a stop outside the door, and with a heavy *ka-chunk* it was thrust open. And then there was no denying it: two people entered the darkened gym.

The girls had planned to do things differently, but instinctively they both moved at the same time, reacting to the new circumstances.

"Now!" yelled Sam as she jumped out from behind the castle, holding the Colt in front of her with a tight double grip. "Freeze, assholes!"

Alice followed a split second later, snapping on the flashlight and blasting it out into the dark, cavernous space.

"Jesus!" someone yelled. "Don't shoot! It's me!"

It took Alice a second to realize it was Levi, and another to realize that it wasn't Levon standing next to him. It was, of all people, Joey O'Day.

Sam dropped the gun to her side.

"What's going on?" Alice asked.

Joey began to speak in a scrambled rush, and she struggled to keep up with what he was telling her. A hunch. Email. Kershaw. Their house.

"Joey," said Sam. "Slow down and say that again."

Joey took a breath. "Kershaw isn't coming here. He's going to your house, I think he's planning to confront your dad."

Alice felt the blood rushing to her head. "I don't understand," she said weakly.

"I called the police," said Joey. "Hopefully they'll get there in time to catch him."

"Oh my God!" said Sam. Alice turned to her and realized she was staring down at the gun, her face stricken.

"Wait a minute," said Levi. "Where's Levon?"

Alice looked at him, her eyes widening. "I thought he was with you."

"He came early," said Levi, and there was a tremor in his voice. "In case Kershaw tried to pull something over on us." He raised his voice. "Levon!"

Sam and Joey began calling as well, but Alice didn't join them. She walked a few steps away, training the flashlight on the pile of gym mats against one of the walls. There was something on the floor that caught and reflected the light.

She stepped closer, catching sight of a gooey, glistening puddle of pine-scented floor cleaner coming from behind the pile of mats. She stepped around the puddle, noticing that it was gradually changing color and becoming orange as it blended with a thick, viscous river of blood—blood that was coming from the narrow space behind the mats. She moved a tiny bit closer, and then she saw him.

Levon.

Dead on the ground.

TODAY

TikTok Transcript:

@RealTrueCrimeKid
THE JANITOR KILLINGS
PART 1 - WELCOME TO EDGAR MILLS

[Opening montage: Scenes from a small town. A charming town square. A busy street lined with quaint shops and restaurants. A couple walking their dog on a trail beside a river.]

[Cut to host, @RealTrueCrimeKid, standing in front of a sign: WELCOME TO EDGAR MILLS.]

@RealTrueCrimeKid (excited, engaging tone): "If you were around in the year 2000, you probably heard about the Teen Detectives of Edgar Mills, Massachusetts. In a town of fewer than 8,000 people, somehow *two* sets of young sleuths made headlines!"

[Cut to headline in *Teen Scene!* magazine: "Teen Detectives Crack the Case!" followed by yearbook photos of Samantha and Alice Van Dyne, then Joey O'Day.]

@RealTrueCrimeKid: "First, there were the Van Dyne twins—Alice and Sam, the daughters of the town's beloved police chief. They cracked a drug smuggling ring in their high school! And then there was Joey O'Day, a computer whiz who made waves solving an internet scam. Classic teen detective stuff, right?"

[Cut to black-and-white crime scene tape overlay.]

@RealTrueCrimeKid: "But then a series of more brutal crimes rocked the town. Two vicious murders. A near-miss attack. And suddenly, Edgar Mills wasn't a wholesome small town anymore—it was *terrified.* And the Van Dyne twins? They weren't just solving low-stakes mysteries anymore. They were *chasing a serial killer.* But they had no idea what they were up against."

[Cut to dramatic slow zoom on an old newspaper: "NIGHT OF TERROR! Edgar Mills Police Chief William Van Dyne Killed in Tragic Confrontation. Local teen also found dead. Janitor captured."]

@RealTrueCrimeKid: "It's been twenty-five years since the Janitor killings. In this new true crime series, I'll be diving deep into the story. We'll be learning about Bruce Philip Kershaw, from his solitary childhood through to his unmasking as the brutal serial killer known as the Janitor. We'll be digging into the stories of his victims. And of course, we'll be talking a great deal about the Van Dyne twins, whose decision to take on a vicious murderer would change Edgar Mills forever. Thanks for watching, and remember to like, share, and follow along to learn more about this truly fascinating chapter in true crime history!"

CHAPTER ONE:
ALICE

Alice stands in the threshold to the foyer and watches her son pull on his boots. He seems barely aware that she's there.

"Anything fun on today's agenda?" she asks.

"Not really," says Will, tying his laces. "We have a group project due for history class next week and we're meeting before school to talk it over."

"You going to walk to school with Joelle?"

He turns to look at her, an uncomfortable expression on his face. "Dad said he'd drive me. I don't really walk to school with Joelle anymore."

This surprises Alice. The neighbor's daughter is a pretty girl. Friendly too. She's a couple of years older than Will, but the two of them are the only kids on this street who go to the high school, and they've always walked together. She tries to remember when she last saw Joelle and draws a blank.

"I thought you guys were friends," says Alice.

Will shrugs, clearly uncomfortable. "I guess. I don't know. Things don't work like that, Mom. She has her own stuff going on. I think maybe she has a boyfriend now."

"Maybe?"

"Mom, I don't know. Why do you care about what's happening with Joelle?"

He's irritated. Not unusual these days, when it seems like everything out of her mouth is annoying or invasive; still, she senses something else going on beneath the words. Does Will have a crush on the older girl? She knows better than to ask him about it.

He pulls on his other boot and yells up the stairs. "I'll be waiting in the car, Dad!"

The reply comes right away. "Okay, buddy, I'll be out in a couple of minutes!"

Will reaches for the door handle.

"Hang on a minute," Alice says. "Are you going to say goodbye?"

"Bye, Mom," he says now, partially turning back, briefly granting her half of himself.

She knows better than to move in for a kiss, but she allows herself to reach out and touch his cheek briefly with the back of her hand. He flinches slightly but doesn't pull away.

"I love you," she says.

He blushes. "I love you too," he mutters before stepping away and finally escaping out the door.

A moment later her husband comes running down the stairs, pulling a coat on.

"I'm running behind," he says. "I forgot we have an off-site team meeting this morning."

"Are you sure you have time to drop Will off?" she asks. "I could always drive him."

"It's all good," he says as he pulls on an overcoat. "I'm going right past the school, but I have to get moving. I already texted to say I'll be a few minutes late."

"Do you think everything is okay with Will?"

"What do you mean?" he asks, checking his hair in the mirror.

"It just feels like he's pulling away," she says. "He doesn't want to talk to me about anything."

He turns back to her and smiles.

"He's a fifteen-year-old boy," he says, in the cheerfully dismissive way she's become accustomed to lately. "It's all normal."

"You're probably right," she says, although her heart is saying something different.

He smiles. "It'll be fine," he assures her. "You're a great mom, and he loves you. More important, he knows you love him. You worry too much."

"I guess," she says.

He gives her a quick kiss on the cheek and then grabs his keys.

"I love you, Alice," he says as he turns to leave.

"I love you too, Levi."

Alice pours herself some coffee and steps out onto the back deck, inhaling the crisp air and finally feeling herself come awake. She stares across the empty back field that runs behind their subdivision. It's bordered by a row of birch trees that line the bank of the river. There's a trail between the trees and the river that runs into the center of town, where it connects with a footbridge that takes it to the other side and cuts back along the south side of town.

When they bought the house, its proximity to the trail was a main feature. Alice intended to use it for jogging, and for a while she did, but that fell by the wayside with the stresses of child-rearing. But this is a beautiful fall day, and she needs to get out of this house or she'll lose her mind.

She sends a text: You home?

The response appears almost instantly: You bet I am. Come over.

She goes back inside to get dressed, then grabs her purse and coat and leaves through the basement door. As she's locking up, Joelle's mother, Vicki, appears from the direction of the trail with her spaniel mix, Lucky.

"Good morning," says Alice, crouching to give Lucky a scratch on the head. "How's it going, Vicki?"

"Not bad," says Vicki. "Parenting is breaking my heart again, but what else is new?"

"You too?" asks Alice, standing. "Will is growing up too quickly. He doesn't want to connect with me anymore. No more hugs at the door."

"Has he called you a stupid bitch?" asks Vicki.

Alice is so startled by this that she laughs. "Jesus. No. Not yet, anyway."

Vicki laughs as well, ruefully. "Yeah, well, you haven't been blessed with a daughter."

Alice is surprised by this. Joelle has always seemed cheerful and polite whenever Alice has spoken to her. "Joelle is so sweet, though," she says.

Vicki nods. "She's going through a phase. A particularly rough phase."

"I'm sorry," Alice says.

Vicki shakes her head as if trying to dislodge an uncomfortable thought. "Thanks, but it will be fine. It's just been a difficult few weeks. I think she's dating someone, and she's being evasive enough that I'm pretty sure it's an older guy."

Alice remembers her conversation with Will and wonders if he might know more than he's letting on. "I'm sorry to hear that."

"I know it will be fine," says Vicki. "It's just difficult because she and I used to be so close, and now she'll barely talk to me. I don't remember it being like this with my mother. I always hoped she would treat me like a confidant. Did you and your sister struggle with your mom when you were in high school?"

Alice hesitates, and Vicki cringes. "I'm sorry," she says. "I know your situation was . . . different."

Alice waves her off. "It's fine. My mother was always totally present, but I don't know if I'd call her a confidant. She was more of a stage mother, always pushing us to try out for plays or talent shows or sports teams. Then when . . . everything happened, things shifted. Heart-to-heart talks weren't really a priority, you know?"

Vicki smiles and nods, as if she *does* know, but of course she doesn't. There's nothing relatable about what happened to Alice and her sister when they were in high school.

"I guess I just have to wait for it to pass," Vicki says. She glances down at Lucky, who is sitting patiently near her feet, staring up at her lovingly. "I should probably give this good boy his breakfast. Have a great day, Alice." With a little wave she disappears through the basement door.

As Alice crosses through the back field and steps through the trees onto the trail, she resolves to invite Vicki and her family over for dinner soon. It used to be a semi-regular thing, but since Covid it feels like people don't really socialize as much as they used to, and they're overdue. Levi and Kent, Vicki's husband, have always gotten along, and maybe it will be a chance for Will and Joelle to reconnect, if only for a little while.

It takes her about twenty minutes to walk into town, and by the time she gets where she's going, she's worked up a sweat. She enters an alley between a couple of the downtown core's older brick commercial buildings and climbs a metal fire escape before knocking on the door. A moment later it swings inward, and Doug Shiftley is standing aside to make room for her to enter.

"Milady," he says.

"I told you not to call me that," she says.

"You got it, homie," he says.

Alice shrugs off her coat and hangs it on a hook near the door, then she walks across the room and collapses into a battered leather couch. She feels herself instantly relax, the way she always does when she visits Doug.

She loves his apartment. It's a studio built into a large open space with brick walls, high ceilings, and two large windows that look over the back parking lot toward the river and trees beyond. Every once in a while she and Doug venture out for a hike or lunch, but most of the time they just hang out here. Partly it's because Alice is nervous that someone will spot them together, but mostly it's because she feels like she can really relax here.

"So," says Doug, sitting down next to her. "You in the mood?"

She smiles at him. "When have I ever *not* been in the mood?"

"That's what I like to hear," he says. He reaches for a wooden box on the coffee table and opens it, revealing a collection of small plastic bags stuffed with cannabis, along with assorted paraphernalia. "You've got to try this shit. Blueberry Grunt. It's super-mellow but also good for creativity. Twenty percent THC with a nice balance of CBD. It's a hybrid, but—"

"Doug," she says, interrupting him. "I don't care. Can we just get high?"

Doug complies and ten minutes later she is sinking back into the couch, blissfully adrift on a cloud of sweet weed.

If someone had told Alice when she was seventeen that she would someday be close friends with Doug Shiftley she would have been horrified. She was only ever vaguely aware of his existence, primarily as nerdy Joey O'Day's even nerdier friend. Then he was cursed with the world's worst nickname—Dog Shit—and he became the school pariah overnight. She still cringes to think that he has her husband to thank for that particular indignity.

She'd always assumed Doug had left town forever, but then a couple of years ago she ran into him on the river trail. She hadn't recognized him at first, but he'd known who she was and struck up a conversation. It turned out he'd recently returned to Edgar Mills to take a job at his father's real estate brokerage. She'd quickly realized that Doug "Dog Shit" Shiftley was a truly solid guy: funny, interesting, a good listener, and always down to hang out when she needed a break from her real life.

"You hungry?" he asks now.

"Always," says Alice, her eyes still closed. Doug likes to stay active when he's high, cooking or puttering or playing video games. Alice is a more passive kind of stoner. She likes to sit and laugh and have someone feed her stuff.

He begins moving around the kitchen. "Omelets it is."

"Levi thinks I worry too much," she says.

"Fuck that guy," says Doug, as he rummages inside the fridge. "I'll never get over the fact that you married Edgar Mills' worst bully, but the fact that you stay with him really blows my mind."

There's a lot about Alice and Levi's relationship that is impossible to explain to an outsider. The simple truth is that they fell into one another's arms a few months after the traumatic night that defined their lives. At first she felt like she was grieving alone, drowning in guilt. Sam's reaction was to pull away from everyone and everything, and their mother was an absolute basket case. If Levi hadn't stepped in to fill the void, she is pretty sure she would have collapsed entirely.

It was true that Levi had a well-deserved reputation as a bully. He was coarser and tougher than his cheerful, fullhearted brother, but during those awful first weeks and months after Levon and her dad died, they'd opened up to each other and she'd discovered a vulnerable side that surprised and comforted her. Levi had loved and idolized his older brother, but he'd also been outshone by him in every regard. He wasn't as smart or handsome or athletic as Levon, so he covered up his insecurity by becoming the town's biggest asshole.

But that side of him disappeared after their shared tragedy, and he showed her the true Levi. Kind. Hardworking. Honest. Against all odds they'd stayed together, through college, marriage, almost a decade of fertility struggles, and finally the birth of their son.

"Levi's a good man," she says. "But I understand why it's hard for other people to believe that." She hesitates. "For you in particular."

Doug waves it off. "Maybe you should bring him over here for a smoke sesh," he says as he begins chopping a red pepper. "We could see if weed makes him chill out a bit."

Alice forces herself up from the couch and crosses to a stool in the kitchen so she can watch him cook. "Levi is never coming here," she says. "And he is never going to know that I come here. This is my sanctuary, okay?"

He shrugs, pulling a pan down from the wall and firing up the propane burner. "Hey, man, if you want to keep our emotional affair a secret from your meathead husband, that's fine with me."

"This is not an emotional affair, Doug," she says. "We are friends with benefits. The benefits being weed and snacks and nineties movies."

Alice's phone buzzes in her pocket and she pulls it out and checks the display. It's an unknown number, and as much as she wants to ignore it, she considers the possibility that it has something to do with Will and answers.

"Hello?"

The voice on the other end is male and very cheerful. "Hey, is this Alice?"

"Yeah," she responds after a moment. "Who's calling?"

"This is Nash Young. You might not remember me."

Alice smiles, surprised. "Nash. Of course I remember you. I heard you were back in town. You're the new chief, right?"

The question is unnecessary. She knows for a fact that he *is* the new police chief. It was a big piece of gossip when he took the post back in the summer, her female friends making a big deal out of the hot new cop in charge of the town's safety and security. She's been expecting to run into him somewhere, but so far it hasn't happened, so she still pictures the twenty-something rookie she had a major crush on back in the day.

He lets out a gravelly chuckle. Is he a smoker? “That’s right,” he says. “It’s been a busy few months. I certainly have big shoes to fill.”

She knows he isn’t talking about Donald Matterson, the bland, grim man who took over the post after her father died and spent the next twenty-some years aging in place.

“You do,” she agrees. “But I know Dad would be happy to know you stepped into the job. He really liked you.”

“Well, that means a lot coming from you,” he says. “I thought the world of your father. He was a real mentor to me.”

There’s a long pause, and Alice wonders if he just called to catch up, but then Nash clears his throat.

“I’m not quite sure how to say this, Alice,” he says. “But is there any chance you’ve seen the news this morning?”

CHAPTER TWO: JOEY

Joey turns away from his computer and stares out his office window at the people passing by on the busy sidewalk down below. He wonders how so many of them have the time to just stroll along, listening to music or podcasts or chatting and drinking coffee. Don't they have work to do? He rubs his temples and reminds himself that he's just burned out, tired of thinking about *critical paths* and *anticipated outcomes* and all the other business-related bullshit that comes along with his job. He wishes he could run outside and join the kids playing soccer in the park across the street.

He's been with Shoreline Technologies for almost twenty years. He was first hired right out of MIT as a programmer and was quickly promoted to head programmer, then developmental engineer, and for the past several years he's been the chief technical officer, overseeing the apps that have been Shoreline's bread and butter for the better part of a decade. Shoreline's biggest success by far is Brown Bag, a virtual grocery assistant that monitors local sales and stock availability to populate a running shopping list and suggests optimum times to do your shopping, along with meal plans and dietary and nutritional strategies.

Brown Bag was chugging along, showing modest but steady growth, when Covid hit. It just so happened that Shoreline was in the early stages of developing a new personal shopping feature designed to help match senior citizens and busy professionals with people who would pick up their groceries for them. The timing was auspicious and the opportunity was undeniable: suddenly huge numbers of people were stuck inside, afraid of grocery stores, and obsessed with cooking.

Mike Bancroft, Shoreline's CEO, along with trusted first officer Joey, decided to throw everything they had at meeting the moment. When other companies were laying off staff, Shoreline was hiring new programmers and putting them through an intense and abbreviated period of training, so staff was prepared to handle things by the time everyone shifted to remote work.

Joey remembers those days with nostalgia. Long hours spent working from an office he'd set up in the spare bedroom of his condo. The sense that he and the team were doing something new and special and *important*. His husband, Austin, a freelance graphic designer, had always worked from home, but now they were cooped up together, a tiny team of two waiting out the pandemic, focused on work, but finding time for leisurely lunches and plenty of sex breaks. It was kind of great, if he's being honest.

The new app launched during the first week of April—just a few weeks into the first lockdown and almost a year earlier than they had originally planned. It was an instant success, beyond what they ever could have hoped for, and the company scaled up so quickly that by the time the pandemic was over, they were able to move into much nicer digs in Cambridge.

Now those days have receded into a hazy past, and the company has shifted to a new focus on "premium virtual retail experiences," which is shorthand for "getting people to buy more and more expensive shit on the internet." Mike likes to say there's a Goop for everyone, and Shoreline's job is to find it for them. The proprietary architecture they built for Brown Bag is tailor-made for this kind of "online experience," and so far the margins have been fantastic. Mike is happy. The investors are happy. The customers are happy. Shoreline's employees are happy.

And Joey has never been so bored.

He's grateful, of course. He owns a lot of stock in Shoreline, and his compensation package is impressive. Mike has always shared the credit for Shoreline's success, and he makes a point of mentioning Joey specifically in almost every interview he gives. But lately something has shifted. What used to be a series of stimulating challenges has become an endless grind. It's hard to maintain a passion for online sales, no matter how deeply he's invested.

His computer chimes and he snaps back to attention, turning away from the window and checking his notifications. He's due to meet Austin in twenty minutes. The restaurant is only a five-minute walk away, and he debates staying a bit longer to send another couple of emails, but instead he stands and pulls on his coat. The emails can wait, and he could really use some fresh air.

As he steps into the hallway, he almost bumps into Mike.

"There's the man I was looking for!" Mike is a big, jolly guy who loves to chat. "You on your way out?"

"I'm meeting Austin for lunch," says Joey.

"Very nice, very nice," says Mike. "I won't keep you, but I do want to put a bug in your ear about something. You remember I met with that French start-up last month?"

Joey nods. "Vaguely." He tends to stay as far away from business development as possible.

"Well, they reached out again today and it turns out that they're interested in exploring a formal partnership."

"A partnership," Joey repeats.

"They want to join forces with Shoreline to create a new digital platform to bring European luxury goods to the North American market," Mike explains. "You know I've had my eyes on Europe for quite a while now. I'm confident that these guys know what they're talking about, and I think the opportunities are huge, but I want to make sure we have a solid presence on the ground there. How do you feel about Paris?"

Joey blinks. "Paris?"

"You think you could convince that handsome husband of yours to pack up and move to the center of the cultural world?"

"Wait a minute," says Joey. "Are you saying you want me to head up a French division of Shoreline?"

"A European division of Shoreline, headquartered in France," Mike corrects. "But yeah. I've been getting the impression lately that you're a bit bored with the way things have played out, and there's nobody I'd trust more with heading up this kind of expansion." He glances at his watch. "I have a meeting and you have lunch. Why don't you order a nice bottle of French wine at lunch, on me, and talk it over with Austin. We can discuss the details later.

* * *

As Joey arrives at the restaurant, he spots Austin through the window, seated in a booth, scrolling on his phone. As always when he comes close to his husband, Joey's heart rate seems to slow, and he is filled with a sense of inner calm. He reflects for the millionth time on how grateful he is to have found the perfect man, and that the perfect man was willing to share his life with him.

Before Austin, Joey was an anxious workaholic, living a highly structured life that revolved around the office, the gym, and the office again. He wasn't looking for a relationship, but what began as a casual hookup soon turned into something much more intense and fulfilling, and now he can hardly believe that he ever lived without this cheerful, optimistic, fun-loving man.

He pushes through the door, and Austin looks up from his phone and smiles broadly as Joey approaches the booth. Joey bends down to give him a quick kiss before sliding in across from him.

"Hey, you," says Austin. "How's work?"

Mike's proposal is still so fresh in Joey's mind that he doesn't even know how to broach it. He decides to have a drink and bring it up once he's had a minute to settle.

"Work's work," he says. "How's your day going?"

"It's going well," says Austin. He takes a deep breath as if he's preparing himself for something. "So, there's something we need to talk about."

Joey's stomach does a heavy flip.

"Okay," he says. "That sounds ominous."

Austin smiles reassuringly and reaches across the table to grab his hand. "Nothing to worry about. I just wanted to reopen the adoption conversation. It's stalled out."

"It hasn't stalled out," says Joey. "We just agreed that we needed some time to let the idea sink in."

"*You* needed the idea to sink in," says Austin. "And that is totally fair, and I promised you I would leave it for a while and let you bring it up when you'd had time to mull it over."

Joey nods. "That is how the conversation went," he agrees.

Austin takes a sip of water. "It's been eight months, Joe. I haven't brought it up one time in eight months. And neither have you."

"I've been thinking it over," says Joey. Which is true, to a degree. He has thought about it several times, in an *Oh shit, I need to think about this and I don't want to* kind of way. "I don't think this is the kind of thing we want to rush."

"I mean, sure?" says Austin. "But the thing is, you know how I feel, and you know that I'd love to talk about it with you and help you sort out your feelings on the matter, but if I don't initiate the conversation, it literally never comes up."

"Okay," says Joey, unsure how to proceed.

"I love you, Joey, and I know you love me."

"Of course I do," says Joey.

"And we got married because we want to spend the rest of our lives together."

Joey nods. "Yes. Obviously."

"We have a great life," says Austin. "And I think there's room here for us to share it with someone else. I think we could give a child a great, loving, fun home. Children, even."

Joey's eyes widen.

"Child!" Austin laughs, quickly backtracking. "Just one, I promise."

Joey nods. "Okay. What are you proposing?"

Austin takes a deep breath. "My cousin Lacey—you remember her from the wedding, right?"

Joey nods. Austin's midwestern family is a lot smaller than Joey's big Catholic brood, and there were only a few people at the wedding from Austin's side. His parents, an aunt, and a couple of cousins.

"The lawyer, right?"

Austin nods. "She called me last week to tell me she has a friend who used an agency to adopt a kid recently. She had a really great experience, and Lacey gave me her number, so I gave her a call and got her story. I didn't want to bring it up with you before I had a chance to talk it over with her."

Joey nods, a feeling of dread coursing through his veins. "Okay," he says.

"Anyway," says Austin, pushing through, "Lacey's friend and her husband both had great things to say about the agency, and they put me in contact with a local representative. They have worked with a lot of gay couples, and I kind of made an appointment for next week."

"An appointment," repeats Joey.

"It's just a meet and greet," Austin hastens to explain. "No commitment. It'll be kind of an interview—on both sides. No expectations, no commitments, just an opportunity to talk this stuff over with someone who knows all the ins and outs. I think it's good research. You're always saying we should do our research, right?"

Joey knows this would be the right moment to bring up his conversation with Mike, but he feels like *Hey, instead of having a kid, let's leave the country* might not be the right approach right now.

"Okay," he says instead. "Let's talk to her."

Austin claps excitedly and then leans across the table to give Joey a kiss on the lips. Clearly relieved by the results of their conversation, he turns his attention to the menu as Joey tries to shove the feeling of dread down into his gut.

Something across the room catches his eye and he leans forward to stare at the television that's mounted behind the bar.

A reporter is standing in front of some police activity, speaking earnestly to the camera. The volume is down, but something about the backdrop is vaguely familiar, and Joey finds himself standing from the booth and walking closer to the TV.

"Joe?"

He's only vaguely aware of Austin speaking.

"Are you okay?"

As he gets closer to the screen, he realizes what he's looking at. The reporter is standing in front of the police station in Edgar Mills. As he watches, a chyron appears on the screen:

TWENTY-FIVE YEARS AFTER SERIAL KILLINGS, SMALL TOWN ROCKED BY NEW MURDER.

CHAPTER THREE:
SAM

Sam wakes in a tangle of bedsheets to a beam of light slicing through the venetian blinds to land directly on her face. It isn't until she moves to yank the duvet back into place that she remembers she isn't alone in bed.

The guy next to her—Allan? Angus? Alex!—mumbles and twists in the other direction, pulling the blanket back around himself. Sam is already awake and buzzing with morning energy, so she leaves him to the bedclothes and slips out of bed.

She climbs into a pair of sweatpants and a T-shirt and pads across her condo to the kitchen. She glances at her phone and notices that she's missed a few calls, two from an unknown number and two from her sister. There are also a couple of voicemails and a Call me back text from Alice. She doesn't have the energy to check the messages, and she's not about to make a phone call with some dude dozing in her bed a few feet away. She'll deal with it all later.

She kind of resents having to stay quiet, because she doesn't owe this guy a comfortable sleep, but she doesn't feel like stepping into a field of forced chatter this early in the morning, so she moves around the kitchen as quietly as she can. There's no softening the buzz of the Nespresso machine, but Alex only shifts deeper into the mattress.

She takes her coffee out onto the balcony and sits, staring down at the street and letting herself wake up. She runs through her plans for the day: go for a run, do some reading, spend a couple of hours working, and maybe catch the screening of *Chinatown* at the Vista later in the evening.

A day to herself, like most of them. Just the way she likes it. Now if she can figure out how to get rid of the overstayer, she'll be all set. Speaking of which, she figures he's had more than enough sleep. She tosses back the rest of her coffee and steps back into the condo. This time she doesn't bother trying to stay quiet. She moves to the window and opens the blinds.

Alex yawns expansively and rolls over onto his back, stretching luxuriously and smiling up at her.

"Hey, babe," he says.

"Good morning," says Sam, in a singsong voice that she has to force. *Babe?* She met this guy less than twelve hours ago.

"You feel like coming back to bed?" he asks, suggestively patting the comforter.

Alex is hot, no question. Fit and tanned and with a thick tousled mop of sandy blond hair, and last night was fun once he stopped expounding and they finally made it into bed. When she was this guy's age—which is to say almost fifteen years younger—she might very well have ignored all of that for the sake of getting laid just one more time. But these days she's more easily satisfied. Her itch has been scratched, and now this little guy will have to go home and scratch himself.

"Actually, I've got kind of a busy day," she says with an apologetic grimace.

It takes him a moment to register that he's being turned down. "Oh, yeah," he says. "Sure. Of course."

He reaches for the clothes that he discarded on the side of the bed last night and begins to get dressed.

"So you're just in L.A. for the weekend?"

She realizes this might be the first question he's asked her about herself since they first sat down over martinis last night—although, to be fair, he was very busy talking about crypto and seed oils and Elon fucking Musk.

"No," she says. "What makes you ask that?"

He looks around the condo. "I just figured since you're in an Airbnb that you might be in town on business."

She laughs. "This is my place. I've lived here for almost twenty years."

He is visibly surprised. "Holy shit, are you serious? What are you, some kind of minimalist?"

She shrugs. "I don't like unnecessary stuff."

Sam likes her small apartment. She likes the sleek but comfortable sofa and the efficient little kitchen with its set of high-end pots and pans, three good knives, and dinner setting for two—and nothing else. She has spent money on good linens and nice furniture and a pared-back wardrobe made up of expensive and durable pieces.

There is nothing in her life that she doesn't need.

Once Alex leaves, Sam decides to wander out to her favorite morning haunt, Billy's, a breakfast joint a few blocks away where she often treats herself to poached eggs, toast, and fruit salad.

She places her order at the counter, then goes outside to wait at one of the café tables on the patio. She makes the mistake of glancing around at the people sitting nearby and happens to lock eyes with a woman sitting with a friend a couple of tables away. Sam looks away quickly, but not before the woman does a double take. She leans in to whisper something to her friend, and then suddenly they're both staring.

Sam used to be recognized all the time, but these incidents have become increasingly rare over the years. The best thing about being a former reality TV star is that the only people who ever recognize her these days are women and gay men of a certain age, and even then it's usually a discreet surreptitious glance over a produce display at the grocery store or standing in line for a coffee.

As for her *past* past identity, her first famous persona, she can't remember the last time anyone drew that connection. Samantha Van Dyne of the Van Dyne twins was a kid. Seventeen. That was a million years ago, and now Sam is a middle-aged woman who barely recognizes that girl when she sees her in old photographs—and certainly can't find her in the bathroom mirror.

The silver lining of her reality TV era is that if someone happens to recognize her, they remember her as *that* woman, not the seventeen-year-old girl she was during her first bout of notoriety. If it takes being associated with the persona they created for her—a trashy, foulmouthed TV villain with no scruples and a willingness to screw over anyone she can to get what she wants—to get people to forget the girl she was before that, she'll take it.

Sam hopes the women at the other table will leave her alone—that they'll keep their little celebrity sighting to themselves until they can post about it on Facebook. But nope. They seem to come to an agreement, and both stand hesitantly and then walk over to her table.

"I'm really sorry to bother you," says one of the women, "but are you Sammy Vee?"

Sam forces herself to smile up at the woman. "Yes, I am, you suspicious bitch."

There's a pause, and then the woman bursts out laughing. The ice broken, she reaches down and slaps Sam lightly on the shoulder in an *Oh, you* gesture, as if they're old friends.

"Best catchline ever," she says.

Sam smiles. "It comes in handy."

"Oh my god, are you kidding me?" says the woman. "I mean, I find myself thinking it all the time when someone's pissing me off. Anyway, I don't want to bother you, I just wanted to say I was obsessed with *Rebel House* back in the day, and I totally loved you."

"Did you?" asks Sam, with a raised eyebrow.

The woman cringes a little bit.

"You hated me," says Sam.

"I hated you," the woman admits. "But, like, in a fun way. You were just so, pardon my French, fucking evil."

"I'll take that as a compliment," says Sam.

"Omigod, yes, of course," says the woman. "It's a total compliment. You were, like, the queen of reality show villains. And to stand out like that in a house *full* of reality show villains takes something special. I mean, that guy with the nose ring? The heavy metal guy?"

"Jack the Bastard," says Sam.

"That's him!" says the woman, pointing as if Sam has won a prize. "I mean, that guy boasted about giving cocaine to his cats, and you made me feel bad for him!"

Sam smiles but doesn't respond, and the woman gets the hint.

"It was so great to meet you. I'll let you get back to your breakfast."

She turns to leave, but her friend, who has been standing by quietly, pipes up almost uncertainly.

"You were also that teen detective, right? You tracked down that serial killer back East?"

Sam freezes, unsure how to respond.

"Oh my God," says the first woman. "What? Really?"

"Bruce Philip Kershaw," says her friend. "I had forgotten all about it until I saw some guy talking about it on TikTok recently."

"On TikTok?" Sam asks, unable to hide the surprise. She avoids social media entirely, but she thought TikTok was for sharing dances and skin care regimes.

"Oh yeah," says the woman. "True crime is huge on TikTok. I think the guy I saw was called True Crime Kid or something like that? He's been posting a series about your case for the twenty-fifth anniversary of the murders. It's such a crazy story. I can't believe you were able to reinvent yourself after everything you went through."

Sam just stares at her, dumbfounded.

The other woman has been watching this exchange with interest, and now she pipes up again. "I remember this now. That's how you got on the show, right? You were a villain because you screwed up and people got killed."

"Your sister's boyfriend," says the second woman, "and your dad." She whispers the second part, placing a hand on her heart and shaking her head solemnly for emphasis. She turns to her friend. "I'll send you a link," she whispers.

Sam's heart is beating so fast, she's worried it will rip through her chest. She's done pretending to smile for these women.

"That was a lifetime ago," she says flatly. She wants them to leave her alone.

"What happened, anyway?" asks the first woman, not taking the hint. "Didn't you leave a door unlocked or something?"

"Come on, Deena," says her friend, clearly aware that they've overstayed their welcome. "Let's leave her be. I'm sure this is the last thing she wants to talk about."

"It was the gun," says Sam. "I took my father's gun to confront Kershaw, but Kershaw was a step ahead of us and went to my parents' house and killed my dad, who didn't have his gun to defend himself."

The women stare at her and she stares right back at them, almost daring them to push the conversation further. Mercifully, her food finally arrives and they take advantage of the distraction to scurry back to their table.

Sam's appetite is gone, so she pushes away her plate and reaches for her phone. A quick search for "TikTok," "True Crime Kid," and "Van Dyne Twins" brings up a list of videos from an account titled @RealTrueCrimeKid. After a moment's hesitation, she plugs in her AirPods and loads the one at the top of the list, titled THE JANITOR KILLINGS, PART 2-THE VAN DYNE TWINS.

A photo of her father appears, the official portrait taken when he was promoted to police chief. He's smiling broadly, young and handsome and alive, and even though she has a framed print of the same photo on the bookcase in her apartment, she feels a sharp stab of pain as she looks at it.

Superimposed over the lower corner of the photo is a teenager wearing a button-down shirt and thick eyeglasses. His hair is slicked back and his voice, when he speaks, is jarringly earnest.

"You're watching the second installment in my series on the Janitor killings, one of the most notorious and dramatic crime stories from the turn of the century. Remember to like, share, and subscribe for more fascinating details, insights, and theories about what really happened in Edgar Mills in the year 2000."

Sam frowns. *Theories?*

"This is Edgar Mills chief of police Bill Van Dyne. Twenty-five years ago, Chief Van Dyne was *this* close to stopping Bruce Philip Kershaw in his tracks when everything went horribly wrong."

The photo of Sam's father is replaced by some highly stylized black-and-white footage of Birch Crest Elementary. From the extremely dilapidated appearance of the building, Sam guesses the footage is recent.

"It's one of the most mysterious pieces of this complicated puzzle: Who or what tipped Chief Van Dyne off to the abandoned school that Kershaw had been using as a lair? For some reason, Birch Crest Elementary School was on Bill Van Dyne's radar. Unfortunately, he never got the chance to act, because his own daughters got there first."

A newspaper headline scrolls across the screen behind the boy: "Edgar Mills Police Chief and Local Teen Killed in Night of Terror."

"To this day, people wonder—if the twins had gone to their father first instead of confronting Kershaw, would he still be alive? Would Alice's boyfriend Levon Brakes still be alive? Would the case have ended differently? Today I'll be asking those questions and many more as we do a deep dive into Samantha and Alice Van

Dyne, the twin teen detectives who took matters into their own hands, with tragic consequences."

Sam has heard enough. She swipes the screen so that the video disappears, and as she's about to flip her phone upside down on the table, it vibrates with an incoming call. It's Alice, and she remembers the missed calls and texts from earlier with unease. Her sister never calls this early in the day.

"Hi," she says, answering. "Everything okay?"

"Oh, thank God I got hold of you." Alice definitely sounds out of sorts.

"Is it Mom?" Sam asks, and she realizes that she's been half expecting this call for years. But Alice surprises her.

"No," she says. "Did the police not call you?"

"Police?" Sam remembers the missed calls. "I missed a couple of messages this morning . . . What's going on?"

There's a long, deadly pause on the other end of the line, and Sam feels her veins fill with ice. Suddenly she dreads what's coming.

"Just tell me."

"Someone's been murdered in Edgar Mills," says Alice.

Sam sits up straight.

"Who?"

"A teenage boy," says Alice. "I don't know a lot of details, but the police want to talk to us." There's a long pause before Alice continues. "They say they want our help."

TikTok Transcript [excerpt]:

@RealTrueCrimeKid
THE JANITOR KILLINGS
PART 3 - WELCOME TO EDGAR MILLS

[Opening montage: A series of still images slowly dissolve into one another: a vintage postcard of the Edgar Mills town clock, a black and white photograph of Cordova's Diner, a colorful snapshot of a parade moving down Main Street in the mid-'80s, etc.]

[Host, @RealTrueCrimeKid, appears superimposed in corner of screen.]

@RealTrueCrimeKid: "You might think this looks like the quintessential New England town, the kind of place where people dream of moving, whether to raise a family, open a small business, or settle into a calm and peaceful retirement. It's not the kind of town where you would expect to find a monster. But in the beginning months of the new century, that's exactly what it was. This is Edgar Mills, Massachusetts, and twenty-five years ago this charming, close-knit little town was the hunting ground for notorious serial killer Bruce Philip Kershaw, better known as the Janitor."

[Cut to news footage from 2000. A middle-aged woman is interviewed on the sidewalk.]

Woman: "This kind of thing isn't supposed to happen in a place like Edgar Mills. It's horrible. Everyone is in a state of shock. I guess we can just be grateful they've got the monster locked up."

Reporter (offscreen): "Do you think what's happened will change Edgar Mills moving forward?"

Woman: "How can it not? How can we ever look at ourselves the same way? Before this, I never used to lock my doors. Now I lock them whether I'm home or not, and I doubt I'll ever leave them unlocked again. This is a small town, everyone knows everyone. There was never any reason to be suspicious of our neighbors, but now . . . I don' t know. I think it's going to be a lot harder to trust people. I guess you just never know what's going on behind closed doors."

CHAPTER FOUR: ALICE

Alice cranes her neck to stare out the window at the throngs of people streaming out of the terminal. Finally she spots Sam moving briskly toward her Suburban. Alice watches her approach in the rearview mirror. Her sister looks as good as always, with her stylish haircut, jeans that fit like they were tailored, and a black T-shirt under a beautiful leather jacket, an expensive but slightly battered overnight bag slung over her shoulder. She's clearly still working out regularly, as evidenced by her strong, confident stride, and how her perfectly fitting clothes hang on her the way they're supposed to, and those chiseled cheekbones.

Alice has cheekbones like that somewhere. Her vision shifts to herself in the mirror, and she stares at the woman she has become, a woman she barely recognizes. Then the passenger door opens and her sister slides inside and the two of them are hugging across the center console and it's like she's complete again.

"Hello, gorgeous," says Sam when they pull apart.

Despite Alice's best efforts, her face crumples and she begins to cry. Sam's face twists in dismay. She was never comfortable around displays of emotion.

"Come on, take it easy," she says, reaching out to wipe a tear away. "You aren't that bummed to see me, are you?"

Alice laughs, a kind of gurgling, snotty snort. "Are you kidding? This is the best thing in a long time. I'm so happy you came."

"I don't think I had much of a choice," says Sam. She reaches around and tosses her duffel bag in the back seat. "So, what do we know? Who was the victim? His name hasn't been released yet, as far as I can find online."

Alice shakes her head. "Not officially, but word is out around town. His name was Justin Beagle. He was a senior, a popular kid, athletic, nice family, lots of friends. A man out walking his dog found his body in the woods along the river trail. The cops have managed to keep the rest of the details under wraps, but I got the impression from Nash that we'll learn more when we get to the station."

"Nash Young?" says Sam. "That's a blast from the past. I didn't realize he still lived in Edgar Mills."

"He's only been back in town for a few months. Apparently he was working in Florida, and when his marriage broke down he applied for Dad's old job and moved back."

"I wonder if he's still as hot as ever," says Sam.

"I wouldn't know," says Alice, avoiding her sister's eyes. "I haven't seen him yet." She doesn't mention that she's tried, and failed, to find him online. Apparently Nash Young doesn't do social media.

"Well, we don't want to keep him waiting," says Sam. "Let's go find out what he wants."

* * *

The Edgar Mills Police Department is as prominent in their childhood memories as Birch Crest Elementary, but it's been kept in decidedly better shape. A fresh coat of paint has been applied to the exterior, the landscaped planter boxes are trimmed and well maintained, and the front door swings open easily when they enter.

They're greeted just inside the front door by a large, framed photograph that catches Alice off guard, even though she and her mother were here to unveil it fifteen years ago on the tenth anniversary of . . . everything. She feels the familiar well of tears in her eyes, and she glances at Sam, expecting a similar reaction, but her sister is just staring at it thoughtfully.

IN LOVING MEMORY OF EDGAR MILLS CHIEF OF POLICE WILLIAM CHARLES VAN DYNE, says the plaque underneath the large photo of their beaming, uniformed father.

"He looks good," says Sam. She reaches out and briefly touches the plaque with the tip of her index finger, then turns away briskly and claps her hands. "Okay, let's get this show on the road."

At the front desk, they announce their arrival to a receptionist, who leads them down a hallway and into a meeting room. "They'll be with you shortly," she says before slipping out and closing the door behind her.

They aren't alone. There's a man sitting at the table, looking at his phone. As they enter, he glances up and lays it down, then stands to greet them.

Sam recognizes him before Alice does.

"Holy shit," she says. "Joey?"

Alice can't remember the last time she saw, or thought about, Joey O'Day. She vaguely remembers hearing that he lives in Boston and made a bunch of money in tech, but beyond that he might as well be a historical figure. One thing is for sure: he's aged beautifully. The short nerdy boy from their high school days has swanned into a fit, handsome, well-put-together man. He's still short, but that only enhances the illusion that he's ten years younger than his true age.

"Hello, Van Dyne twins," he says. He stands and comes around the table, giving each of them a somewhat awkward hug.

"You're looking good," says Sam, assessing him. "What are you doing here, anyway? Do you have any idea what this is about?"

"No more than you do," says Joey. "Nash wouldn't say much on the phone, but he was persuasive. Said it was really important, so I agreed to take the day off work. Civic duty and all that."

There's a knock on the door and then a slight, elderly man in a dated suit steps into the room.

"I hope I'm not interrupting," he says.

"Perry?" asks Sam. "What are you doing here?"

Perry looks at Alice. "You didn't tell her?"

"Tell me what?" Sam asks, casting an accusatory look at Alice.

"I forgot to mention that I asked Perry to join us," says Alice. The truth is that Sam has never liked Perry Lemire and Alice didn't want to rock the boat.

Perry turns to Joey. "I'm the Van Dyne family lawyer," he explains.

"You're not my lawyer," says Sam. She looks at Alice. "Is he your lawyer?"

Perry straightens his posture. "I was your family's lawyer for many years," he says with dignity, "and I still manage some of your mother's affairs. I was also a trusted friend and advisor to your father. Maybe you think I'm meddling, but the police reached out to me to help bring the two of you here, and so I feel as if I bear some responsibility. But if you'd prefer for me to leave . . ."

"It's fine, Perry," says Alice. "I invited you. You can stay."

Sam gives Alice an irritated look, but before she can say anything the door opens again and a man and a woman walk in. The last time Alice saw Nash Young was at their father's memorial service. He was a baby-faced rookie, tall and fit and as green as they come. Like Sam and Joey, he's kept himself in good shape, but there's no avoiding the lines around his eyes and the gentle downward slump of his cheeks. He's far from the wide-eyed newbie he used to be, and there's a worldly expression in his baby-blue eyes.

He gives them a warm smile. "The teen detectives," he says. "Together again. I'm happy you were all able to come at such short notice." He gestures at the woman beside him. "This is my colleague Angela Corvallis. She's a special investigator with the state and she's helping us with the current investigation."

The woman with him appears to be in her late thirties, and to say she's neatly put together is an understatement. She's wearing a crisply tailored gray pin-striped suit, her dark hair is pulled back into a tight bun, and she stares at them unsmilingly from behind wire-rimmed glasses. She gives them an obvious once-over, and Alice gets the strong vibe that she isn't pleased to be there.

She pulls out a chair in a move that somehow indicates she's in control. "Have a seat," she says. It's a command, and Alice can sense Sam bristling beside her.

The room instinctively divides itself in three. Alice, Sam, and Joey sit at the table across from the detectives, and after a moment's consideration Perry drags another chair into the corner. He sits and pulls a notebook from his briefcase.

"I am going to cut right to the chase," says Nash. "You're all busy people and we have an investigation to run. How much do you know?"

"We know that a teenage kid was murdered," says Sam. "But it's impossible to find out more than that online."

"Yesterday morning, a man walking his dog came across the body of eighteen-year-old Justin Beagle in the woods that run along the Edgar Mills River Trail," says Angela Corvallis. "He had been shot once. Straight through the heart."

Alice lets out a small gasp.

"Where on the trail?" asks Sam.

"A clearing not too far from the north entrance," says Nash. "Notably, there was cleaning fluid found on the body. Heavy-duty pine-scented floor cleaner. It had been poured all over his legs and torso."

The room falls into a deathly silence that's only broken when Joey lets out a long, slow whistle.

"What does this mean?" asks Alice.

"Copycat killing," says Joey.

Nash looks like he's about to speak, but Corvallis cuts him off. "I can see why you'd think that, but there were several significant differences. For one thing, nothing about the scene resembled the Janitor's crimes. There was a struggle, and guns weren't Kershaw's MO."

"He used a gun once," says Sam.

"Yes," says Corvallis, unfazed. "Of course. But that was an outlier, not part of his typical routine."

"So you think the cleaning fluid is just a coincidence?" asks Sam.

Corvallis is quick with an answer. "The cleaner seemed to have been thrown on as an afterthought and the jug was left behind. The entire thing reeked of a decoy, as if the fluid was left to muddy the scene and throw investigators off the trail. Let's say there was a dispute of some sort, perhaps a drug deal gone wrong. Someone gets shot, and the killer decides to create a distraction by trying to tie the crime to Bruce Philip Kershaw."

"Who's been in maximum security prison for the past twenty-five years," says Joey.

"Are we sure?" asks Sam. "Has anyone checked for a hole in the wall behind his Rita Hayworth poster?"

"We can assure you that Kershaw is still very much locked up," says Corvallis.

"In fact, that's why we wanted to talk to the three of you," says Nash.

They go silent at this, as a tense expectation fills the air. This is why they all came in the first place, isn't it? Curiosity.

"Yesterday afternoon," Nash continues, "less than twelve hours after the discovery of Justin Beagle's body, Bruce Philip Kershaw told a guard he had information to share about the murder. He refused to disclose what he knew or how he obtained the information, but the fact that he knew about the murder before it had even been made public caught our attention."

"We are understandably very suspicious of anything Kershaw has to say," says Corvallis. "But Chief Young strongly argued that we should at least listen to the man, and so we drove to Bay State Penitentiary, where Kershaw is being held, and we met with him."

Alice realizes that she's on the edge of her seat.

"What did he tell you?" she asks.

"Nothing," says Corvallis.

"Not exactly nothing," corrects Nash. "He said he has information, but he'll only share it under certain conditions."

"What kind of conditions?" asks Sam.

Nash glances at Corvallis, who gives him a slight nod. "He wants to speak to the three of you."

"Us?" asks Joey. He sounds as surprised as Alice feels.

Nash nods. "His exact words were 'I'll tell the teen detectives what I know or I won't tell anyone. And it has to be all three of them or I'll keep my mouth shut.'"

"What would this look like?" says Sam.

"He wants to meet with all three of you in person, at the prison," says Corvallis. "No phones. No videoconferencing."

"So you expect us to sit across a table from the monster who murdered our father?" says Sam. "Just a friendly catch-up?"

"We don't expect you to do anything," says Corvallis. "Realistically, nobody thinks he really has any information. I think he's bored and looking to stir up some shit, and he saw this murder as an opportunity to do that."

"What do you think, Nash?" asks Sam.

"I have a slightly different perspective from Angela," he says, and Alice senses that Nash is treading carefully. "I don't want to give you the wrong impression: we're talking about a very manipulative man, and I think chances are that he doesn't know anything. But there are a few things worth noting. For one, Kershaw has been a model prisoner for his entire stay. No fights. No drama. He keeps his head down and he doesn't look for attention or controversy."

"That's fabulous," says Sam. "I wonder if there's a greeting card for that."

Nash ignores this. "My point is that it seems very out of character for Kershaw to begin playing games. I have no idea what he wants to say to the three of you, but I think it might be worth hearing him out."

Alice looks at Corvallis. "You don't agree."

Corvallis nods. "To put it bluntly, I think the man is full of it and this is a waste of police resources, but Chief Nash here felt strongly enough about the matter that I agreed to float the idea with the three of you. If you want to walk away, you can walk away and we can get back to investigating the case on the ground, where I'm confident it will be solved."

They sit silently for a moment, considering this. Finally, Joey turns to Nash.

"You really think there's a chance he might know something?" he asks. "You think he wouldn't bother going through this fuss if there wasn't something behind it."

"I do," says Nash. "I think it's a tiny chance, but it's not nothing. Kershaw barely spoke to investigators back in the day. He didn't take the stand in his own defense. He has never given an interview. There might be details he's been keeping to himself all this time, and if so, I think we should take advantage of this willingness to talk."

Joey nods, seems to make up his mind. "I'd see him. I mean, I definitely get it if the twins don't want to go through with it. I don't have the personal connection like they do. But if they're amenable to it, I'd go just to hear what he has to say. Then at least we'd know."

"Would that be good enough?" asks Alice. "I mean, if Joey is willing to talk to him on our behalf, maybe that's enough for him."

Corvallis shakes her head. "He was very clear. He'll only talk if all three of you show up or he won't talk at all."

From the back of the room, a thin voice speaks up, and Alice realizes she has completely forgotten that Perry is here. "Girls," he says, "as your lawyer, I would strongly recommend that you turn down this offer. I think Special Investigator Corvallis makes an excel—"

Sam slams her hands down on the table.

"Jesus Christ, Perry, I'm forty-two years old. I am not a girl and you're not my lawyer." She turns to Nash. "Do you know what? To hell with it. Let's do it. Let's go see the bastard, let him spin his fairy tale, stare him right in the fucking eyes, and let him know that we aren't scared of him one little bit."

Perry lets out a quiet, indignant huff but doesn't speak up again.

The room goes silent and Alice looks up, suddenly aware that everyone is watching her, waiting for her decision.

"I don't know," she says, shaking her head. "If we meet with Kershaw, I worry I'll see him in my nightmares every night for the rest of my life."

"Hasn't he already been in your nightmares?" asks Sam.

She holds Alice's gaze until finally Alice nods.

"So let's give him nightmares instead," says her sister.

Alice looks at her sister and Joey. She sees a spark of expectation in their eyes as they wait for her decision, and suddenly she's reminded of how she used to feel, how she wanted to ask every question, turn over every stone, follow every lead, listen to every hunch. She's scared of what this means, but underneath the fear is a stronger feeling, a tight, muscular knot in her gut telling her to do what needs doing.

"Okay," she says. "When do we go see him?"

TikTok Transcript [excerpt]:

@RealTrueCrimeKid
THE JANITOR KILLINGS
PART 4 – BRUCE PHILIP KERSHAW

[A still image of a man's face fills the screen. His small, squinting eyes appear to be avoiding the camera, his mouth is twisted into a deep frown, and his thinning hair sits limply on his head. The image pulls out to reveal the man is in a prison jumpsuit, his hands cuffed behind his back, as two grim-faced bailiffs guide him into a courtroom.]

[Host, @RealTrueCrimeKid, appears superimposed in corner of screen.]

@RealTrueCrimeKid: "This is Bruce Philip Kershaw, better known as the Janitor. Was he always a monster, or did Edgar Mills *create* him?"

[Cut to old photos of Kershaw's childhood home, then a yearbook photo of young Bruce, looking awkward and withdrawn.]

@RealTrueCrimeKid: "Kershaw was the younger of two kids, raised by loving parents who owned several buildings in town. But socially anxious, he struggled to fit in. People who knew him said he was 'intelligent but profoundly introverted.'"

[Cut to a newspaper clipping: "Tragedy Strikes: Local Couple Killed in Car Accident."]

@RealTrueCrimeKid: "When he was just nineteen, his parents died in a car crash. Along with his sister he inherited their sizable estate, including several properties, but despite the fact that he didn't need a job he began working in his early twenties as—you guessed it—a janitor at Birch Crest Elementary School in Edgar Mills."

[Cut to darkened footage of an abandoned school hallway, eerie music in the background.]

@RealTrueCrimeKid: "In 1999, Birch Crest Elementary was closed down, and Kershaw began working at Edgar Mills High School. But he kept a set of keys that gave him access to the abandoned building and his old custodial closet. In that closet? Gallons of pine-scented cleaner—cleaner that he would eventually use to douse his victims."

[Cut to a grid of four photos: a young man, smiling and giving a thumbs up; a middle-aged woman standing in front of a palm tree; a handsome teenage boy in a football jersey; a professional headshot of a police officer in uniform.]

@RealTrueCrimeKid: "By the time the Janitor's reign of terror had ended, he'd claimed four victims: video rental clerk DJ Cartwright, mail carrier Mary Ellen Spakalitis, high school student Levon Brakes, and Edgar Mills chief of police Bill Van Dyne. For his crimes, Kershaw was ultimately sentenced to four consecutive life sentences at Bay State Maximum Security Penitentiary. If the victims' loved ones can take solace in anything, it's that Bruce Philip Kershaw will die behind bars."

CHAPTER FIVE: JOEY

When Joey looks back on that night, it's as a bystander, someone who witnessed an awful event but wasn't directly involved, the driver of the first car to come across a horrible crash.

In reality, he knows he played more of a central role than that. He'll never fully forget the vivid horror of finding Levon's body or the awful drive to the Van Dyne house with the twins and the chaotic scene they found there. Of course he gave a detailed statement to police, and there was even talk of him testifying in court, but that never amounted to anything. Somehow the story of his involvement wasn't picked up by the media, and he was able to slip out of the spotlight before anyone really seemed to notice that he'd been there at all.

Thinking back on it now, it's amazing that he managed to come out of the entire episode basically unscathed. In some ways it was likely just self-preservation. He saw how damaged the twins and Levi were, floating like ghosts through the hallways of Edgar Mills High when they finally returned, and he knew he wanted to avoid that kind of trauma. But it was more than that. He was a teenager trying to figure out what his life would look like, dealing with the burgeoning, terrifying realization that he was gay, and determined to become the person *he* needed to be. He knew instinctively that he couldn't afford to become tied to this tragedy.

So he thanked his lucky stars that he and his family had slipped through unharmed and unrecognized, kept his head down, and focused on his schoolwork. As soon as he graduated, he headed for Cambridge and MIT, and the whole thing slipped behind him.

It had never been his story, after all.

Which makes it all the more bizarre to find himself entering Bay State Maximum Security Penitentiary to meet with one of the most enigmatic serial killers in Massachusetts history.

He would have been an asshole to say no, but he'd be lying if he didn't admit some real curiosity about the whole thing. What does Kershaw *want*?

After a quick briefing with Corvallis and Nash Young, he and the twins are ushered into a nondescript room with a sofa and a couple of armchairs and a television mounted in the corner near the ceiling playing ESPN on mute.

"Make yourselves comfortable," says the guard who has accompanied them. "We'll be back with the inmate shortly."

"Where will he be sitting?" asks Alice nervously.

The guard shrugs. "He'll sit in one of the chairs, I guess."

He leaves and Sam drops onto the sofa. "Weird shit, am I right? Do they expect us to hang out and watch *Seinfeld* reruns together?"

Despite her wisecracking, Joey can tell that she's nervous. Alice takes a seat next to her and Joey takes one of the armchairs. Nobody speaks. Even Sam appears struck quiet by the reality of the meeting they're about to have.

Fortunately, they don't have long to wait. Just a few minutes pass before the door opens again, and then there he is, the monster himself, Bruce Philip Kershaw: the Janitor.

A different guard, wearing an incongruously cheerful expression, leads him into the room, directing him to a chair across from them, directly underneath the television. Kershaw is wearing chains on his wrists and ankles, and the guard uses them to lock him to his chair, then grabs a remote from a side table and turns off the TV.

Joey regards Kershaw curiously. He didn't attend the trial, so he hasn't seen Kershaw in person since he worked as a school janitor, and he's much smaller than Joey remembers. He's slight and frail looking, with sagging jowls and a thin flop of gray hair. This morning he revisited what he knows about this case, skimming Wikipedia and reading through a few blog posts and old newspaper articles. The pictures accompanying them—the photo of Kershaw being brought into the courtroom, his affectless mug shot, and a school ID photo in which he looks manic and wide-eyed and unhinged—are much more chilling than the insubstantial little man sitting in front of them.

"Okay, then," the guard says as he makes his way to the door. "If you guys need anything, I'll be out in the hallway."

"Wait," says Alice. "You're not staying? You're leaving us alone with him?"

She is going out of her way to avoid looking at Kershaw even though he's sitting just a few feet away from her. Sam, on the other hand, is staring so hard at him that she seems to have forgotten how to blink. Joey thinks lasers might very well shoot out of her eyes and incinerate Kershaw on the spot.

"You've got nothing to worry about with old BK," says the guard, smiling. "He's the best-behaved prisoner in the entire joint." He smiles fondly at the prisoner.

Sam scoffs at this. "BK," she says to the old man. "Cute. Is that your nickname? Do they put it on your birthday cakes?"

"Sam," says Alice. "Don't antagonize him."

Sam just shakes her head in disgust. "Look at him," she says, contempt dripping from her voice. "He doesn't have a spine. If anyone should be afraid of anyone, it's him who should be afraid of us."

The guard's cheerful smile instantly disappears. "Do I need to be worried about this?" he says.

"No," says Joey quickly. "We just want to hear what the man has to say and then we'll be out of here."

The guard looks skeptical, his glance flipping between Sam and Kershaw as he measures the situation, and for a moment Joey is convinced the plug is going to be pulled on the entire thing. But then the guard relaxes. "Okay," he says. "I'll be right outside."

He leaves, and the four of them are finally alone together.

The instant the guard leaves, Kershaw's demeanor changes dramatically, his hangdog expression shifting into something resembling a sneer. Without warning, he lunges forward, the chains rattling as they hold him back.

"Boo," he says, before bursting into laughter and dropping back into his chair.

Joey feels a shiver of uncertainty run down his back. Beside him, Alice actually yelps.

"I'm going to get the guard," she says. She stands, but Sam reaches up and grabs her arm.

"Let the freak talk," says Sam. "If we don't hear him out, we'll never get past this. He can't move."

"Your sister's right," says Kershaw, rattling the chains to show he's restricted. "I didn't mean to scare you, I'm just playing around."

Reluctantly, Alice sits, but she pulls her chair back to widen the gap between herself and Kershaw.

"No more games," says Sam.

"Yes, ma'am," says the prisoner, adopting a little boy's voice that makes Joey's skin crawl. He's beginning to wonder if he made a mistake coming here. What happened to the model prisoner?

"You killed our father," says Alice. She's looking directly at Kershaw for the first time.

"I did," he says. He shrugs and looks away. He clears his throat. "What, you want an apology?"

Alice opens her mouth to respond, but Sam holds up a hand. "We didn't come here for apologies," she says. "We came here because a kid is dead, and the police asked us to help them, and we feel an obligation. We don't need to waste time on what happened back then."

Kershaw gives her a sly look and lets out a low, knowing chuckle. "But what if it's all connected?" he says.

Joey feels a frisson of exhilaration at the words and leans forward in his chair. "What do you mean?"

Kershaw drops his gaze, smiling coyly. "It's just a question. I'm only speculating."

"Listen," says Sam, and Joey can tell that she's reached the end of her rope. "I'm going to count to three. Either tell us what you have to say or we're fucking leaving."

Kershaw doesn't make her count. "A little bird told me that there are some . . . similarities, between this murder and the deaths back then."

He looks at them as if waiting for confirmation. When none of them speak, he continues.

"If this was a copycat murder," he says, "it makes me wonder. That's all."

"Wonder about what?" asks Alice.

"It makes me wonder if it was the same copycat who was operating back in 2000."

Joey hears Alice gasp, and his own mind scrambles to understand what Kershaw is saying.

"What do you mean by that?" he asks.

"You disappoint me, Mr. O'Day," says Kershaw. "You're supposed to be some kind of computer genius, yet you're telling me you can't figure out such a basic equation? Let me spell it out for you. I didn't commit all the murders that were pinned on me, and I think that there's a decent chance that the copycat might be up to their old tricks."

Sam scoffs. "Cut the crap," she says. "They aren't going to let you out of prison. You are a cold-blooded serial killer. It's a bit late to change your story now."

"I've never told my story," says Kershaw calmly. "The police and the lawyers and the media told *a* story, but I kept my own story to myself, and I can promise you it hasn't changed."

"Okay," says Joey. "Just to be sure we're clear, you're saying you killed *some* but not all of them. So which ones *did* you kill?"

Infuriatingly, Kershaw only shrugs.

"We know you killed our father," says Sam. "You can't sneak out of that. But the old lady? The video clerk? Levon?"

"I can't give you any more details," says Kershaw. He grins devilishly. "It's up to you to figure out who I killed and who I didn't."

Sam throws her hands up in frustration. "This is all just a game to you, isn't it?"

"Why us?" asks Alice. "Why didn't you just tell the police about this?"

Kershaw's demeanor grows serious. "Because I know they wouldn't give this a second thought, but I think the three of you will. I expect you'll leave this room asking whether what you believe happened is actually true. You can't help yourselves."

Alice stands, and as she begins to speak, Joey realizes she's shaking with rage.

"You just wanted to mess with us," she says. "You're admitting it right now. You wanted to plant an evil little seed, just for kicks. You're a sick fuck, but I think you know that."

She turns and leaves the room. After a long, scathing glance at Kershaw, Sam follows.

Joey stands, about to follow them out, but he freezes when Kershaw speaks again. "I wanted you to come with them because I know you're rational. You'll do the thinking that they're too emotional to manage."

Joey turns back to the man. "You mean because they're women? Jesus."

"No," says Kershaw calmly. "Because I killed their father. I didn't take anything from you. I hope you can help them, because I don't trust anyone other than the three of you to figure this out."

* * *

"Well, now we know I was right," says Corvallis. "The guy is full of shit. What a waste of time and resources."

They're in a briefing room in the prison's administrative wing, filling Nash and Corvallis in on their meeting.

"Shouldn't we consider the possibility he's telling the truth?" asks Joey.

"He's not telling the truth," says Corvallis. "He's either desperate for a new angle to help him drum up an appeal or he's looking for attention. Either way, he's a scam artist, and I am just really sorry that I put the three of you in front of him."

She glances at Nash with an expression that doesn't indicate regret at all, and Joey gets the distinct impression she's happy that things didn't turn out the way he expected they would. This is some kind of win for her.

"It's okay," says Alice. "I actually feel better now than I did going into the room."

Joey feels differently.

"It just doesn't make sense to me," he says. "If Kershaw was trying to use this as an excuse to get out of prison, wouldn't he have just said the copycat committed *all* of the murders back then? He even admitted in the room that he killed Chief Van Dyne. What does he hope to gain from this kind of lie? It doesn't make sense."

"It doesn't need to make sense," says Sam. "He's a homicidal maniac."

"I know that," Joey replies, trying to explain himself. "I just think it's worth examining all options, and one of them is that he's telling the truth, or at least partly telling the truth. How did he know about Justin Beagle in the first place? It hadn't even gone public yet."

"You'd be surprised how much information leaks into prisons," says Corvallis. "All it takes is for one guard to be buddies with a cop who has some inside information, and word trickles around. Gossip is currency around these kinds of places."

"I did some digging around online this morning," Joey admits, almost reluctantly. "There are some rumors out there that would back up what Kershaw was telling us."

"Let me guess," says Corvallis drily. "Reddit detectives. We love them in law enforcement."

Joey gives Alice an apologetic look before elaborating. "People say that the timing around Levon's death doesn't line up."

"What do you mean, the timing?" asks Sam.

"The state's case claims that Kershaw drove to the elementary school to retrieve his backpack *after* receiving the twins' email," Joey explains. "At the school he unexpectedly came face-to-face with Levon, killed him, and then drove home to his apartment, where he dropped off the bag of evidence, and *then* emailed the twins to cancel on them before heading to the Van Dyne home, where he killed Chief Van Dyne."

"Yeah," says Sam, "so?"

"So the theory—and this is *just* a theory—is that it wouldn't make sense to do everything in that order, and the timing would have been almost impossible."

"The key word being 'almost,'" says Nash. "I drove that route myself with some detectives during the investigation, and we were able to pull it off. It was tight, but we did it."

"So you also think Kershaw is lying, Nash?" asks Alice.

Nash nods. "Yeah, I do. The simplest solution is the best solution nine times out of ten, and in this case the simplest solution is that Kershaw did it, prosecutors proved it, and until today he has never once tried to push back and make an alternative argument for himself. I'm just sorry that the three of you had to face that asshole for us to figure this out. I should have never let myself believe that he had something worthwhile to tell you. What a total waste of time."

"You see this all the time with these guys," says Corvallis. "The implications of what life in prison really means begin to sink in and they start revising history, hoping some alternative theory will stick to the wall and set them free."

She stands and gathers up her papers. "I think the best takeaway is that we've ruled something out here. If there is a connection between his crimes and this crime, it's surface level, someone using the Janitor's notoriety to cover his tracks. That's been our primary theory, and this just helps us narrow some things down as we try to track down the culprit. And on that note, we have a lot of work to get back to, so you're free to head out and live your lives again."

From the corner of his eye, Joey catches Nash open and then close his mouth, as if he was about to say something but thought better of it.

There's a slightly awkward round of handshakes with Corvallis, and then Nash sees them out of the building.

"I'm sorry about that," he says when they're standing outside. "I thought it was worth a shot, but I guess I just ended up reopening some old wounds."

"It's okay, Nash," says Alice. Joey notices that she seems a lot less uptight than when she was going into the room. "I think maybe it helped a little to see him in person. He really is a pathetic creature."

Sam nods. "You can say that again. Now we can shove him to the back of our minds and forget about him forever."

"I just wish he had something valuable to tell us," says Nash.

Alice reaches out and puts a hand on his shoulder. "You followed your gut. Dad would have been proud of you."

Nash drops his head, thoughtful. "Maybe if we can catch whoever did this, I'll have earned that."

He's about to turn away but stops. "I don't pretend to understand how the three of you worked things out back in the day, but if any theories or hunches occur to you at any point . . . I'm all ears, okay?" He grins wryly. "I mean, I have three of the greatest teen detectives in history here; I'd be crazy not to listen to them, right?"

"We're hardly teens anymore," says Alice.

"You're only as old as you feel," says Nash with a wink. Then he turns back to the door, lifting an arm in a goodbye gesture as he disappears inside.

Joey turns back to the twins.

"Well, it would have been nice to catch up under different circumstances," he says.

"Look me up if you're ever in L.A.," says Sam.

He nods. "I'll do that." They both know he won't.

Without warning, Alice steps in for a hug, squeezing him tight.

"The teen detectives," she says, and there's a note of sadness in her voice. "Our final case over before it begins."

"We never actually worked a case together," says Joey. "I wasn't really a detective. Not like the two of you."

"You played your part in putting that asshole behind bars," says Sam. "We all did, even if it came with a price. Now we can finally get on with our lives."

But as Joey walks across the parking lot, it isn't closure he's feeling but something closer to distraction. And as he climbs into his car and pulls out of the parking lot and gets back on the road, something the Janitor said to him hums in his mind.

I hope you can help them.

CHAPTER SIX:
SAM

"So," says Sam, once they're a few miles away from the penitentiary and have both had a chance to process what just happened, "what do you think? Do you buy his story?"

Alice laughs. "Not even a little bit." Her expression shifts and she turns away from the wheel to examine Sam's expression. "Why, do you?"

"No," says Sam. "He's a pathetic little man grasping for attention. But I'm glad I came. I'm glad we did that."

"Me too," says Alice. "It was really intense to be in the same room with him, but also kind of satisfying. I feel lighter all of a sudden. Does that sound crazy?"

Sam shakes her head. "No. I feel the same way. I think we were both desperate for some closure. Now I just want to go back to your house, pour a big glass of wine, and pester that nephew of mine for all the high school gossip."

Alice doesn't respond, and when Sam turns to look at her, she's smiling awkwardly ahead at the road.

"What?" asks Sam, although she already knows what her sister is thinking.

"Speaking of closure," says Alice, "I wonder if you have any interest in making one more stop before we go home?"

Sam is definitely *not* interested in making that particular stop, but something about her sister's voice taps into her well-hidden reserve of guilt. She sighs. "Fine," she says. "I've already faced one monster from my past today. I might as well face the other one. Take me to Grey Gardens."

Alice parks across the street from 15 Bluebonnet Lane, and Sam climbs out of the car and stares at her childhood home. From this distance, the large Craftsman bungalow prompts a wave of nostalgia: the huge old chestnut tree in the front yard where she and Sam spent hours on the swing their father hung for them, the wide front porch where her father liked to sit with a beer at the end of a long day.

It's only upon closer examination that the neglect becomes obvious. Peeling paint. Empty, weed-filled flower beds. Moss growing in patches on the roof. There are a million reasons why Joanna Van Dyne should have left this house years ago, but for some reason she insists on staying.

The last time Sam saw her mother was a few years ago, when Alice convinced her to return to Edgar Mills for Christmas. The experience was not pleasant, and she barely made it through Christmas dinner intact. She hasn't been back since.

She knows that their mother struggles with intense PTSD and that the things she witnessed on the night their father died loom large at the front of their mother's brain. She has compassion for her mother and she isn't willing to cut her out entirely, so she still sends birthday cards and Christmas gifts and struggles through a monthly phone call, but she's done her best to distance herself emotionally.

So it's with a lot of trepidation that Sam follows her sister through a tangle of overgrown grass to the front porch.

"Levi and Will used to take care of the lawn," says Alice. "But she asked them to stop, God knows why. I've stopped trying to understand her."

"You're sure she doesn't know I'm here?" Sam asks. "It might set her off."

Alice gives her head a firm, confident shake. "No. She avoids the news like the plague. She only watches streaming, and she stays away from the internet. She doesn't even have a smartphone. I doubt she even knows what year it is. We'll just tell her you were in Boston for business and decided to surprise us."

She pushes open the door and steps into the house.

"Mom!" yells Alice. "Where are you? I've brought a surprise!"

There's no reply, and Sam stares down the hallway with mounting horror. Alice has warned her that their mother has become a hoarder, but she's still caught off guard. The house, once her mother's pride and joy, neatly organized and sparkling clean, full of sunlight streaming through windows to kiss houseplants and shine on immaculately scrubbed floors, is now thick with the funk of neglect.

The houseplants are still there, sitting on their windowsills, but they are long dead, just desiccated husks and dried leaves poking out of pots. There are boxes and random piles of things everywhere, and stacks of old books and newspapers covering every other available surface. The house doesn't stink, beyond the flat, dull smell of old paper, and it doesn't seem particularly dirty, but it has a distinct aura of disorder.

Sam stops in the dining room and stares at the antique china cabinet, still stocked with their grandmother's best dinner set. Her eyes move to the middle of three drawers, where her father's gun used to live in a small, locked box. For the first time since the night her father died, she wonders what happened to the Colt. Is it sitting in a plastic bag deep in an evidence room, or was it returned to her mother only to be tucked back into its drawer?

"Mom?" Alice calls again, and Sam picks up on a note of trepidation in her sister's voice that sets off alarm bells.

"We should go," she says. "She's obviously not—"

The girls jump in unison at the sound of something smashing against the wall in the kitchen, followed by a loud, guttural scream that goes on for a lot longer than it should.

"Oh, for crying out loud," says Alice, marching toward the kitchen door. For a split second Sam considers calling an Uber and having it take her straight to the airport. Instead, she follows Alice into the kitchen.

Their mother is on the floor, surrounded by broken pottery. Perched on a chair at the kitchen table, looking like he wishes he could disappear into thin air, is Perry Lemire.

Alice moves to crouch next to their mother, approaching cautiously as if she's examining an injured animal. Joanna looks dazed and unmoored, but then her eyes lock on Sam.

"So you decided to visit me after all," she says.

Sam pins Perry with a glare. "You told her I was here? You couldn't leave that to me?"

Perry doesn't answer; he just squirms uncomfortably in his chair.

"That's not all he told me!" says Joanna, her voice shifting fluidly from manic to angry. "In fact, he had a fine story to share about the two of you going to see that monster without even having the courtesy to warn me first."

"What the hell, Perry?" Alice stares at the lawyer in disbelief.

"What the hell indeed," says Joanna, swatting away Alice's hands and getting to her feet. "You two and your stupid detective nonsense. If you'd only left well enough alone and stuck with figure skating or volleyball or needlepoint, your father would still be here."

Sam closes her eyes. This has been a common theme through the years since their dad died, but it never stops stinging.

"Maybe we would have stuck to figure skating, or volleyball, or fucking *needlepoint* if you hadn't been such a frigging stage mother," she says. She turns to Perry. "Are you proud of yourself for shoving your nose into our business?"

The man clutches at his wide, dated necktie. "I thought your mother deserved to know what was happening," he says weakly.

"Oh yeah?" Sam asks. "How did that work out?"

"Don't talk to him like that," Joanna snaps. "He's a trusted friend and our family lawyer."

Sam scoffs. "You aren't my lawyer," she says to Perry. "And I think it's about time you canceled your association with this family. I don't feel comfortable with you involved in our affairs."

"You have no say over this, Sam," says Joanna. "This is my business."

"Oh, I think I have plenty of say," says Sam. "Unless old Perry here wants me to make an official complaint to the state bar about how loose and free he's been with confidential information, he'll agree right now to step away from whatever kind of parasocial arrangement the two of you have going on."

"Sam," says Alice, "let's take it easy for a minute. We're all just a bit upset."

"No," says Perry, standing, "she's right. I overstepped my bounds. I'll see myself out. I'll be in touch, Joanna."

He exits the kitchen and walks down the hallway to the foyer.

"You're fired!" Sam yells as the front door closes.

"Why are you so hostile towards Perry?" Joanna asks.

"You mean beside the fact that he's feeding you confidential information?" asks Sam. "How about the fact that the guy is a creep? He was always poking around after Dad died, showing up unannounced and hovering on the edges."

"He did a lot for this family," says Joanna. "He's been my only friend for many years. It's so typical of *you* to turn up out of the blue after who knows how many years and start bossing me around. I bet this was all planned for one of your TV shows, wasn't it? You wanted to stir up some shit so you can sell our dirty laundry to the highest bidder."

Sam feels herself heading in the direction of a meltdown and forces herself to hold it in. She moves to the back door and shoves through it onto the porch, slamming it behind her. She grabs onto the railing with both hands, her jaw clenched and her eyes shut tight. Inside the house, she can hear the muffled sounds of her mother speaking and Alice soothing her in even, quiet tones, and she longs for the calm, peaceful minimalism of her condo.

"You okay?"

Her eyes snap open at the unfamiliar voice. It takes her a moment to find where it's coming from. On the other side of the fence at the back of the yard, partially shrouded by her mother's overgrown willow tree, is a boy. He's short and slight, with sandy blond hair and thick eyeglasses.

She considers waving him off, telling him she's fine and walking around the side of the house to wait in Alice's car, but she realizes she's desperate for a distraction. She walks down from the porch and crosses the yard to the boy. At first glance she thought he was just a kid, but up close she thinks he might be a bit older than that, maybe thirteen or fourteen. He also looks vaguely familiar, although she can't place him.

"I'm fine," she says.

From behind her comes another piercing scream and the sound of more dishes being broken.

"Sounds like your mom isn't fine," he says. He glances back at the house behind him and then drops his voice conspiratorially. "My house gets like that sometimes. At least you can leave when you feel like it. I assume you have a place of your own in Los Angeles?"

She squints at him. "How do you know that? How do you know Joanna is my mom and I live in Los Angeles?"

He laughs. "You're Sam Van Dyne, right? One of the Van Dyne twins? Alice still lives in Edgar Mills, but you've been on the West Coast since you moved there right out of high school. I'm a big fan."

Sam stares at the boy more closely and suddenly it comes to her.

"Oh my god," she says. "You're that kid from the internet. True Crime Kid."

"Real True Crime Kid," he corrects. He grins, clearly pleased that she recognized him. "Evan, in the real world. Are you a subscriber?"

"Hell no," she says. His smile drops and she softens her reaction. "I don't have TikTok and I'm not into true crime, for obvious reasons. But I saw one of your videos about my family recently."

If she's expecting an apologetic or even sheepish response, she's disappointed. "Yeah!" he says excitedly. "My videos on the Janitor killings are blowing up! I've gained almost a hundred thousand new followers since I started posting them!"

"Are you serious?" asks Sam, taken aback.

"There are lots of super-young influencers," he says, slightly indignant, "even in true crime."

"Is that what you are?" she asks. "An influencer?"

He considers this. "I consider myself more of a storyteller. My dad used to live in Edgar Mills, before he met my mother. He told me the story when we moved here and I did a Wikipedia search. After that, I kind of fell down a rabbit hole. There is so much information about the case online. Did you know there's even a dedicated Wiki? You can find crime scene photos, full court transcripts, you name it. I have a ton of material to work with, and since I'm here in town it's easy to get cool footage."

"Where were you before?" she asks, hoping to change the subject.

"Upstate New York. My dad got laid off from his job and we decided to move. I say 'we' but I didn't have a lot of say in the matter.

What about you? Are you in town to figure out what happened to Justin Beagle?"

The question catches Sam off guard. "No. What would give you that idea?"

"I don't know," he says, shrugging. "Maybe because you haven't been back to town in a long time, and now the first murder in twenty-five years happens, and all of a sudden here you are. Pretty big coincidence, don't you think?"

"You sound like you're interviewing me," says Sam.

"Would you be open to an actual interview?" asks Evan, without skipping a beat. "On camera?"

"Not in a million years," she says. Something occurs to her. "You're not planning on posting videos about Justin Beagle, are you?"

"Why shouldn't I?" he asks, and Sam can't help but marvel at how self-confident this kid is.

"Well for one thing, the police are still in the middle of their investigation.

"That never stopped you from asking questions when you were in high school," he counters.

"I was older than you," she says, "and besides, you probably know better than anyone how that turned out. If I were you, I'd stick to the history lessons."

He considers this before pushing back. "I'm not the only person in Edgar Mills who is obsessing about what happened to Justin, you know. There are a lot of rumors circulating."

"Oh yeah? What are people saying?"

His eyes glitter and she can tell he's picked up on her poorly veiled curiosity. "Oh, you know, typical stuff. That he had a secret lover, or he was addicted to drugs, or he owed money to some bad guys and he got got." He pauses, weighing his next words like a ball before tossing them. "The big one is that there's some connection to the Janitor."

He watches her carefully, waiting for her to respond.

"Of course people are going to say that," she says. She's not about to point out that she's heard that *from* the Janitor. "Which is why you should keep your nose out of things and avoid spreading unsubstantiated rumors. You have a responsibility with that many followers."

"Come on," he says, "are you telling me you've never questioned the official narrative?"

"The official narrative?" she repeats. "What is this, QAnon?"

Evan appears unfazed by her sarcasm. "I'm just saying, the guy never testified, never gave an interview, never said a single thing about a single thing. There are lots of unanswered questions floating around out there."

Sam knows she should disengage herself, but she can't help it. "What kinds of unanswered questions?"

"Levon Brakes for one," he says. "It would have been impossible for Kershaw to kill him, get home, and then make it to the Van Dyne house in time to kill the chief."

"Not impossible," says Sam, the memory of their conversation with Nash still fresh in her mind. "The police did the drive and proved it was possible."

Joey shrugs. "You'd know better than me," he says, in a tone that suggests he doesn't believe that for a minute. "Did you know that his stuff is just sitting there?" he asks.

"Justin Beagle's stuff?" asks Sam, confused.

"No, Bruce Philip Kershaw's," he says. "His apartment is still just locked up tight with all his crap still in it, untouched."

"That's not true," says Sam. This is the kind of urban legend that would circulate in a town like Edgar Mills. "He had to sell all his properties to cover the civil suits."

He shakes his head and smiles at this, like the cat who swallowed the canary. "That's true, but half of the properties his parents left behind when they died actually went to his sister, and his apartment just happened to be inside one of them. Apartment 308, the Santa María building."

She raises an eyebrow. "How did you figure that out?"

"I sent a few emails to his sister, pretending to be an insurance representative. She confirmed the apartment was still unoccupied. It wasn't all that complicated."

Sam is impressed despite herself. "That's some pretty good detective work."

"Thank you," he says. "I would love to get inside there. It would make for a killer video. But it would be pretty stupid to post evidence of a B and E."

She's about to ask him for more details, but their attention is pulled away by the sound of a battered old minivan pulling into the driveway of his house. When Evan turns back to look at her, she realizes that his expression has changed dramatically. The precocious, confident young man of a moment ago has been replaced by someone timid, almost nervous.

An adult couple climbs out of the van: a tall, thin bald man and a plain-looking woman in a drab housedress who is even shorter than Evan.

"Come help with these groceries!" the man calls over in a sharp, unfriendly voice as he moves to pop the trunk.

Evan turns back to Sam and gives her a small, apologetic smile. "Nice to meet you," he says before turning and running to meet his parents at the car. His head bowed, Sam watches as he grabs several bags of groceries and then follows his mother into the house. The father lingers by the car for a moment, and once his wife and son have gone inside, he turns and stares in Sam's direction. She turns away, pretending to examine her mother's neglected garden, and when she looks back, he's disappeared as well.

Back inside the house, Sam finds that the broken dishes have been cleaned up and there's a pot of tea sitting on the table. Even more surprising is her mother, who seems to have pulled herself together and is sitting at the table, cradling a mug. She smiles brightly as Sam enters the kitchen.

"There's my darling," she says. She pats the table. "Come have a seat and catch me up."

Sam looks at Alice, who is wiping down the counter. "Did you give her a shot of horse tranquilizer?"

Joanna frowns. "Okay, that's enough. You know how easy I get set off by anything to do with . . . you know. Now, come and sit down with your mother."

"Okay, Mom," says Sam. "I accept your apology." She sits at the table and reaches to pour herself a cup of tea.

"Your sister was about to tell me about your meeting with . . ."

"Kershaw?" asks Sam.

"That man," says her mother. "If I'd known about it—if Perry had called me *before* instead of after the fact—I would have put a stop to it."

"No you wouldn't have, Mom," says Sam. "Because Alice and I are grown adults with agency."

Joanna ignores this. "I've lived the past quarter century in fear of that man coming back here to finish the job he started."

"He's in prison, Mom," says Alice. "He can't hurt you."

Joanna doesn't look convinced. "Well, are you going to tell me what he had to say?"

The sisters exchange a look. "Is this going to set you off again?" Sam asks.

Joanna stands, and for a moment Sam thinks she's going to storm out of the room, but instead she walks to the refrigerator and pulls a bottle of vodka from the freezer. Without a word, she pulls some glasses from the cupboard, pours three healthy drinks, and brings them to the table.

She sits and takes a slug. "Okay," she says. "Lay it on me."

"He didn't really say anything so much as imply it," says Alice.

"What did he imply?" Joanna has fixed her daughters with a steady gaze. She takes another drink.

"That he didn't kill all of the victims," says Sam. "Of course, he didn't have any details about who he killed and who he didn't. He was just talking out of his ass."

"That's absurd," says Joanna. "He killed your father in cold blood. I was there, remember?"

"He didn't dispute that he killed Dad," says Alice. "Just that he didn't kill all of the rest of them."

Sam looks at her surprised. "You're not falling for his story, are you?"

"Of course not," says Alice. "I'm just repeating what he said."

Joanna slams her empty glass onto the table and reaches for the bottle. "I don't care what he said. I was there. That man is exactly where he belongs, and I hope he rots."

"Tell us what happened that night, Mom," says Sam. From across the table, Alice shoots her a warning look, but Sam has never heard her mother talk about that night, and she isn't going to let the opportunity to learn more about her father's final moments pass her by.

"You know all of this already from the trial," says Joanna.

"Yeah," says Sam. "But I've never heard it directly from you." She turns to Alice. "Have you?"

Alice just gives a gentle shake of her head. Joanna purses her lips, but after a moment, relents.

"I was in the kitchen, cleaning the pantry, when I heard the doorbell. Your father called out that he was going to answer it, and then suddenly there was a commotion."

"What do you mean, 'a commotion'?" asks Sam.

Joanna shuts her eyes, remembering. "The door banged open, and I heard heavy footsteps and an unfamiliar raised voice. I was about to come out to see what was going on when I heard your father yell from the door to stay exactly where I was. I froze just inside the door and I could hear them talking but I couldn't make out what they were saying."

"Could you tell it was a man?" asks Sam.

"Yes," says her mother, a note of intense weariness entering her voice. "It was Kershaw. But their voices began low and gradually became more heated. Then I heard him yell, 'Stay in there, Joanna!' and I heard a shot, and when I pushed through from the kitchen, your father was on the floor and Kershaw was running out through the front door. I went to him and the blood was just . . . it was pouring out. I dropped to the floor and pulled him to me and I was aware of sirens and people yelling . . . At some point Perry showed up, and then you girls were there, and it was all just . . . chaos. I'm telling you girls, he's an evil man and he killed your father, and that's all any of us need to know."

A chill descends on the room, and Sam realizes that Joanna has shared as much as she's going to. Alice deftly guides them on to safer subject matter, and they scrape through a half an hour of painful small talk before they finally manage to make their exit.

Joanna follows them to the door, where she gives Sam a brief hug. She pulls back and reaches up to cup Sam's cheek in her hand for just a second.

"You'll be in touch," she says.

Sam nods. "Yeah, Mom, of course." She's about to turn away when she remembers something. "Oh, I see somebody finally moved into the McCoy house."

"The Stevenses," says Joanna, her lips pursing. "Parson and Isobel. They keep to themselves, and I don't blame them. The fighting that goes on over there, you wouldn't believe it. You can hear them screaming at each other and slamming doors at all hours. You met them?"

"I met their son," says Sam.

Joanna smiles. "Evan. He's a different story. Smart as a whip and could chat the hind legs off a grasshopper. Precocious. I feel bad for him, so I pay him to do small chores around the house. Change light bulbs and so on. He had his father come over one day when the dishwasher was on the fritz. He fixed it, but I didn't care for his attitude. He barely spoke, grunted when I offered him a drink. Couldn't get out of here fast enough. He was clearly annoyed with the boy for asking him to help."

Sam thinks back to how quickly Evan's demeanor shifted when his parents returned home. She might have been imagining it, but she could have sworn the man gave her a dirty look.

"What about the mother?" she asks.

"I've spoken to Isobel exactly once," says Joanna. "I introduced myself across the back fence a few days after they arrived. Caught her by surprise, I think. She managed to choke out a few words before disappearing into the house, and she's avoided eye contact with me ever since."

"Sounds like something's off in that house," says Alice. "The poor kid."

Sam feels a bit bad for the way she dismissed Evan's interest in the Janitor case. From the sound of things, the kid just needs an outlet, and she figures true crime isn't any worse than violent video games.

She half wishes she'd had a few more minutes to ask him about the rumors he claimed are circulating around town, but she knows it's for the best. Her short-lived involvement in the Justin Beagle murder case is over, and she intends to keep it that way.

CHAPTER SEVEN: ALICE

"I don't know how you handle it," says Sam as they drive back to Alice's house. "I don't know how you can just take that kind of abuse."

"It's fine," says Alice. "She needs somebody around, and that just happens to be me."

"Why does she act this way?" Sam closes her eyes and presses her head back against the headrest. "Doesn't she realize that she'd be so much happier if she was able to just get out of her own way?"

"She's grieving," says Alice. "She'll be grieving until the day she dies."

"We didn't have the luxury of grieving for that long," says Sam. "We were forced to move on with our lives."

Alice pulls into the driveway of her house and parks. She looks across at her sister. "It's not like that, Sam. You have to see things through her eyes. She'll never get over what happened to Dad, so there's no sense trying to change her."

"You're so Zen," says Sam. "I thought I was supposed to be the chill one."

"When it comes to Mom, Zen is the only approach worth taking," says Alice.

As they climb out of the car, a voice calls out from across the street.

"Alice!"

They turn to see a tall, lithe woman in athletic wear and a full face of makeup wave and then cross over to them in a light jog.

"Hi, Drea," says Alice. "This is my sister, Samantha. Sam, this is my neighbor Drea Parker."

"Oh my gosh, hi," says Drea, pulling off a Lycra glove to extend a hand. "So nice to finally meet the other half of the dynamic duo! Are you here to help solve a mystery?" She laughs cheerfully at her own joke.

"Just a quick visit to see family," says Sam, and Alice can tell she's reaffirming her decision to avoid following in Alice's suburban footsteps.

"God, so tacky of me," says Drea, grimacing. "I wasn't even thinking about poor Justin."

"Did you know him?" asks Sam.

"No, but I have friends in common with his mother." Drea drops her voice to a respectful whisper. "It's just so awful. Do you know they're saying he might have been involved in organized crime?"

"Sounds like there are lots of rumors floating around," says Sam. "We should be careful which ones we spread."

Drea looks taken aback but quickly recovers. "One hundred percent. Detective's rules, am I right?" She drops into a husky lower register. "Stick to the truth!" She turns back to Alice. "Anyway, that's kind of why I wanted to chat. There's a meal train going around for the Beagle family. If you're interested, you can find the sign-up on my Facebook."

"Thanks," says Alice. "I'll do that."

"Okay, I'd better head out before it gets any darker," says Drea. "I'm going to try to squeeze a couple of miles in before I have to make dinner for the gang. Have a great night, you suspicious bitches!" She winks and then turns and sprints coltishly away down the street.

"Jesus Christ," says Sam as they watch her disappear around the corner.

"She's fine," says Alice. "A bit high-strung, but nice enough."

"That woman is far from fine," says Sam, moving to grab her luggage from the Suburban.

For the first time in as long as Alice can remember, everyone eats together in the dining room. To his credit, Levi has come home from work early to cook for them, and Will, usually anxious to retreat to his room with a plate, cheerfully plunks down at the table next to Sam.

Alice is happy that they're both so fond of her sister, but as she watches them interact with her so willingly, cracking jokes, asking about life in Los Angeles, and opening up to her questions about what's been happening in their lives, she can't help but feel a bit stung. Is it her fault that the house is usually so stale and flat and joyless?

"Will," Sam asks suddenly, "do you know this Evan Stevens kid? The one who lives behind Grandma?"

Will looks slightly uncomfortable, and Alice's attention perks up. "Not really. I mean, I know who he is, but we aren't friends or anything." He pauses, debating whether to say something. "He wanted to know about you guys."

"What?" asks Alice. "Why?"

"He has a TikTok channel," Sam explains. "True crime stuff. He's been doing videos about . . . the Janitor."

"Jesus Christ," says Levi. "Tell me you didn't talk to him, Will."

"No, of course I didn't," says Will. "I wouldn't anyway, but even if I wanted to it's not like I know a lot about that stuff, just that you were kind of famous."

"We weren't famous," says Alice. "We had some notoriety for a while, and I wouldn't wish that on anyone. Now can we please talk about something else?"

"It was your mother's biggest dream to be famous," says Sam.

Will looks at Alice, genuinely surprised. "Famous for what?"

Alice waves off the question, suddenly embarrassed. "God, I don't know. I used to talk about it the way people say they want to be an astronaut."

"She was a triple threat," says Sam. "A great actor, dancer, and singer. She made me take singing lessons with her."

"Mom made us take those lessons," says Alice. "She hired some wacky lady to come to the house every week and give us singing lessons. Brenda Regent—you remember her?"

"How could I forget?" says Sam, laughing. "That hair."

"So why didn't you ever pursue it?" asks Will, and Alice can't remember the last time he seemed this interested in her. "Aunt Sam became the famous one."

"Don't remind me," says Sam. "Early aughts reality TV show fame is not the kind of fame I'd wish on anyone."

Alice is surprised when Levi reaches out to take her hand. "Your mom and I decided that staying here in Edgar Mills and raising a family was more rewarding than any kind of fame could ever be."

None of that is true, thinks Alice. There was no decision. There was only a path clearly laid out in front of her one minute and gone like a mirage the next. But she smiles and squeezes Levi's hand back.

"Best decision of my life," she says.

After dinner, the sisters take a bottle of wine downstairs into the rec room, curling up under blankets on the large sectional. Alice finds a '90s music station on YouTube and pours them hearty glasses.

"The guys seem to be doing well," Sam observes.

"It was nice to spend more than five minutes with Will," Alice says. "You should come visit more often: it coaxes him out of his room."

"He's at that stage, hey?"

"I didn't have a stage like that," says Alice. "I just wanted to hang out with my family all the time."

"I did," says Sam, taking a sip. "I couldn't stay in the room with you losers. I think you only played nice because you wanted to show me up."

"That's probably true," says Alice, laughing. "But you *were* a total bitch from fourteen to sixteen. What changed?"

"You know what changed," says Sam. "The blue van."

Alice takes a long sip of her Chardonnay, savoring it as she sinks back into the cushions, remembering their first case. It was like a gift, the way they had found themselves swept up in the mystery, as if the gods had placed it in front of them to help dictate their destiny.

Their father was ripping his hair out trying to pin down the source of a drug supply chain that had been infiltrating Edgar Mills, flooding the area with dirty ecstasy that was starting to make its way into the high school. Some twenty-year-old kid had almost OD'd, and none of the usual low-level dealers who they pulled in for questioning had any idea what was going on.

But one of them—a pot dealer, disgruntled at how quickly his business had fizzled—dropped a clue. He mentioned a blue van, and then, realizing he should have kept his mouth shut, claimed he'd made a mistake and clammed up. Their father—who spent a lot of his evenings in his favorite easy chair, half an eye on the TV as he doodled on the daily newspaper, working through the details of his latest case—wrote BLUE VAN over and over on the paper, and Sam spotted it on his side table the next day and mentioned it to Alice on their walk to school.

Sam always knew that it was all about the story. *Where* had the blue van come from? *When* did it make its deliveries? *How* were the drugs distributed after that?

And Alice always knew that it was all about the characters. *Who* did the van belong to? *Who* was driving it? *Who* were the drugs being delivered to in Edgar Mills?

Their first case seems so quaint now, almost archaic. A drug dealer in a van, no less. But at the time it felt momentous. Doug has teased her about it more than once, calling her a narc as they've passed a joint back and forth in his apartment, but at the time the stakes couldn't have felt higher.

She sits up now, an urgency jabbing at her heart through the soft fog of wine. She remembers the thrill of adventure as they began to work out theories together in their shared bedroom, as they strategically went about breaking the town into a grid, using their mother's little grey Toyota Tercel to patrol and keep track of the various areas. She remembers the intense jolt of energy that had crackled between them when they'd finally spotted the van, the excitement as they'd tracked it, the euphoria of *solving* the crime. Most of all, she remembers the look on their father's face when they presented their findings to him, as he slowly realized they'd figured it out.

She had never felt that good, that proud, that *invincible* in her life.

"Do you ever want to go back and do it all again?" she says.

Sam looks at her askance. "I want the exact opposite of that," she says. "I want to go back and start over and stop the whole thing before it even got going."

Alice waves this off impatiently. "Yeah, I know: of course we wouldn't have engaged with Kershaw. I mean, if none of that had happened and Dad had lived. What if we'd kept going, stuck with it?"

"It would have sucked," says Sam bluntly. "We would have fizzled out and missed out on the chance to become who we were really supposed to be."

Alice isn't so sure. She's a disaffected housewife, straight from central casting. Sam is a washed-up reality TV star with obvious avoidance issues. Would the detective route really have been so much worse?

"Do you miss it at all?" she asks.

Sam considers this. "I miss . . . being young and living in the moment. But I don't really think about what could have been. There's too much water under the bridge."

"It's funny," says Alice. "I hate talking about it. Levi and I never discuss it, and when it comes to Will I just pretend it never happened. It was bad enough that we had to go through it, I don't want to pass it on to him like some kind of traumatic inheritance.

But some days I just feel overwhelmed by all the things I missed out on. It was as if I had this big sparkling future laid out in front of me, and then overnight it all disappeared, and I settled for something different. You know I wouldn't trade being a mom for the world, but sometimes I just wonder what my life would have looked like if things had played out differently."

"What about being a wife?" asks Sam. "Would you trade that?"

Alice shrugs. "I honestly don't know anymore."

"Levi's a good man," says Sam.

"I know." Alice sighs. "But things aren't the same. Something is off with him lately. I can't put my finger on it, but he's been . . . distant. And do you want to know the worst part?"

"What's that?" asks Sam, reaching for the bottle.

"I don't care all that much. Isn't that awful?"

Sam shrugs. "I assume it's normal for people to have ups and downs in their marriages."

"I know that," says Alice. "I've just found myself drifting lately. Wondering if I should have made different choices. I didn't have a chance to make a clean break like you did, you know?"

"My break hasn't been half as clean as you imagine," says Sam. "Did you forget I was America's most hated reality show villain of 2003?"

"*I* didn't hate you," says Alice.

"All I'm saying," says Sam, "is that a boring, repetitive, comfortable life has a lot going for it. Don't lose sight of your blessings."

Alice smiles sadly. She knows Sam is probably right, but even so, once they've polished off the bottle of wine and Sam has carried herself off to bed, she decides to settle in and sleep on the couch anyway.

* * *

Alice awakens with a start, and for a split second she thinks she's only been asleep for a few minutes, until she registers the light streaming through the blinds.

There's a loud banging on the front door, and she realizes the noise must have woken her up. By the time she gets to the top of the stairs, yawning and rubbing the sleep out of her eyes, Levi has already made it to the door, pulling a T-shirt on above his flannel pajama pants.

"Mom?"

Alice turns and looks up the stairs at Will, looking down from the railing. Behind him, Sam steps out from the spare room, pulling a robe around her. "Who is it?" Will asks.

She shakes her head and turns back to Levi, who is undoing the lock and opening the door.

A uniformed policeman is standing on their front step in the early morning light.

"I'm sorry to bother you folks," he says, "but we're canvassing the neighborhood to find out if anyone heard or saw anything suspicious last night?"

"Why?" asks Alice. "What's going on?"

"I'm afraid I'm not able to share any information just yet, ma'am," he says, but Alice isn't listening. She pushes past Levi and the cop and stares out at the street in shock. There are emergency vehicles parked against the curb, their lights flashing, and she's just in time to see some grim-faced paramedics wheel a stretcher out of Vicki and Kent's house next door, the shape of a body clearly visible beneath a white sheet.

CHAPTER EIGHT: JOEY

Joey wipes his last chunk of toast over the empty plate in front of him, cleaning up the remaining egg yolk and bacon grease. He chews and swallows, then takes a last swig of coffee and leans back in his chair, belching softly.

"Delicious, Ma," he says.

"You're too skinny," says his mother, Marion, coming over with the coffeepot to give him a refill. "Now, when are you and that man of yours going to bring me home a baby to snuggle? You've got lots of money; you could pay for a surrogate."

"You have six grandkids," he points out.

"You can never have enough grandkids," she says. "Besides, they're all grown up. I can't pick them up anymore."

The shrill blast of the vintage landline in the corner fills the room, saving Joey from the conversation at least for now.

"That'll be Cheryl," says his mom, hurrying to grab the phone. Joey is pretty sure she's the only person in Massachusetts with a working landline. She has a cell phone as well, which she uses with alarming regularity, but she refuses to give up the phone number they've used for almost fifty years.

"Hello?" his mother answers, almost yelling into the receiver. There's a pause as she listens, her mouth hanging open and her eyes wide, then she lets out a gasp, followed by a drawn-out and portentous "No!"

Joey knows enough not to be alarmed. His mother and her friend Cheryl phone each other regularly to exchange news and gossip, and it always sounds like this, at least on his mother's end of the line. She's as likely to have just learned that there's an excellent sale on oranges at the neighborhood grocery as she is to have heard some other, more salacious gossip. He tunes out the conversation and pulls his phone from his pocket. He notices that there's a text from Mike Bancroft.

Let's get together this afternoon and talk about what I proposed the other day.

Joey inwardly curses. In all the chaos around the trip home to meet with Kershaw and the upcoming adoption appointment, he hasn't had a chance to discuss Paris with Austin. Maybe a meeting with Mike will help clarify a few things. He's about to text back and suggest this afternoon when he's yanked away by the sound of the phone being slammed down.

"You are not going to believe this," says his mother, and something in the tone of her voice tells him she isn't talking about the price of oranges. "There's been another murder."

Joey feels his heart give a little stuttering flip. "What? Where?"

"Here!" she says. "In town! A woman named Vicki Williamson. Do you know her?"

Joey shakes his head, bewildered. "I don't know anyone here anymore, Ma."

"You're more connected than you think," she says. "Anyway, she's married to a doctor, and they have a teenage daughter. Cheryl says the father and daughter were away for the night and came home and found her dead."

She pulls her cell phone from her pocket and begins to tap away, no doubt heading to Facebook for more information. "Imagine the shock. What a sin."

Joey stands, the implications of this revelation muddying up his mind. There's no indication yet that this new death was in any way connected to Justin Beagle's, but it's an awfully big coincidence. His brain is fizzing, asking questions he doesn't necessarily want answered. He needs to get out of here before his curiosity takes over.

"That's really terrible," he says. "Keep me in the loop, okay? I've got to hit the road."

"You just got here!" his mother protests.

"I told you last night: this was just a quick trip to do some market research," he says. "Now I have to get back to the office." He's not proud that he has lied to his mother about his reasons for being in town, but if he had told her he was here to meet with the police, let alone the Janitor, the news would have made it through town and across the nation in record time. He grabs his jacket from the hook by the door.

"Don't think I haven't noticed that you didn't answer my question," says Marion. "Your biological clock is ticking."

Joey gives her a kiss on the cheek and reaches for the door. "We'll talk about it next time," he promises.

Joey climbs into his car feeling unsettled. Twenty-five years without a murder and suddenly two in less than a week? He thinks back to the moment when he and Kershaw were alone in the interview room. As crazy as the man looked, Joey could have sworn there was some truth behind what he'd told them.

A knock on the car window startles him and he screams.

"Sorry!" says a familiar face standing outside.

"Jesus Christ, Doug," he says. "You scared the shit out of me."

Joey can't remember the last time he saw Doug Shiftley. He didn't exactly have a lot of friends when he still lived in Edgar Mills, but he and Doug grew up together and were tight all the way through. He's embarrassed to admit just how little effort he's made to maintain the connection over the years.

His old friend has aged into himself. He looks like he's been working out a bit, and although he's still a bit shaggy around the edges, what used to read as messy and Pig-Pen-ish has mellowed into a sort of attractive unkemptness. He's wearing jeans and a Talking Heads T-shirt, green Converses and a vintage corduroy blazer. He actually looks hip, which is something nobody in their school years would have predicted about the future Doug.

"I'm glad I caught you before you skipped town," says Doug.

"How did you know I was *in* town?"

"Alice told me."

"Alice Van Dyne?" asks Joey, surprised.

"It's kind of a long story," says Doug. "Listen, I know you're a super-busy guy, but do you think you could spare an hour or so to swing by my apartment? There's something I want to show you. It's kind of important."

Joey knows he should leave town and get back to the city to start putting out fires, but he's intrigued. Besides, he misses his old friend.

"Sure," he says. "Hop in."

Doug lives above a pharmacy in an old brick building downtown. He leads the way up a metal staircase at the back of the building and unlocks a heavy metal door.

"Holy shit," Joey says when he's standing inside. "This is, like, our dream apartment as fourteen-year-olds."

"Thanks," says Doug, who is moving around turning on lights. "My old man owns this building. He let me renovate the space in exchange for supervising a few commercial buildings he owns downtown. I guess I kind of work in real estate now." He opens the fridge and pulls out a couple of beers, holds one up. "You down?"

"It's not even ten a.m.," says Joey.

"They're light," says Doug, cracking them both and bringing them over and taking the seat across from Joey.

Joey shrugs and takes the beer and they clink.

"I'll cut right to the chase," says Doug. "Alice told me all about your meeting with Kershaw."

"Doug," says Joey, "are you having an affair with Alice Van Dyne?"

Doug laughs. "Hell no. Not at all—nothing like that. We're friends. We hang out every couple of weeks and we text a lot. She comes over here, we smoke weed, order pizza, watch movies. That kind of thing. She's kind of my best buddy."

"I thought I was your best buddy," says Joey.

"You're my best buddy emeritus," says Doug. "But you haven't really been around all that much in, I don't know, twenty-five years. To make a long story short, Alice and I are tight, but we have an unspoken agreement to not talk about it, because if her husband found out he'd probably come over here and kick my ass. So don't mention it to anyone, especially not your mother, no offense."

"Fair enough," says Joey. "So Alice told you what Kershaw had to say."

Doug nods. "She said he was grifting you guys, looking for attention or whatever. And maybe it would have been easy to just accept that and write it off, but last night another woman was murdered."

"Vicki Williamson," says Joey.

"Let me guess," says Doug. "Your mom got a call about it?"

Joey nods.

"Okay," says Doug, "so word is traveling. And if people are on edge now, they are going to freak out when they learn she was also found with cleaning fluid soaking through her clothes. Just like Justin Beagle."

Joey feels a familiar and not especially welcome tingle run down the back of his neck. The fizzing in his brain returns.

"Shit," he says.

Doug nods. "So if it was just one kid with some detergent on him, it might be possible to pass it off as a coincidence. But *two* murdered victims found like that? Shut the front door."

"Okay, Doug, what exactly are you trying to say here?"

"This is all getting really heavy really fast," says Doug. "Did you know that Vicki Williamson was Alice's next-door neighbor? Like, in the actual adjacent house? Ten feet separating them?"

"I didn't know that," says Joey, slowly. He is trying to keep his reactions restrained, but the fizzing is quickly evolving into an impossible-to-ignore clanging.

"It just doesn't sit right," says Doug. "Almost exactly twenty-five years after a series of murders, someone targets a woman who lives directly next door to one of the primary figures from the last round of killings. That's quite a coincidence, don't you think?"

"Yeah, it is," Joey admits. "But I'm sure that hasn't escaped notice. If the police weren't assuming this was a copycat before, they definitely are now."

Doug doesn't answer. Instead, he sits and chews his lip for a long moment. Then he stands abruptly and goes to a bookshelf that runs along the back wall. From a stack of nondescript papers on a lower shelf, he pulls out a notebook. It's the kind Joey remembers using in school: cheap and flimsy, bound with a bright yellow cover. Doug sits down again, and when he drops the notebook on the coffee table in between them, Joey is able to tell that this one has been well used. It's thick with bits and pieces of paper sticking out from the sides, some elastic bands holding it all together.

"What is it?" asks Joey.

"Okay," says Doug. "So, back then when you guys were starting to become famous but before the shit hit the fan, I was kind of obsessed with the whole thing. I mean, you were my only friend in the world and suddenly you had this big, flashy persona. I was still home looking at the bra section of the Sears catalogue, and you were getting your picture taken with the gorgeous Van Dyne twins."

"'Flashy' is a bit of a stretch," says Joey. "I was never really famous, like the twins."

"That's not the point," says Doug. "You were living this cool second life, and people respected you. I even benefited from being your friend. People stopped calling me Dog Shit, for one thing. But it was also just really weird."

"Sure," says Joey. "I *can* see that."

"Anyway," says Doug, "I was jealous. I wanted so badly to be part of the action, but I knew that was never going to happen. So instead I decided to start chronicling everything." He pulls the rubber bands off the notebook and pushes it across the table. "Take a look."

Joey grabs the notebook and begins flipping. Sure enough, it's full of information about the teen detectives. From local newspaper articles to glossy spreads in *Seventeen* and *Teen Beat*. Random ephemera fills the gaps, like an old take-out menu from Cordova's, and an embroidered Edgar Mills High School patch. He pulls out a playbill for the EMHS production of *Oklahoma!* and stares.

"I had forgotten all about this."

"You took that guy down," says Doug. "It was awesome."

During the production Joey, who was working backstage as a tech, discovered that the director of the show—hired from out of town by the school administration—had been using his position to steal expensive office equipment from the school. Once he was exposed by Joey, it came out he had done the same at several other schools, and he was eventually convicted of major theft and identity fraud.

"I didn't do much," says Joey. "I just noticed something."

"Yeah, well nobody else noticed it," says Doug. "You *were* a detective, man. You undersell yourself."

Joey places the playbill back in the scrapbook, uninterested in reopening that discussion. "Okay, so what's this all about?"

"Do you remember when Levi confronted you at school that day?"

"Of course I remember."

"Do you remember that I was with you?"

Joey frowns. "I don't think so, Doug. I know we had plans, and I had to cancel on you."

"Yeah, that's right," says Doug. "It was a Friday and we were leaving school. We had rented *Event Horizon* and we were going to watch it and order Domino's and you were going to crash over. But then Levi just kind of appeared. At first I was worried he was approaching *me* and he was going to inflict some fun new gratuitous humiliation. But he didn't look at me. Instead he confronted *you*."

"Is that really how it happened?" asks Joey.

Doug nods. "Yep. Then he left and you bailed on me."

Joey nods slowly as the memory begins to come back. "I remember now," he says. "You *were* there."

"Levi caught you off guard," says Doug. "You muttered something about going home and then you just took off. But I'd heard everything Levi said to you, and I knew something was up. Something big. And I decided that I wanted to be part of it. So I went to the police station."

Joey stares at him, his eyes widening.

"You went to the cops? Are you serious?"

"I didn't really have a plan," says Doug. "But I remember having a strong feeling that something serious was about to happen and adults should be involved. So I went to the station, but when I got there nobody was at the reception desk. I figured maybe they were in the bathroom or something."

Joey has no idea where this is going, but Doug has his full attention. "So what did you do?"

Doug closes his eyes, thinking back to that day. "About halfway down the hallway there was a window looking into a conference room, and I could see that some kind of big meeting was going on. Van Dyne was at the front of the room, talking to a bunch of cops, and it looked very serious. I started second-guessing myself. It's not like I was going to knock on the door and interrupt the meeting. I didn't even have any information, just a bad feeling. But I noticed that Van Dyne's office was right there."

Joey nods, remembering this from his time spent at the station. The chief's office was right behind the reception desk.

"The door was open," Doug continues. "I thought maybe I would leave the chief a note, so I walked in and over to his desk, and it was covered with crap: paperwork and empty coffee cups and just a bunch of *stuff*. I spotted a notepad and picked it up, and there was some writing on the top page, so I was about to pull the blank page out from beneath it, but then I heard footsteps."

Joey realizes that he's shifted to the edge of his seat.

"It was the receptionist," Doug continues. "I was caught off guard, and I ripped the top pages off and shoved them in my pocket right before she discovered me. I pretended I was lost and asked for the bathroom. Then I hightailed it home, where I finally had a chance to take a good look."

"What did it say?" asks Joey.

In response, Doug grabs the scrapbook and flips to the last page, revealing a small, unassuming piece of paper, torn along one edge.

Joey leans down to examine the paper. In blue ballpoint pen, someone has written a short list, which reads:

Goldfish
Call Perry

And at the very bottom, in capital letters, underlined twice, Joey reads:

BRUCE PHILIP KERSHAW DIDN'T KILL MARY ELLEN SPAKALITIS.

"What the hell?" asks Joey.

"I know," says Doug. "I don't know what it means, but—"

"So you're telling me that Bill Van Dyne wrote this on the day that he died?" says Joey.

"I mean, we can't be sure it was that exact day," says Doug, "but it probably was. It was right on top of his desk."

"Did you tell anyone about this?" asks Joey.

Doug shakes his head. "No, because by the time I'd even processed it, Levon Brakes was dead, and Kershaw had been caught red-handed after shooting Chief Van Dyne . . ."

He trails off, and Joey picks up the thread. "And you figured the case was solved, so this didn't mean anything."

Doug nods. "But now, considering everything that's happening . . . I wonder if maybe it did."

CHAPTER NINE:
SAM

Sam knows that the world thinks her time on *Rebel House* is a stain on her past. The person she became inside that stupid, trashy mansion in Brentwood couldn't have been more different from the smart, poised, and attractive young sleuth who had only recently been solving crimes and posing for magazine spreads with her sister.

Sammy Vee. The man-stealing, double-crossing, shit-talking wild child, complete with the nasty but memorable catch phrase. She was everything Samantha Van Dyne wasn't. She was an unexpected villain. A wolf shedding her sheepskin. And if there's one thing more popular than a redemption arc, it's a fall from grace. Suspicious bitch indeed. The public ate her up.

As much as Sammy Vee was a role, a character she slipped into, there was nothing insincere about presenting herself as a villain, because it was true. She'd done an unforgivable thing when she took her father's gun. She'd taken away his opportunity to defend himself. She might as well have pulled the trigger herself.

That awful detail was only briefly mentioned at the trial, during her mother's testimony, but it was just the kind of revelation the hungry media loved. It was just another salacious detail in a story that was full of them, but it was true, and she knew she needed to be punished. Transforming into someone who America loved to hate was a good start.

She lasted about ten years on the reality show circuit, moving from *Rebel House* to a spinoff, then to guest appearances on other shows. Eventually she stopped getting callbacks because producers were looking for a "younger vibe" and she realized with some relief that her fifteen minutes of fame had come and gone. By then the break from her former self seemed permanent.

Fortunately she was prepared. Onscreen she may have acted a mess, but she'd been wise with her earnings. She had savings, she owned her condo outright, and she made a decent living as a freelance copywriter. She had built a life in Los Angeles, there was no reason to return.

Of course nothing is ever that simple.

Sam knew the moment her sister phoned to tell her about the murder that she was being asked to walk through a door into the past.

They say they want our help.

Hadn't she felt it immediately? A sparkle? A promise? An invitation to get the band back together? It was a once-in-a-lifetime chance to go back in time and return to the person she had been. Who in their right mind would ever turn down such an opportunity?

When it turned out that Kershaw was bullshitting them, the relief had landed on her like a bucket of cold water—snapping her awake and out of the trance. Now she could say goodbye to Edgar Mills once and for all and move back to L.A. and the future she had spent twenty-five years preparing for.

She should have known it wouldn't be so easy to turn back, but she tries.

She sits next to Alice and Levi and Will as the police ask a round of questions. When they leave, she makes breakfast for the family and sits through it all, chatting cheerfully with Will and Levi as if nothing out of the ordinary is going on. All the while, she tries not to notice her sister's pale, haunted face.

There's a flurry of hugs and goodbyes and promises to visit, and then Levi and Will are gone.

"Well," says Alice, "I should get dressed. We'll want to get on the road soon if you're going to catch this flight."

There's an edge to her voice, but Sam knows that acknowledging it will only make everything more difficult.

"I'll pack my bag," she says.

They don't speak much on the way to the airport. Alice is clearly distracted by the murder next door, and Sam doesn't want to talk about it for fear of where that line of discussion will lead. She pretends to catch up on work emails as they leave town, and Alice puts on the radio, and the trip passes mostly in silence.

At the terminal, Sam gets her bag out of the back seat and Alice comes around to the sidewalk to hug her goodbye. They hold on for a long time, and when Sam finally pulls away, her heart sinks when she sees that Alice is crying.

"Oh Jesus," she says. She puts her bag on the ground and pulls a Kleenex from her pocket, handing it to Alice. "You cried when I showed up; you're crying when I leave. I'm going to start feeling guilty if you don't cut this out."

"I'm sorry," says Alice. She wipes her eyes and then blows her nose loudly. "I know. It's just . . . I don't want you to leave."

"You know I'm happier on the West Coast, right?" Sam says. Alice nods. "And you're always, always welcome to come see me. Come alone. Will and Levi will manage without you for a couple of weeks. We can drive to Napa!"

Alice smiles blearily. "Yeah. That sounds nice."

Sam reaches for her sister's hand and squeezes. "Alice," she says. "I don't know what happened to your neighbor, but I promise you it was a coincidence, okay? Kershaw is in jail for what he did. It's over."

Alice takes a deep breath and collects herself. "I know you're right," she says. "But there's just an awful feeling in my gut that keeps telling me otherwise."

Sam stands on the sidewalk, waving until her sister has disappeared out of sight, and then she throws her bag over her shoulder and makes her way into the terminal.

The security line is long and snaking, and Sam takes her spot behind a couple shepherding a pair of young kids and begins to shuffle along with the crowd. She thinks back to her mother, stuck in that horrible time capsule of a house, reliving the past on a loop. She thinks of her nephew, and her brother-in-law, and Joey O'day, and Nash Young, and the dead boy and the dead woman, and the many unanswered questions that have settled like a gray haze on Edgar Mills.

She thinks of her quiet, empty apartment. Its west-facing windows. Its small balcony and its expensive espresso machine and its half-empty closet containing nice, classic clothes.

She thinks of Alice, left behind to deal with everything on her own.

She does her best to keep her mind from analyzing what she's learned, but it's no use. Two murders in just a few days after all this time is too big of a coincidence to ignore. What if Kershaw wasn't lying? Joey and the kid, Evan, both mentioned the theories online about Levon's death.

If she allows herself to assume for the sake of argument that Kershaw was telling the truth, and there *was* a second killer, and that killer is active again, where does that bring her?

It brings her to who might be next, and on a list of possibilities her sister and her mother are at the very top.

"Fuck," she says. The couple in front of her turn and give her a dirty look. "Sorry," she says. She hoists her bag over her shoulder and steps away from the line.

Half an hour later, Sam is in a rental car, headed back in the direction of Edgar Mills.

The Niña, Pinta, and Santa María are unremarkable low-rise apartment buildings in a newer part of town. The buildings sit along the river, across the street from a series of cookie-cutter bungalows that have seen better days.

Bruce Philip Kershaw's father developed this patch of land in the early '80s. Sam knows this because it came out during the trial. The Janitor, as it turned out, was a very wealthy man. His parents died unexpectedly in a car accident when Kershaw was just out of high school, and the entire real estate empire was left to Kershaw and an older sister who lived in Boston and managed the business.

Sam had always assumed that Kershaw's notorious apartment, where he had planned his crimes, had been sold to help cover his legal bills and civil suits, but she had forgotten about the sister. She has only a vague memory of the woman, a decade older than her brother—a starched, grim-looking person who sat behind the defendant's table for a few days during the trial before disappearing one day and never returning, the reality of her brother's crimes apparently too much for her to handle.

Thanks to Evan Stevens, she now knows that the woman didn't abandon her brother entirely. She kept a home for him. For what? In case he ever went free? There's not much chance of that, considering he's working his way through multiple consecutive life sentences.

One thing Sam does remember from the trial is the location of the apartment. He occupied the top corner unit facing the river in the Santa María, the easternmost building. His second victim, Mary Ellen Spakalitis, lived in the Pinta next door, and he had an unobstructed view of her ground-floor apartment from his living room window.

She watches the building from the rental car, parked across the street. It's gloomy and rainy, and in the middle of this weekday there aren't many people around, but eventually she spots a young mother pushing a stroller laden with shopping bags down the sidewalk. When the woman turns the stroller onto the front walkway, Sam gets out of the car, hurrying through the rain and timing things so that she arrives at the front door just as the woman has unlocked it and is trying to maneuver the stroller inside. Sam reaches out for the door and pulls it wide.

"Thank you," the woman says gratefully. She reaches back to hold the door open for Sam, who steps inside.

"No problem," says Sam as she makes a show of shaking the rain off, doing her best to make it appear as if she belongs there. "Looks like we picked the wrong day to go outside."

"No kidding," says the woman. Before she has the chance to say anything else, the baby begins to cry and her attention is diverted. Sam uses the opportunity to slip into the stairwell.

She climbs to the third and top floor and steps into the hallway. It's dim and dingy, with gray industrial carpet bearing a worn footpath and fluorescent lights flickering erratically along its length. Sam glances at a small plaque pointing out the unit numbers, and before anyone else steps out and sees her, she walks quickly to the end of the hallway and the doorway to apartment 308.

Sam tries the door. As expected, it's locked. She pulls the eyeglass repair kit she picked up at a service station on the way over and removes the tiny flathead screwdriver. With a quick twist of her wrist, she unlocks the door, another one of her father's lessons coming in handy. She steps inside, closing the door quickly and quietly behind her.

She steps out of her shoes and through the darkened entryway into a simple kitchen, a counter and appliances along one wall, a round table with two chairs in the middle of the room. Through an archway is a living room with corner windows that look out onto the river and provide the space with a dim, watery light.

Sam stands in the archway and takes in the space. The first thing that strikes her is how clean the apartment is. She was prepared for something gruesome and demonic, like Buffalo Bill's basement in *The Silence of the Lambs* or maybe some leftover crime scene tape and a general sense of disarray from the investigation. At the very least she expected layers of dust and grime, a sense of entropy.

But this place has been cleaned—maybe not recently but within the past few months. She steps to the window and runs her finger over the sill. It comes up clean. Behind the door in the bathroom, similarly tidy, she finds a bucket and mop and some cleaning supplies that are distinctly modern. She adjusts her expectations in her mind and arrives at the easiest solution: if the sister still owns the apartment, she is paying someone to keep it clean.

Sam stands and looks around the room, calling up her father's advice about how to assess a crime scene.

You have to think like this is your *space,* she can still remember him telling her. *Every day, you come home to this house, or walk through this parking lot on your way to work, or sit in this particular spot on this particular beach. You have to imagine yourself being there and looking around and recognizing what doesn't fit. Once you've had that conversation with yourself, begin to look around, beginning with the perimeter.*

Beginning with the entryway, Sam proceeds to carefully examine the edges of each room. Moving slowly and methodically, she makes her way around the space, shifting furniture away from the wall, then replacing it. Pulling back curtains, using the light on her phone to peer behind and beneath the heavy cast iron radiators that sit under each window.

As she moves around the apartment, she begins to notice the signs of vacancy that had originally evaded her. The calendar above the small desk in the living room is from twenty-five years ago. The books on the shelves are similarly dated, as are the DVDs and, for that matter, the fact that there *are* DVDs.

She's struck by how neat and orderly everything is. This isn't the maniac's lair she's always imagined.

In the kitchen, she stops and stares at the refrigerator. It's unplugged and there's a phone book holding the door open to keep it from going moldy. She bends down and checks underneath, confirming that the fridge is on wheels, before pulling it halfway out with a bit of effort. Using her light she leans in to look behind it.

Whoever has been cleaning out this apartment has clearly never bothered to move the fridge. Thick grimy dust bunnies fill the corners of the cavity, and a ballpoint pen and a few coins sit exposed on the floor after who knows how many years in the dark. She spots a tiny triangle of white sticking out from beneath the fridge. She pulls it the rest of the way out, then reaches down and picks up a small piece of paper.

It's a receipt. She imagines Kershaw coming home and emptying his pocket: he tosses whatever random detritus he's collected throughout his day—receipts, candy wrappers, ticket stubs—onto the counter. This receipt must have slipped over the back and into the gap.

Is it really possible that the police missed it during their investigation? She considers this. A lot of evidence was collected in this apartment and used in Kershaw's trial. Bags of bloody clothing and other items linked to the crime scenes had been stuffed under the bed and into the backs of closets. It seems plausible that the police and prosecution had so much to work with that they didn't feel it necessary to overdo their search.

She moves to a window to take a closer look.

It's from a restaurant. She doesn't recognize the name—Bonnie's Roadside Motel and Grill—but the bill informs her two people ate breakfast together: *1 lumberjack brkfst, 1 standard brkfst, 2 coffee*. The date at the top reads, "November 17, 2000."

Her Spidey sense tingles. That's the date that the second victim, Mary Ellen Spakalitis, was presumed to have been murdered. She pulls her phone out of her pocket and does a quick search. The only Bonnie's Roadside Motel and Grill she can find is in Vermont, a three-hour drive away.

Sam stares out the window as she thinks everything over. Outside, the river runs by, dark and muddy with runoff from yesterday's rain and the decay of autumn.

This doesn't prove anything about anything. If the receipt *is* Kershaw's, there's no reason why he couldn't have killed Spakalitis and then driven to Vermont, but she knows the trial inside out, and there was no mention at any point of Kershaw being out of town that day.

The way she sees it, there are three options. One is that this receipt doesn't belong to Kershaw and he was never in Vermont that day. The second is that Kershaw *was* in Vermont, and told his lawyers, and they chose not to use that evidence. The third is that Kershaw was in Vermont and *didn't* tell his lawyers or use it as evidence of innocence.

But why would he do that?

Sam wonders if it might have something to do with the other person who was with him.

CHAPTER TEN:
ALICE

"This all seems a bit unnecessary," says Levi as he adjusts his collar at the entryway mirror.

"Our friend and next-door neighbor died," says Alice. "We have to go show our support. Everyone is going to be there."

"You make it sound like a party," he says.

Alice bites her lip. Levi has been acting like a petulant child since he got home from work and she told him that Drea and some of the other neighbors have organized a drop-in at the Williamson house.

"We don't want to be the only assholes who don't show up," she says.

"I just don't think it's right for us to be trampling all over the place so soon after she died," Levi says. "Don't the police have an investigation to carry out?"

"Drea spoke to Kent to arrange things and he told her the police wrapped their sweep of the scene yesterday afternoon."

"You always know all the lingo," he says. It's not a compliment. "You sound like a cop from *Law & Order.*"

"Should I come?"

They turn to see Will standing at the top of the stairs, looking down at them uncertainly.

"Oh, honey," says Alice. "That's sweet, but I don't think you need to worry about it. It will be really grim and sad."

She remembers what things were like at her house after her father died. Her father's sisters and their families set up camp, making the house feel crowded and suffocating, and she had to talk to streams of neighbors as they came through offering hushed, earnest condolences. It was tough enough on her that she doesn't ever want to subject Will to that kind of experience if it isn't totally necessary.

"I don't know," says Will. "I thought maybe I should be there to help Joelle out."

"Bad idea, buddy," says Levi. "Believe me, that poor girl is overwhelmed right now, and the more people she has to interact with, the more stressful it will probably be for her."

Alice is relieved that at least she and Levi can agree on one thing.

"Yeah," says Will. "You're probably right." Without another word he turns and disappears back into his bedroom.

Alice and Levi make the short trek to the house next door. Unsure of what to bring, Alice spent the afternoon baking a lemon loaf, which she's holding now, wrapped in a fresh tea towel.

The door is opened by Drea.

"Hi," she says, stepping forward to give Alice a hug. "Why don't I take that. Kent's in the living room."

Alice hands the loaf to Drea and then takes Levi's hand and guides him into the living room.

Kent is a tall, fit guy in his late forties, about a decade older than his wife. At neighborhood barbecues he tends to congregate with other men, drinking beer and talking confidently about sports. Today he's in a chair in the corner, looking completely exhausted as another couple from down the street murmur their condolences. As Alice and Levi approach, they step out of the way, obviously happy that their turn is over.

Alice crouches next to the chair so she's face-to-face with Kent.

"Hi, Kent," she says softly. "We're so sorry for your loss."

"How are you holding up, buddy?" asks Levi, reaching down for a handshake.

Kent shakes his head. "It's a nightmare. We don't know what the hell is going on. The police haven't told us much of anything."

Alice has a million questions, but she's tactful enough not to pry. Besides, if there's one of her father's lessons she remembers, it's that the most successful way to get the answer to a question is to not ask it. She stares at him sympathetically, without saying anything, until he speaks again to break the silence.

"She was in the entryway," he says. "Joelle and I were out of town for the night visiting my parents. When we got home in the morning, we found her. She was just lying there . . ."

He breaks down now, weeping, and Levi shoots Alice a look that says, *Look what you did.* Alice crouches next to Kent and puts a hand on his knee.

"I know what you're going through," she says. She grabs a tissue from a box on the side table and hands it to him. "I've been there."

He blows his nose and takes a deep breath. "I know you have," he says. He looks up at Levi. "You both have. I mean, it's one thing for someone to die, but to die like *this*? I just can't believe it."

"You have to trust the process, buddy," says Levi. "That's the best advice I can give you. Let the authorities handle it. The last thing you want is to get caught up in trying to do their job for them. That will make you crazy."

Alice wonders if it's a dig. Levi has never blamed her for what happened to his brother, but the fact that he's bringing up such pointed advice seems to be saying something. It's not as if Kent Williamson is suddenly going to start investigating his wife's murder.

Another couple has appeared behind them, and Alice gives Kent's knee one final squeeze before standing. "We're here for anything you need," she says, and then she and Levi gratefully step away.

Levi joins some men in the den on the other side of the front hallway, where there's a football game on the TV. Alice heads to the kitchen; Drea is set up at the counter and is repackaging the mountain of food that's been dropped off, presumably for the deep freeze.

"Do you want a coffee?" she asks. Alice nods gratefully and accepts the mug.

"What a mess," she says.

"Did you see anything weird that night?" asks Drea. "I mean, you're right next door."

Alice shakes her head. "We didn't see anything. What have you heard?" Drea is always a reliable source of inside information.

"Well," she says, glancing around the corner to make sure there's nobody within eavesdropping distance. "The story is that someone rang the doorbell in the middle of the night, woke her up, and totally took her by surprise. They struggled in the front entryway and he overpowered her." She lowers her voice. "Apparently there was cleaning fluid everywhere. The cops spent hours but they didn't find much, not even a fingerprint on the door. And they've canvassed the whole neighborhood and nobody saw a thing. There are obviously doorbell cameras here and there, but nothing was caught on video."

"Awful," says Alice.

"You're telling me." Drea turns back to the food. "Is your sister back in town? Maybe the two of you can dust off your detective shoes and start looking into these murders."

Alice manages a laugh. "She's gone back already. I dropped her off at the airport yesterday."

"Aww," says Drea. "That's too bad. You'll miss her, I bet. I guess California is a lot more appealing than Edgar Mills in dreary old November. But really, Alice, what do you think? Is it a copycat killer? I heard through the grapevine that Justin Beagle's body had cleaning fluid on it too."

"I have no idea what the police are thinking," she says. She's not about to tell Drea about the meeting with Nash and Corvallis, let alone Kershaw.

"But I want to know what *you* think," says Drea. "*You're* the detective, after all."

Alice smiles weakly. "That was a long time ago, Drea."

"But aren't you worried? Everyone is freaking out, Alice. John bought a gun, and I didn't argue with him about it. And we're not even . . ." She trails off, looks away.

"You're not even what?" Alice asks.

"We're not even involved," she says. "Not directly, I mean. Whoever is doing this could just be randomly choosing people, but don't you think it's kind of a wild coincidence that the murderer chose someone right next door to you? What if that was a mistake?"

"A mistake?" It takes Alice a couple of seconds to catch what Drea is suggesting, and then her mind breaks open and she finds herself holding her breath. "You mean maybe he meant to target me?"

The thought of it is like an attack. But spoken aloud, it sounds obvious. Alice wonders how she didn't consider it herself.

"I'm not trying to insinuate anything," says Drea. "But if the police don't present a believable theory soon or show some kind of progress, we're considering taking the kids and getting out of town. We'll work remotely from my parents' house until things are resolved. You might want to consider doing the same thing."

Alice remembers a similar exodus when the Janitor was still on the loose. In the end, it didn't much matter. She wonders what Levi would think if she suggested it.

"I'm just saying," Drea continues. "Whatever is going on, it's not worth fucking around with. Pardon my French."

Alice finds Joelle in the basement. She's sitting in the corner of a large, battered sectional, surrounded by a few sad-faced girls. To her mild surprise, there's also a boy in the mix.

"Hi, Joelle," she says gently, approaching. "How are you doing, honey?"

The other girls instinctively pull out their phones, unwilling to meet the eyes of another concerned adult. Joelle must realize that she doesn't have the same option, so she just stares at the older woman, bewildered and dazed.

"I'm okay," she says in a tiny voice.

Out of the corner of her eye, Alice is aware that the boy is watching this exchange with interest.

"Well, if you need anything, don't hesitate to ask," she says. "There's lots of food upstairs. I know anyone would be happy to bring you a plate."

"Thanks," says Joelle in the same barely perceptible, almost babyish voice.

Alice turns away, and she can almost feel a wave of relief from the sofa. By the time she gets to the bottom of the basement stairs, she can hear their light whispers resuming.

Out of sight of the girls, she looks down the corridor next to the stairway, where a door opens into the backyard. It was this door that Vicki used to take her dog for a walk. Next to the door, lying quietly and glumly on the floor, is Vicki's dog, Lucky. Above him, Alice recognizes Vicki's ratty old dog-walking jacket hanging on a hook with Lucky's leash.

Lucky looks sad in the way only a dog can look sad. He doesn't lift his head as she approaches, but the tip of his tail wags a couple of times out of instinct or politeness as she crouches beside him.

"Hello, sweetie," she says, giving him a scratch behind the ears. "Do you miss your mom?"

"Are you investigating?"

She jumps at the sound of a voice directly behind her.

She turns to see the boy, Joelle's friend, standing at the foot of the stairs. He approaches as she stands.

She's taken aback by the question. "No," she says, "I'm just talking to the dog."

He nods, but there's something about his expression that tells her he doesn't believe her.

"I'm Evan," he says. "My family lives next to your mom. Or behind her, I guess. I met your sister the other day."

It's the TikToker, Alice realizes. The boy who was digging for information with Will.

"You're friends with Joelle?" she asks, trying not to sound too suspicious.

He nods. "She's the first person I started hanging out with when we moved to Edgar Mills. The other kids weren't very welcoming, but Joelle kind of took me under her wing."

"How do you think she's doing, really?" she asks.

He glances over his shoulder, drops his voice. "I mean, how would *you* be doing?"

"Fair enough," says Alice. She remembers what her mother said about the kid. *Precocious.*

He moves to the door and peers out the window. "This is pretty much completely hidden underneath the deck," he says. "It's basically obscured. Do you know if they use it much?"

"They mostly use it to take the dog out onto the trail," she says.

The boy chews on his lip, clearly thinking something through.

"Joelle told me you live next door," he says. "Which side?"

She points in the direction of her house. "Right there," she says. "West. It sounds like I should ask if *you're* investigating."

He grins. "Guilty. I guess I couldn't get that past a seasoned sleuth like you."

Alice has always been suspicious of people who are overly familiar, and this kid is grating on her nerves. She knows she should dissuade him—that she should leave the investigation to the police and go back to her house and forget any of this has happened—but she can't help herself. The tingling feeling that comes along with a new case—even just *talking* about a new case—is too hard to ignore.

"I'm not a sleuth," she says. "But I'll bite. What's your assessment?"

He chews on his lip again, considering. "Well," he begins, "it just seems very brazen and convenient to me that the killer was willing to walk right up to the front door, ring the doorbell, walk right inside and kill Mrs. Williamson, then turn around and leave from the front door *again*, and feel confident they wouldn't be seen."

"It was the middle of the night," counters Alice.

"Sure," says Evan, shrugging. "But it still seems risky, right? If this guy is going to do this so methodically, you'd think he wouldn't take big risks like that. If he came through the front, he'd have to either park on the street or walk up the street, and both are a huge gamble."

"And that's why you're back here," she says, "looking at this door."

He grins, sheepishly. "I'm back here because I followed you to see what *you'd* uncover. You're the professional. But now that I see this door . . ."

He looks at the coat, mulling things over. He reaches out to touch the leash, and Lucky's ears perk up excitedly.

"The trail is right back there," he says. "If he was watching her, following her, had her in his sights, wouldn't that be the perfect place to begin understanding her rhythms?"

Alice doesn't want to follow this line of thinking, but again she can't help it.

"Okay," she says, playing along. "Then what?"

"Well," he says, "he gets used to her routine and watches her until he confirms that she uses this door to get in and out of the house, and then . . ." He falters. Alice waits. "He comes in through the back door in the middle of the night, surprises her in the front entryway, kills her, then slips back out this door."

"Okay," she says, "so you think that he broke in through this door and staged the front door?"

Evan's confidence begins to waver as he sees her point.

"There's no sign of a break-in," he says.

"Doesn't look like it," she says.

He considers this. "Maybe . . . maybe she left the door unlocked?"

Alice shakes her head. "Not a chance. She was home alone that night. I bet she triple-checked those doors. I think it's safe to say that the police have the right idea here."

He looks a bit crestfallen, and she feels guilty.

"Don't feel so bad," she says. "It's worth examining every theory, and you had a good one. But if you want my advice, let the cops do their job and stick to your homework."

"That's basically what your sister said," he tells her. She notices that he doesn't intend to let anything drop. She remembers this so well, the feeling of being swept up in some grand investigation. Tossing aside reservations and ignoring the warnings of adults. He wants to be caught up in something big, and she knows that nothing is going to change his mind. At the end of the day, he isn't her kid and it isn't her business.

"I should go upstairs," she says. "And you should go be with your friends."

He nods and steps around her on his way back into the rec room. "You know," he says, "it's amazing what you and your sister did. Totally amazing."

Alice smiles. "We should have known to leave well enough alone."

He doesn't respond, but she can tell by the look on his face as he disappears around the corner that he doesn't agree.

Alice is crouching to give Lucky a final pat when something occurs to her. A handful of times over the past few years, when Vicki had an early appointment or some other scheduling issue, she asked Alice to walk Lucky. She would let herself in through the basement door, using a key that was hidden beneath a planter, and Lucky would always be there waiting for her, excited for his walk.

She stands and checks to make sure nobody else is around before unlocking the basement door and slipping outside. She finds the planter and looks underneath it.

The key is gone.

CHAPTER ELEVEN: JOEY

For the second morning in a row, Joey wakes up in his childhood bedroom.

After Doug showed him the note, the two of them went out for a beer, which turned into many, many beers, which led to him calling Austin and saying he was going to crash with his mother for an extra night. Austin didn't mind—he's always telling Joey he should spend more time with friends and family—and his mother was predictably delighted when he stumbled in late in the evening and announced that he'd be sticking around a while longer.

He can hear her banging around downstairs now and he knows he should get out of bed, join her for a quick breakfast, and get on the road to drive straight back to the office, but instead he reaches for his phone. He can't get Doug's secret note out of his mind, and he has some questions.

He realized while he and Doug were discussing the case over beer and wings last night that he doesn't really know much about the Janitor's victims. Like most of what happened back then, he's done his best to push it all back into the recesses of his mind. If it's true that Mary Ellen Spakalitis was the victim of another killer, is there perhaps some clue floating out there that was never picked up on?

He does a simple Google search for "murder + edgar mills" and is surprised by just how many hits pop up. It appears that the deaths of Justin Beagle and Vicki Williamson have kicked off a wave of refreshed interest in the Janitor murders, and this time the scrutiny isn't just coming from outliers and true crime junkies. There are stories in *The New York Times*, in *The Washington Post*, and even on the BBC.

He reads through several articles, skimming to the spots where they discuss the older set of killings, but they all have the same sparse details, the names of the victims and then a more fulsome account of the night when Levon and Chief Van Dyne were killed and Kershaw was arrested.

He alters his search, adding "spakalitis," and some new results pop up. At the top of the screen is a still shot from a TikTok video posted by @RealTrueCrimeKid: "THE JANITOR KILLINGS, PART 5 - BRUCE PHILIP KERSHAW'S VICTIMS."

He clicks on the link to open the video and watches as a young teenage boy sitting at a desk in a bedroom begins to speak.

"The Janitor's first victim was twenty-five-year-old video store clerk Dennis James 'DJ' Cartwright. Cartwright worked at Hollywood Nites, a video rental store that sat about halfway between Kershaw's apartment building and Birch Crest Elementary, where Kershaw worked for several years until it closed. I'll be discussing the significance of Birch Crest Elementary in an upcoming TikTok so don't forget to like, share, and subscribe so you don't miss it."

Joey can't help but marvel at the TikTok kid's delivery. He's as smooth and professional as a seasoned television anchor.

"Multiple witnesses would later recount seeing Kershaw conversing with DJ Cartwright during his weekly Friday afternoon visit to Hollywood Nites. By all accounts, the two appeared to be friendly and could often be overheard discussing movies at great length, but there's no indication that the relationship extended beyond this. Kershaw's second victim was closer to home, literally. Fifty-seven-year-old mail carrier Mary Ellen Spakalitis lived in the building directly across from Bruce Philip Kershaw's. From his top-floor living room window, he had a clear view into her ground-floor apartment. He could well have watched her for months, even longer, planning his entry, scoping the scene. Spakalitis was originally from New Jersey and had moved to Edgar Mills a decade previously after the death of her husband. Not much is known about her, but neighbors said she was a friendly but quiet person who kept to herself. Spakalitis had no close living relations, and police were unable to discover whether she and Kershaw had ever had any kind of significant interaction or connection. Twenty-five years later, it's unlikely we'll ever know."

Joey pauses the video. The kid has just hit the nail on the head. What makes this case so complicated—maybe any cold case—is the way time has brushed away the facts and the details, warping and erasing peoples' recollections, so that there's nothing left but fuzzy memories and conflicting impressions.

He glances across the room at the simple pine desk his father built for him when he was a kid. His old computer is still sitting there, a giant, clunky beige Dell with a tube monitor, still protected by a heavy plastic slipcover. The comparatively tiny smartphone he's holding has orders of magnitude more power and access to an infinity of information, but he'd trade it all in for a chance to slip back in time for just a couple of hours of digging around on his old computer, looking for clues as things were still unfolding. He knows it's ridiculous, but he can't help feeling that he might have better luck finding answers under those circumstances.

He presses Play and watches the rest of the video as the Real True Crime Kid describes the Janitor's unsuccessful attempt to claim a third victim, the profoundly lucky teenager Lizzie Carroll. Her story is straightforward: she was walking home from a sleepover when someone jumped out of some bushes and grabbed her by the arm. Fortunately for her, it had rained the previous night, and the ground in that particular stretch of woods was slippery. As she twisted in shock, the would-be captor slipped in the mud and lost his grip, giving her just enough of a window to run. Risking a quick glance back, she saw a chilling sight: a figure dressed in a full-body hazmat suit, running in the opposite direction.

A hazmat suit, complete with traces of mud that were eventually confirmed to have come from that same spot on the trail, was later found in a trunk in the apartment of Bruce Philip Kershaw.

"There's nothing to indicate that the attack on Lizzie was in any way planned or organized," says the kid on TikTok. "But one thing is undeniable: Lizzie Carroll was by far the luckiest person to come into contact with the Janitor when he was on the prowl."

Joey turns off his phone and gets out of bed. He can smell coffee and he needs some.

In the kitchen, his mother is cheerfully sliding a turkey into the oven.

"You're making that for yourself?" he asks.

"No," she says, avoiding his eye. "I told the family you were here and they're all coming over for dinner."

"Ma," he says, "I have to go home. I need to go to work."

"Well, go, then," she says. "We'll eat without you. We all need to eat."

He sighs. "They're all coming?" Joey's two sisters and his brother all still live in Edgar Mills, and they all have kids.

"They love to come for dinner," she says. "They'll be grateful I made them a turkey, even if you aren't."

"Jesus Christ, Ma," he says, squeezing the bridge of his nose and willing himself to float high into the sky, far above the guilt trip. "Fine. I'll stay for one more night."

"Good," she says. She comes over to pinch his cheeks. "I'd make you breakfast but you slept in for too long and I have to get myself ready for church. There's cereal and bread for toast and I just put on a pot of coffee."

"It's Wednesday," says Joey, puzzled. "Why are you going to church?"

"That poor Beagle boy is being buried today," she says, making the sign of the cross. "His family goes to Holy Redeemer. I'm helping with the lunch after the service."

Kershaw implied that there was some connection between the old murders and the new murders. If Joey can't go back in time, maybe he needs to start looking at what's happening right here, right now.

"I'll come with you," he says.

The church is surrounded by news vans, and reporters are clustered together on the sidewalk across from the church.

"Bunch of vultures," says Joey's mother as they push through the crowd and up the walkway into the church where he was baptized, received his First Communion and his confirmation, and spent three years as an altar boy. He hasn't set foot in a Catholic church since his younger sister's wedding a few years back, but the scent and aura of the place are almost the time machine he was wishing for earlier.

His mother is clearly proud to have him on her arm, and she stops to reintroduce him to about a dozen old ladies he hasn't seen in years before they finally grab a seat in one of the side pews. He watches as the church fills up, wondering if a mysterious stranger in black might show up to stand at the back and stare at the proceedings through sunglasses, but as far as he can tell it's just the expected collection of grieving family, a large contingent of Justin's school friends, and general members of the congregation in attendance. There are a few reporters in the back rows discreetly jotting down notes, but beyond that nobody looks out of place.

The funeral mass is as sad as you'd expect for a popular young person taken down in his prime, and Joey is relieved when it finally comes to a close and they can transition to the reception room in the basement. It's a large wood-paneled space with a faded red carpet that felt extremely retro even back when Joey was a kid, and the impression is heightened now.

"You had your First Communion party here," says his mother. "Do you remember? All you kids were so cute in your little outfits. There's nothing like kids, you know."

Joey laughs. "If I did have kids, they wouldn't be doing their Catholic sacraments, Ma."

She pats his arm. "I'm going to help out in the kitchen for a bit. Why don't you go find someone to talk to?"

He fetches himself a coffee from an ancient urn in the corner and stands against the wall, trying not to look too obvious as he checks out the crowd. Various conversations are taking place around the room, from the teenagers quietly chatting in the corner to a group of old women gossiping at a table, but the general focus is the back of the room, where a long line of people wait to extend hugs and condolences to Justin's extended family. Nearby, Angela Corvallis stands watching over the interactions like a hawk.

"Didn't expect to see you here."

Joey turns to see Nash Young, out of uniform and in a dark blue suit, stepping up to him.

"I brought my mom," says Joey. "I decided to stick around for a few days since I was in town anyway. Are you here on official business?"

Nash shakes his head. "Just paying my respects. I'm on a pretty short leash at the moment. I'm still involved in the investigation, but I'm definitely not calling any shots after setting up that interview with the three of you and Kershaw. It didn't go over well with the state."

"You mean Corvallis," says Joey.

Nash does a quick check over his shoulder to make sure she's still on the other side of the room and then leans in and drops his voice. "Let's just say the focus of the investigation hasn't really changed since the second murder."

"What do you mean?"

"When Vicki Williamson's body was found covered in cleaning fluid, I thought we would have immediately shifted focus to finding connections to the original murders. But nope. She insists it's all a distraction."

"So you're carrying out your own investigation," says Joey.

Nash shrugs. "I don't know if I'd go that far, but obviously if I happen to pick up any interesting or useful information while I'm chatting with people, and that information supports a different theory . . . Well, I can't stop my brain from working, can I?"

"Why are you telling me this?" Joey asks. "Isn't this all highly sensitive?"

Nash nods. "You're right. I'm taking a chance here, but it's worth the risk if you've got some information of your own to share. So how about it, have you learned anything worth mentioning?"

Joey gives him a funny look. "I'm not sure I know what you mean."

"Come on, man," says Nash. "You're telling me you're not wearing your sleuth hat? You told me you were driving back to Boston right after the interview the other day, yet here you are."

Joey has to give him credit: he has a point. But for some reason—maybe the fact that he doesn't feel like it's his place to tell Nash about Doug's note—he isn't prepared to admit it. "I was never a detective, Chief," he says. "I'm just spending some quality time with my mother."

Nash regards him curiously for a long moment, then shrugs. "Fair enough. Well, it was good to see you. If you *do* have any insights, let me know."

He pulls a card from his pocket and hands it to Joey before heading to join the sympathy procession.

Joey is about to go look for his mother when his attention is caught by a whispered conversation happening around the corner in the stairwell. He can't make out what's being discussed, but he can tell that it's a heated exchange, and he steps a bit closer, pretending to examine a bulletin board near the exit.

"This isn't appropriate, Jerry, and you know it," one of the men is saying.

"What do you expect me to do? Keep my mouth shut?" The other guy's voice has enough of a slur for Joey to assume he's been drinking. "Nobody wants to face the facts about this thing."

"I'm not getting into that with you again, Jerry," says the first man firmly. "You need to go for a walk and sober yourself up."

Joey pretends to be carefully examining a leaflet advertising an upcoming rummage sale as one of the men strides out of the stairwell and walks back across the room to where Justin's family is gathered. A moment later he hears heavy footsteps ascending the stairs and then the loud *ka-chunk* of an exterior door opening. Joey gives it a few seconds and then slips into the stairwell and follows the other man outside.

It's gotten colder since they entered the church, and a light flurry is beginning to descend. A heavyset man in his late fifties, bald and red-faced, is lighting a cigarette in the shelter of the door. He nods at Joey and holds out the pack.

"No, thanks," says Joey. "Just getting some fresh air. Funerals always stress me out."

"You can say that again," says the man. "How did you know Justin?"

"I didn't," Joey explains. "I'm in town visiting my mother and offered to drive her. She's helping out in the kitchen."

"God love her," says the man. "I was his uncle."

"Oh no," says Joey. "My condolences. It's tough."

"What kind of bastard would—" The guy chokes on the words and blinks back tears, then sucks hard on his cigarette, pulling himself together. "That kid was a straight arrow. Phenomenal athlete. Honor student. Believe me, he didn't get his brains from his uncle Jerry, but we were buddies. He liked to talk to me about sports and cars and stuff."

He takes another puff on his cigarette. "You know what's crazy, though? A while back he starts asking me about the Janitor. 'What was it like back then, Uncle Jer? Did you know any of the victims, Uncle Jer? Did you ever meet the Janitor, Uncle Jer?'"

"Are you serious?" asks Joey.

"Dead serious. You think that's a coincidence? This kid starts to obsess about those murders and then he ends up dead the same way? Bullshit. That's no coincidence. But nobody wants to hear it. I guess they all think I'm trying to stir shit up for the fun of it, like I'm that kind of guy."

He shakes his head at the insult.

"Did you tell the cops about this?" asks Joey.

"Of course I did," he says. "I told the state investigator who is running the show. She said she'd 'look into it' and that was the end of that. Who knows, maybe they *are* looking into it. But I can tell you one thing: nobody's come back to ask me any more questions."

He finishes his cigarette and crushes the butt under his heel. "I'm going to walk to the pub down the block for a beer. Care to join me?"

Joey considers it, but he isn't sure what he'd ask the man that hasn't already been answered. If Alice Van Dyne were here she'd probably have some ideas, but he thinks he's gotten about as much out of the guy as he ever will.

"I should stick around and wait to drive my mother home," says Joey.

"Suit yourself," says Jerry. "It won't be the first drink I had by myself."

CHAPTER TWELVE:
SAM

As Sam drives down the main street of Edgar Mills, she's struck with the strangest vibe, as if she's stepped into an alternate reality. At first glance it's all as recognizable as the back of her own hand. The rows of neat brick and stone commercial buildings lining both sides of the street, the Catholic church and the Presbyterian church sitting kitty-corner to one another across the town square, the small park with its bandstand and manicured rhododendrons and hydrangeas, and the town hall occupying the other quadrant.

But on closer inspection, everything is a little bit different. What used to be a family-owned drugstore is now a franchise. The restaurants and clothing stores she grew up with are gone, their signs replaced by those of unfamiliar businesses. A shiny new playground takes up the entire corner of the park where she used to play ultimate Frisbee.

She turns a corner, and her heart swells as her destination comes into view. Cordova's, the diner that has been occupying the same corner for the better part of a century. At least some things never change.

She parks outside, and when she steps through the front door and the bells jingle overhead, it's like walking into a time capsule. The smell of grease and coffee greet her like an old friend. The interior hasn't changed a bit since she used to hang out here with her sister and their friends as a teenager. The chipped Formica counter with its chrome edge, the worn linoleum, the bulky stools, the row of booths along the far wall—they all combine to prompt a wash of intense nostalgia. The only notable difference is the lack of cigarette smoke.

The place is basically empty, which is a relief. The last thing she wants is to run into some face from the past. She hasn't reached out to Alice yet to let her know she's still in town, let alone Joanna, so it's a bit risky to be out in public, but she needs to do some serious thinking and her shitty highway motel room doesn't cut it.

She orders a coffee at the counter and takes it to a booth at the back of the diner. She pulls a notebook and a pen from her bag and begins to doodle as she works through the details of the case she's learned so far. Her father always said that he did his best thinking with pen and paper, and it's a technique that she has firmly adopted.

She begins absentmindedly drawing small flowers and vines that merge into rabbits and butterflies and skulls and tiny mandalas. Her hand takes over, and she finds herself writing THEN on one side of the page and NOW on the other side, creating two columns.

Underneath THEN she writes the names of the Janitor's victims:

DJ Cartwright
Mary Ellen Spakalitis
*Lizzie Carroll (got away)
Levon Brakes
Chief Bill Van Dyne (Dad)

On the other side of the page, she writes the two names of the latest victims:

Justin Beagle
Vicki Williamson

She stares, thinking through the connections between the victims. Mary Ellen Spakalitis and Vicki Williamson were both found at home, Spakalitis in her kitchen and Williamson in her front entryway. They'd each been doused with cleaning fluid and stabbed.

She knows the least about Justin Beagle, but she does know he was attacked on the river trail, just like Lizzie Carroll, the only person known to have gotten away from the Janitor. She underlines Justin's name three times.

Levon and Sam's father were killed less strategically. The case laid out by the state was that Kershaw, tipped off by the email sent by the twins, had rushed to retrieve the evidence he'd hidden at the school and was surprised by Levon, who he overpowered and stabbed before dumping the evidence at his apartment and then driving to the Van Dyne house and committing his final crime.

There were several signs of a struggle in the gymnasium where Levon had been discovered. This crime scene had also been amended with cleaning fluid, but less carefully than in the other cases. It had been poured over the floor and body haphazardly, in what seemed to be a hasty attempt to obscure evidence.

Finally, there's the first victim, DJ Cartwright. He was a twenty-five-year-old clerk at a video rental shop that lay halfway between Birch Crest Elementary and Kershaw's apartment. He hadn't been killed at home, like Mary Ellen and Vicki, but he *had* been stabbed, and cleaning fluid had been poured over the body. Her eyes jump between the names and details, trying and failing to spot a common thread that has so far been overlooked.

The bells on the door ring, and when Sam glances up from her paper she sees Evan, the TikTok kid, slipping into the diner. His face is drawn and tense and he glances over his shoulder as if he's concerned that he's being followed. He hurries to the back of the diner and slides into the booth next to hers, his head down. She isn't sure what is going on with Evan Stevens, but she feels a pang of compassion for him.

"Evan?" she asks.

He jumps in his seat, startled at the sound of his name. "Oh," he says when he registers her. "Sorry. I didn't see you there." He laughs awkwardly and seems to be trying to hide his nervousness. Now that she's looking directly at him, she notices a large bruise on the side of his face.

"Are you okay?" she asks.

"Yeah!" he says. "I'm fine!" He catches her skeptical expression and his face falls. "There are some people who don't . . ." He pauses for a long time, and the look on his face is so miserable that Sam feels a stab of sadness. "It doesn't matter," he finishes quietly.

"Do you want to join me?" she asks after a brief hesitation. She was hoping to spend this time by herself, but it's clear the kid is going through some stuff, probably being bullied, and she can't very well ignore him. His face lights up at the invitation, and she adjusts to the change of plans.

"Sure!" he says. He grabs his backpack and slides into the booth across from her. He immediately clocks her open notebook, and she regrets not closing it.

"You're investigating," he observes.

"No," she says. "I'm just thinking."

"Isn't thinking ninety percent of every investigation?" he asks.

"An investigation would require me to follow up my thinking with some kind of action," she says. "Not everyone who theorizes is investigating."

He gives her the kind of look that only a teenager can pull off, halfway between skepticism and pity, and she is reminded, suddenly and unexpectedly, of her own teenage self pushing back against her father's proclamations. He shrugs.

"Okay," he says. "Why do you have Justin's name underlined?"

"Did you know him?" she asks, dodging the question.

"Everyone knew him," he says. "He was one of those guys. You know, the 'big man on campus' type. I thought he was kind of a dick, but girls loved him."

"If high school is anything like it was when I was a teenager, that tracks," says Sam.

"You didn't answer my question," he says. "Why is his name underlined and the others aren't?"

She sighs. The kid is too smart to pull the wool over his eyes. "I'm curious whether there are any similarities between the older murders and the newer ones. Justin Beagle is the only one where I don't know exactly where he was murdered. I mean, I know he was found on the river trail, but not exactly where."

Sam is surprised when Evan smiles. Whatever has been bothering him seems forgotten, and he leans across the table, his eyes twinkling.

"I know something the cops don't," he whispers.

Sam feels the hair on the back of her neck stick up.

"What is it?" she asks.

"It would be easier to show you," he says.

Following Evan's directions, Sam drives him to the small parking lot about a mile outside of town that marks the beginning of the Edgar Mills River Trail. As she gets out of the car, she notices some remnants of crime scene tape fluttering on a wooden railing.

"He wasn't killed here in the parking lot, was he?" she asks.

"No," says Evan. "But the working theory is that the killer parked here and took his supplies into the woods: a gun and a bottle of cleaning fluid."

"How do you know this?" asks Sam, surprised.

He shrugs. "There's a lot of speculation online," he says.

Evan walks to the trailhead that leads from the parking lot into the forest and Sam follows. As they step into the trees, the sounds of traffic disappear behind them, replaced by the gentle rush of water from the river flowing just a few feet away, beyond a shallow embankment.

There has clearly been a lot of activity along the trail. More crime scene tape and arrows painted on seemingly random trees in neon orange paint indicate that a serious investigation has taken place here.

"The police lifted the barricades yesterday," says Evan as he leads Sam along the path. "So I came down to check things out for myself."

Sam is struck by how confidently the teenager leads her along the path, the broken, damaged young man from less than an hour ago replaced by someone who seems entirely in his element. In spite of herself, she thinks that maybe the kid does have the makings of an effective sleuth.

"Let me guess," she says. "You were here to shoot some video."

"I'm not posting anything about Justin and Vicki just yet," he says defensively. "I'm not stupid, I don't want to interfere with the investigation. But eventually someone will get caught for the crimes, and I want to be ready to take advantage of it. So yeah, I'm capturing as much footage as I can in the meantime."

"You think they'll catch the killer?" she says.

"Absolutely," he says. "They'll slip up at some point."

He steps off the trail and into a small clearing. It's been heavily trampled, and there's more crime scene tape fluttering from the trees. It's clearly been the site of an intense police investigation in recent days.

"Is this where the body was found?" she asks.

Evan nods. "This is where the cool kids come to drink and smoke weed and make out. I don't hang out here."

In the middle of the clearing is a bonfire pit, surrounded by a random collection of beat-up old chairs and a battered, weather-worn sofa. Hanging from one tree is a tattered old tarpaulin that has been tied into place to form a makeshift rain shelter. She remembers partying in places like this when she was young. There was an old gravel quarry on the far side of town where just this kind of makeshift living room had been assembled. An image flashes briefly in her mind: her sister sitting on Levon's lap, laughing at some clown's antics. She smiles at the memory.

"From what I've heard," says Evan, "nobody really uses this place except on weekends. Justin was found by a dog walker shortly after dawn on a Wednesday morning, so he likely came late on Tuesday night or very early in the morning, which is an odd time to be here in the woods."

"Do you think he might have been here for a drug deal?" Sam asks, remembering Angela Corvallis's theory.

Evan shakes his head. "I think he was meeting someone, but not for drugs. By all accounts, Justin was totally clean and didn't touch drugs or booze. But come look at this."

He moves to the back of the clearing and stands next to a thick cluster of low, scrabbly spruce trees.

Sam joins him. "What am I looking at?"

"Follow me," he says. He crouches and pushes aside some lower branches, then disappears into the trees. Sam follows, cursing to herself as she shoves through the hard, scratching branches. A moment later, she breaks through and finds herself in a small hollowed-out space under the trees, face-to-face with Evan, who is grinning like he just aced an exam.

"Pretty cool, hey?" he asks.

"So, what is this, your clubhouse?"

He rolls his eyes. "It's a pretty great hiding place," he says. "Or, more to the point, a great spying place." He points behind her, to the space where they pushed through, and when she turns, she can see that there is a small gap in the trees at eye level that gives a full view of the clearing.

"Okay," she says, "you think the killer hid here while he was waiting for Justin to arrive, then caught him off guard."

Evan nods. "Yup."

"That's a solid theory, buddy," she says. "But I hate to break it to you: the cops have definitely figured this much out already."

She feels bad about crushing his enthusiasm, but his self-satisfied smile doesn't fade.

"I'm sure they have," he says. "But I'm pretty sure they haven't figured out the rest."

Evan speaks with a confidence that Sam finds compelling, and she finds herself listening intently to hear what he has to say next.

"The theory the police have settled on," he says, reciting the facts like a crime reporter on the local news, "is that Justin Beagle's killer confronted him in the clearing and shot him through the chest, killing him instantly. Then they doused the body and the area with cleaning fluid and left the way they came, along the river trail. Footprints moving in both directions, along with trace amounts of cleaner found along the trail, would appear to heavily back that up. The footprints would indicate a man, shoe size 10, wearing boots with thick heels."

Sam nods. "And the killer quite possibly hid in here and waited for Justin to arrive. So the big question is whether he knew Justin would be here, or if he was just waiting for anyone to arrive and he chose his victim at random."

Evan tilts his head back and forth in a *yes and no* gesture. "Okay, so that is a big question for sure, but what I'm wondering is whether the killer actually used the river trail to get here."

Sam is confused. "What do you mean?"

"I mean it would have been really easy for someone to stage their entrance and exit," he says. "To make it look like they'd parked where we did, then walked in and out on the river trail. The weather was nice, and there would have been no chance of rain washing away footprints that had been preplanted."

"So, what, you think the killer dropped down from the sky?" Sam asks.

Evan grins and shakes his head, then he turns and wriggles his way through the trees on the back side of the den. Once again Sam follows.

The rear of the spruce thicket opens into the forest. It's a mix of trees, mostly pine and maple, with various shrubs and ferns filling in the space. Unlike the carefully maintained river trail or even the roughly stamped-down space that defines the clearing, the forest proper is untamed.

This is not a human place. Even at the height of a sunny day, this dense corner of the forest seems to consist entirely of shadows. Sam has the strange impression that the woods are unsettled. Are they angry about being disturbed, or is this the aftermath of the violence that occurred just beyond the trees only a few days ago?

"All the evidence pointed to an altercation in the clearing, with both individuals—victim and murderer—using the river trail to get there," says Evan. "But look at this."

He leads her over a fallen tree and carefully steps through a small, sun-dappled field of ferns. Finally he stops and points, and Sam sees it: a narrow path through the trees.

"It would have been easy for the cops to miss this," says Evan. "But somebody could have used this trail to come and go from the clearing, and there would have been almost no risk of being spotted."

Sam has to agree: the trail is almost invisible unless you're looking for it.

"It's probably a deer path," she says.

Evan nods. "Quite possibly, but that doesn't mean a human can't use it." He moves to the trail and begins to walk, and Sam hurries to follow him. He moves confidently through the trees and they walk for about ten minutes, neither of them speaking. Occasionally the muffled intermittent rush of cars reaches them through the trees, and at one point a lawn mower starts up in the distance, reminders that they're still close to civilization, but in the depths of the forest they might as well be invisible.

Finally, the woods begin to thin, and more light trickles down through the thick canopy as the evergreens and maples give way to tall, stately birch trees rustling in the breeze. Evan stops and waits for her to catch up, then turns and steps out of the forest.

Sam has already figured out where they've been headed, but it doesn't stop her breath from catching in her throat as she emerges onto the gently sloping hillside and stares down at the dilapidated remains of Birch Crest Elementary.

"Seriously, Evan," Sam says, "you need to promise me you'll stay away from that building."

They're back in Sam's car, heading to Evan's house so she can drop him off. Evan tried and failed to convince her that they should follow through and break into the school, but she quickly put that suggestion to rest. It's been twenty-five years since she last came close to that building, and she isn't interested in revisiting it.

"I just don't get what the problem is," he says, a bit sulkily. "We were on a roll. Why didn't we keep going and see what we could find in there? Isn't that what you would have done when you were in high school?"

"Evan," she says, "I should never have gone into the woods with you in the first place. It was totally inappropriate. But breaking into the school with you would have been completely negligent. That building is a hazard, and it's liable to come crashing down on anyone who is stupid enough to go inside. We'll tell the police, but I don't think they're going to find anything. There's no indication that Justin's murder, or Vicki's for that matter, has any connection to Birch Crest."

"It's a pretty big coincidence, don't you think?" he asks. "A secret path directly from the Janitor's lair to the scene of a copycat killing?"

"Yeah, you're right!" says Sam. "It's a coincidence, and that's all it is. A stupid, random coincidence. This is a really small town, Evan. That deer path could have led to the grocery store or the football field."

"But it didn't," he says stubbornly. "It led to the epicenter of the Janitor's massacre."

"Part of the skill of analyzing a scene," Sam says, forcing herself to remain patient, "is knowing what to disregard."

He turns to stare out the window, clearly disappointed.

"I know what it's like to become obsessed with an investigation," she says. "I know the feeling of that specific kind of thrill, how it makes you want to put everything else aside and just keep digging until you find an answer. But that kind of obsession leads to stupid risks, and those risks can have consequences that will haunt you forever."

He stares at her, clearly waiting for her to continue. She sighs. "With all the research you've done into the case, you probably know about how I took my father's gun."

"Yeah," says Evan. "I've heard about that."

"I had been taking gun safety lessons and doing practice shooting with my father since I was a kid," she explains. "I was comfortable with guns, and it seemed like the smart thing to do. But what

I didn't count on was that my father would need that gun and it wouldn't be there for him. Do you understand what I'm saying?"

He chews on his lip. "You feel like you're responsible for your father's death?"

Sam flinches at the blunt way he says it, but then she nods. "Not entirely, but I'll have to live with that question for the rest of my life. If we had gone to our father from the start . . . if we hadn't gotten out over our skis . . . if I hadn't taken that gun . . ."

"Maybe things would be different," says Evan.

"Yeah," says Sam. She releases a breath. "Exactly."

He nods slowly. "I get that," he says. "It's just . . . people are dead, and their loved ones deserve answers."

"You're absolutely right," Sam says. "They do deserve answers, and we have to give the authorities time do their job and figure things out. It's one thing to make a bunch of TikToks about old cases, it's something else entirely to insert yourself into an ongoing investigation. I need you to promise me you'll take a step back, okay?"

He nods, but she can tell he isn't convinced.

"Promise me," she presses.

He nods, holding her gaze this time. "I get it. I promise."

"Good," she says as she turns onto his street. "I'll talk to the police and tell them about your discovery so they can check things out more carefully, okay?"

"The police?" he asks, and the alarm in his voice is palpable. "You won't mention my name, will you?"

She looks at him, surprised. "Why not? What's the matter?"

Evan doesn't answer. Instead, he drops down low in his seat. "Can you just keep driving? For another block or two?"

She's confused until she turns back to the window and sees that Evan's father is standing in their front yard, smoking a cigarette. He's scowling out at the world, but she doesn't think he's spotted them.

"No problem," she replies. She drives for another couple of blocks and pulls over when they're safely out of sight.

"Evan," she says, choosing her words carefully, "is everything okay at home?"

He stares at her, his eyes wide but opaque. "You mean with my father?" he asks. "Yeah, everything's fine. He's just a weird guy, and I think . . . I think losing his job kind of messed him up, if you know what I mean. I just don't want to get a call from the cops, because I know it would piss him off."

"Of course." Sam hesitates, trying to decide what to say next. She probably shouldn't even have him in her car, let alone press him for personal information. She doesn't want to overstep yet another boundary. Finally she settles on rummaging inside her purse and pulling out a piece of paper and a pen. She scribbles her number down and gives it to him. "I won't mention you to the police, but if you need anything at all, get in touch, okay?"

He takes the paper and gives her a pitifully grateful smile.

"Okay," he says, shoving the paper into his pocket. "Thanks." He climbs out of the car, and as Sam pulls away, she sees him in the rearview mirror just standing there, watching her leave.

She feels bad for him, but the time for kid stuff is over. She needs to see her sister.

CHAPTER THIRTEEN: ALICE

Alice stands at the counter ignoring the pile of dishes that need washing, staring instead through her kitchen window at the Williamson house next door. She can't help thinking about what Drea said about the killer maybe mistaking Vicki for *her*. Could that be possible? If so, why is Vicki's back door key missing? Wouldn't that imply someone was watching her? And if so, doesn't that throw the wrong-victim theory out the window?

For a while after they left Kent and Vicki's house, she considered asking Levi for his opinion, whether he thinks they should pack up and leave town for a while like other people are doing. But she didn't bring it up, because she was worried he'd agree. Alice's overriding emotion right now isn't fear; it's curiosity.

She doesn't want to flee. She wants to get to the bottom of things.

She really wishes she could talk to her sister about all of this, but Sam couldn't get out of town fast enough. She's tried texting Doug a couple of times since yesterday, but he hasn't responded. That's not entirely out of character, since Doug can be a bit of a flake, but it's another reminder that she's on her own.

She hears the front door open and a moment later Levi enters the kitchen. He loosens his tie and reaches into the fridge for a beer without even acknowledging her.

"Well, hello to you too," she says.

"Don't start with me, Alice," he says, before tipping the bottle and downing half of it in one swallow.

"Don't start?" she asks. She's used to her communication with Levi being tight lately, but this feels especially hostile even for him. "I guess we've just reached the point where we don't even bother to go through the motions of asking how each other's day went."

"Oh, for Christ's sake," he says. "I ask you every single day how your day went, and every single day you make some passive-aggressive little comment about how boring your life is."

"Well, it *is* kind of boring," she says.

"Right." He downs the rest of the beer in one long frat-boy slug and slams the bottle down on the counter. "Well, I truly love my daily grind of shoving numbers around in a spreadsheet and pretending to like the assholes I work with. At least you get to spend some time in your own head, which is just how you like it, isn't it?"

Alice feels the argument enter a tense new phase and freezes. "What's that supposed to mean?"

He laughs bitterly. "I'm not an idiot, Alice. I know who I married. Do you forget that I was there all those years ago? You just can't help inserting yourself into this, can you?"

"Into what?" she asks, although she knows exactly what he's talking about.

"Don't give me that shit," he says. "You've had your head in the clouds for days, obviously fantasizing about solving this new case.

Didn't you learn your lesson the last time? This isn't a game, Alice. My brother and your father are dead. Isn't that enough for you?"

Alice stares at him, shocked. She remembers how much they supported each other after the tragedy. They had worked through the trauma together. Helped each other heal. Created a family.

And now, twenty-five years later, it's as if they've returned right back to where they started, only this time Levi has decided he wants to do things differently.

The anger in his face melts away, and he just looks tired and unhappy.

"I'm sorry," he says. "I shouldn't have said that."

"What the hell is wrong with you two?"

They turn to see Will in the doorway, glaring at them.

"What are you doing home, honey?" asks Alice. "I thought you had French tutoring after school."

"It got canceled," says Will. "You guys never used to fight like this. It sucks. If you're going to get divorced, just get fucking divorced, okay?"

"Watch your language," says Alice. "We are not getting divorced."

"Yeah, well maybe you should," says Will. They follow him into the entryway, where he grabs his coat and backpack.

"I'm going to the library." He yanks the front door open and freezes at the sight of Sam on the doorstep.

"Hey!" she says, with forced cheerfulness. She notices Alice and Levi hovering behind Will and must see the tension in their faces. "Is everything okay?"

Will shoves past her without speaking.

"Hang on," calls Levi, "I'll drive you."

He grabs a coat from a hook by the door and hurries after Will. After a beat Sam steps into the house.

"What's going on?" she asks.

But Alice is in no mood to talk about it. "What are you doing here?"

Sam looks sheepish. "It's kind of a long story . . . The truth is I didn't actually go back to Los Angeles."

Alice stares at her sister in disbelief. "What are you talking about? I dropped you off at the airport two days ago."

"I know," says Sam. "I was about to leave, but . . . I just couldn't stop thinking about everything going on back here, and I decided to stick around."

She smiles, but Alice is in no mood to play nice.

"You're telling me you had me drive you all the way to the airport just so you could *pretend* you were about to fly back to L.A?"

"I wasn't pretending," Sam protests. "It was a spur-of-the-moment decision. I decided to stay and look around a little bit."

"What do you mean, 'look around'?" asks Alice. "Is that what you've been doing for the past two days? Looking around?"

Sam looks sheepish. "I guess you could say I was . . . investigating."

Alice isn't sure what does it. Maybe it's her sister's unexpected reappearance. Maybe it's the fact that the husband she's been with since she was seventeen years old is beginning to feel like a complete stranger, and their son seems to hate them both. Maybe it's because the sister who was supposed to be her rock, her support, her closest confidante, has decided to just pick up the thread that they dropped all those years ago *on her own*. Whatever it is, she feels something inside herself suddenly break.

She bursts into tears.

She's only vaguely aware of Sam pulling her into an embrace as she blubbers about Levi and Will, and Joanna and their dad, and Vicki, and all the other things that have built up inside her. She cries until she's out of tears, and then she pulls back and wipes her face and takes a deep breath.

"Sam," she says, "are you serious about investigating?"

"Yeah," says Sam, holding her gaze. "I think I am. I've learned a lot in the past couple of days."

Alice nods. "I have too. I think we need to try to solve this, Sam."

Sam takes her hand. "I agree," she says, "but I think we could use some help."

CHAPTER FOURTEEN: JOEY

By the time Joey arrives at Cordova's, Samantha and Alice are already there, sitting in a window booth. He slides in across from them.

"I'm glad we can do this in person," says Alice. "We thought you'd be back in Boston by now."

"That was the plan," he says, "but I decided to take a few days off work so I could spend some quality time with my mom."

He doesn't tell them the truth, which is that he's avoiding Boston, or more accurately, the conversations he needs to have once he returns.

This morning he woke to an email from Mike outlining more details about the Paris opportunity, including photos of a very nice flat in the 8th Arrondissement that comes with the job. "It's yours if you want it," the message said, "but we'll need to start making some plans soon. Hope to see you today so we can discuss."

He knows he needs to bring Austin into the loop so he can give Mike a final decision, but the truth is, he knows what Austin will say and he doesn't want to hear that answer. It's not that he doesn't want kids. It's not even that he *does* want to move to Paris.

It's that he doesn't want to keep doing his job at Shoreline, and he feels stuck at a crossroads between two imperfect paths.

But there's no avoiding reality, and he's decided he'll finally talk to Austin to confirm that Paris is out of the question, and then tell Mike he isn't interested. He had been preparing to head back this morning to do just that when the twins reached out, asking to connect. Something about what that implied seemed a lot more appealing than dealing with his real-life situation, so he texted Mike, alluding to a "family emergency," before calling Austin to say he'd be staying with his mom for a few more days. Now here he is with the Van Dyne twins for the second time in less than a week.

"So what's all this about, anyway?" he asks.

"We'll cut to the chase," says Sam. "We're going to start our own investigation into the murders."

Joey nods slowly and Alice raises an eyebrow. "You don't look surprised."

"I had a hunch it would be about this," he says. "I mean, what else, right?"

Sam pushes something across the table. It's a receipt inside a plastic bag, and as Joey picks it up and examines it, Sam tells him about breaking into Kershaw's apartment.

"We think this proves that Kershaw was out of state when Mary Ellen Spakalitis was killed," she says.

"There's more," says Alice. Joey listens as the twins go back and forth, explaining the missing key to Vicki's back door, and the secret path leading from the clearing where Justin was found dead to Birch Crest Elementary.

"Somebody is trying to orchestrate things to look a certain way," says Sam. "And if this receipt does confirm what Kershaw was trying to tell us, that's the same thing that happened all those years ago. We're not saying it's definitely the same person . . ."

"But it's a pretty big coincidence if it isn't," Joey muses, finishing her sentence.

The twins nod. "Exactly," they say at the same time.

"Okay," says Joey, "so let's say we're all in agreement here. Kershaw was telling the truth, and there's some kind of connection between all of the cases. What's next?"

"That's where you come in," says Alice. "You can help us with digital forensics. I was reading about some of the apps you've worked on, using cellphone data to map people's preferences. Could you find a way to dig into Justin and Vicki's histories so we can retrace their steps?"

Joey laughs. "Oh man, that is absolutely not going to happen. For one thing, the privacy implications are enormous. The police might be able to access some of that information using warrants, but if I tried to pull something like that off, I could go to jail."

Alice frowns, disappointed. "There must be some way you can help us."

Instead of answering, Joey takes a long breath, considering something. "Okay," he says finally. "I have to show you guys something."

He pulls up Doug's note on his phone and passes it across the table to them.

The sisters stare at the image in shock.

Goldfish
Call Perry
Bruce Philip Kershaw didn't kill Mary Ellen Spakalitis.

"That's Dad's handwriting," Sam says finally.

"That's what we thought," says Joey.

"Who is 'we'?" asks Sam.

Joey glances at Alice before answering. "Doug Shiftley took this note from your father's office on the day that he died."

"Wait," says Alice, clearly shocked. "What?"

"Why the hell was Dog Shit in Dad's office?" asks Sam.

"You shouldn't call him that," says Alice, with surprising vehemence. "It's a nasty name."

"Your husband gave it to him," says Sam with a shrug.

Joey relays the story of how Doug came to find the note.

"I can't believe he's kept this to himself for all these years," says Sam.

"Goldfish," muses Alice. "There's something familiar about that, but I can't place it. I don't understand why Doug didn't tell me about this."

"Why would he?" Sam casts an inquisitive look at her sister, whose face flushes a deep red. "Oh. My. God. Are you having an affair with Dougie Dog Shit?"

"Jesus Christ, Sam," says Alice. "Stop calling him that. No, of course I'm not having an affair." She pauses, then sighs. "We've become really good friends lately, but I . . . I kind of haven't mentioned it to Levi. I just can't believe he didn't tell me anything about this note."

"I think we're getting off track here," says Joey. "As far as anyone knew, your father had never even heard of Kershaw before . . ."

He goes quiet, and Sam finishes his sentence. "Before he showed up at our house and shot him to death."

Joey nods. "But Doug's note tells us he *was* aware of Kershaw, if only anecdotally."

"So now we have two pieces of evidence backing up what Kershaw told us," says Alice. "The receipt, showing he was out of town, and Dad's note literally spelling out not only that he knew about Kershaw but that Kershaw was innocent of Spakalitis's murder."

"What we're missing," says Sam, "is some evidence that what happened back then is connected to what's happening now."

Joey sighs, and Alice has the sudden feeling that he's about to tell them something important.

"Okay," he says. "Yesterday I took my mother to Justin Beagle's funeral. Afterwards I spoke to Justin's uncle. He was kind of drunk and really upset, but he told me something interesting. He said a few weeks before he died, Justin asked him a bunch of questions about the Janitor murders. The uncle said it was like he was obsessed and that was totally out of character for him. The kid usually talked about sports or cars. True crime wasn't his thing at all, but then out of nowhere he became fixated and wanted all the details he could get."

Sam is just staring at him.

"What?" asks Joey.

"For someone who likes to talk about how much he hates investigating, you sure are doing a lot of it. Secret notes and uninvited funeral attending?"

"I was just asking some questions," he says.

"So something tuned Justin in to the original murders and then he turned up dead," says Alice. "What are we missing in between?"

Sam points at the note on Joey's phone screen. "I guess we start by figuring out what Dad's note meant."

"Oh my God!" says Alice. "Brenda Regent!"

Sam's eyes widen and she slaps the table. "Holy shit. You're right."

"Who's Brenda Regent?" asks Joey.

"She was our music teacher," says Alice. "Mom hired her to give us voice lessons. Just another step on her obsessive journey to make us famous."

"Brenda Regent was a real weirdo," says Sam.

"Not a weirdo, exactly," says Alice. "Intense."

"Intense," Sam agrees. "I think Mom thought we could be recording artists. We went along with it for a while, but then we started solving cases and we put our foot down and told Mom we wouldn't do it anymore. That was the end of Brenda Regent, better known to us as Goldfish."

Joey raises an eyebrow inquisitively, and Alice explains.

"She had a Ronald McDonald dye job and a wardrobe full of brassy autumn colors. She seemed to only wear tones of red and orange and yellow and gold. So we called her Goldfish." She shrugs. "We were asshole teenagers. I wonder what she could have had to do with all of this."

"Maybe we should try to find her," says Joey. "See what she remembers."

"Even if we could find her," says Alice, "she wouldn't want to see me or Sam. She didn't like us very much after our revolt. But I doubt she'd know who you are."

Joey thinks this over. "I'm not really good at . . . you know, talking to people. That was never my strength."

"I don't think you give yourself enough credit," says Alice. "Sounds like you did a pretty good job with Justin's uncle."

"Fair enough," says Joey. "I'll try to track her down, but I can't make any promises."

"I guess that leaves Perry to us," says Alice. "It wouldn't be unusual for Dad to run things by Perry if he was suspicious of something. It's probably worth a visit. Maybe you and I should go see him, Sam."

"Are you kidding?" asks Sam. "I literally just fired the guy. He's not going to be excited to have a heart-to-heart with me after that."

"Okay," says Alice. "I'll go see him myself. But what are you going to do?"

"There's something I want to look into," says Sam cryptically.

"So"—Joey cocks an eye at them—"have we decided we're just not going to talk to the police about this?"

The sisters exchange a look. "We aren't sure that's a good idea," says Sam finally. "As long as Angela Corvallis is in charge of the investigation, nobody is going to seriously look into the connection between everyone who died then and everyone who is dying now."

"I saw Nash at Justin's funeral. It looked like he was poking around on his own. He gave me the impression that he's on a short leash with Corvallis."

"We could bring him into the conversation," Alice proposes.

Sam shakes her head. "Not yet. Let's see what we can find out on our own first, and then when we have something more concrete to share, we'll bring it to him instead of Corvallis."

"That works," says Alice. "Joey?"

He nods. "I guess it's settled. We're going to work a case together after all."

CHAPTER FIFTEEN: SAM

When Doug arrives home he's laden down with grocery bags and his mind is clearly elsewhere, because he doesn't notice Sam leaning against his building until she says his name. He screams, almost dropping the bags.

"Jesus Christ!" He squints. "Sam Van Dyne? Is that you?"

"The one and only," she says. "You got a few minutes? I need to talk to you."

Doug hesitates, and she smiles, softening her approach. "I don't bite."

"Sure," he says, after a pause. "Come on in." He leads the way up the steps.

She didn't know what to expect from Doug's apartment, but it turns out that it's actually really nice, with a hip but lived-in vibe that she kind of digs. "Cool place," she says.

"Thanks." He places the grocery bags on the island. "Grab a seat, I just have to put a few things away. Do you want a beer?"

"I'd love one," she says, dropping into a low leather chair. She watches him as he moves around, putting away groceries, and she realizes that, like his apartment, Doug himself is looking hip and lived-in. Old Dog Shit seems to have gone through a glow-up in the decades since she last saw and, let's be honest, thought about him. He's grown a beard and let his hair get kind of shaggy, and his Coke bottle glasses have thinned out and been replaced with some interesting frames.

He also moves around the apartment fluidly in a way that indicates someone who is comfortable in his own skin. If there's one thing Dog Sh—Doug Shiftley was *not* in his high school phase, it was comfortable in his own skin.

He finishes putting away his groceries and reaches into the fridge to retrieve two Heinekens. He cracks them and comes over to hand her one.

"Do you mind if I put on music?" he asks.

She shrugs. "Be my guest in your own house."

Still standing, he pulls out his phone and scrolls. Sam realizes they've barely spoken since they entered his apartment. She realizes why a moment later as music fills the room from some speakers in the corner, and he drops onto the sofa across from her and begins to laugh.

"What's so funny?" she asks warily.

"Oh, man, Samantha Van Dyne," he says. "Do you have any idea how high I am right now?"

"What, with weed?" she asks.

"Yeah, man, with weed." He lets out a long laugh and shakes his head, running his fingers through his hair. "I like to get stoned when I buy groceries. It's like playing a little video game in the real world. And then I come home ready to make myself some ramen, and the hottest girl from my high school, who I haven't seen in a quarter century, jumps out from an alley and invites herself into my apartment. Are you here to rope me into some multilevel marketing bullshit?"

Sam laughs out loud. She didn't expect to find Doug this entertaining.

"No," she says. "I'm here to find out if you're sleeping with my sister."

The grin drops from Doug's face. "Jesus, no! What the hell? Did Levi put you up to this? Did he send you here to tell me if I don't lay off, he'll shove my head down another toilet?"

"Wow," says Sam. "Did he really do that?"

"Where have you been?" he asks. "He gave me my nickname too, among other horrors. Do you know how much therapy I had to go through to stop thinking of *myself* as Dog Shit?"

"Levi has nothing to do with this," she says. "So you two aren't having an affair?"

Doug takes a sip of his beer and looks her straight in the eye. "No. I don't make a habit of sleeping with married women, not that I wouldn't like to pull one over on Levi Brakes. But it's not like that with me and Alice. We're buddies."

Sam believes him, and she feels bad for doubting Alice. But that's not the only reason she's here. "If you're such great buddies, why didn't you ever mention to her that you were holding on to important information related to our father's murder?"

Doug lets out a long sigh that braps through his lips. "Samantha Van Dyne," he says. "You sure know how to kill someone's grocery store buzz. The truth is, until very recently it felt like all of that was really behind Alice."

"Behind her," repeats Sam.

"Yeah," says Doug. "Behind her. Behind Joey. Behind Edgar Mills. I don't know about you, because I haven't seen you in literally decades, but the rest of us around here want to put it all behind us and get back to normal. How would it have benefited anyone for me to tell that story? It doesn't change the outcome. It would have only served to drag shit up again, and who wants that? Alice and I smoke joints and watch old movies and eat snacks. There wasn't really an appropriate moment."

"Okay," says Sam, "but now with all the . . . stuff."

"The new murders," says Doug. "Yeah. I confided in Joey because it felt like I could talk to him without it becoming a big emotional thing. Do you . . . are you guys doing something about it?"

"What do you mean, 'doing something about it'?" she asks.

"You know," he says. "Are you *investigating*? If Joey told the two of you about that note, then obviously you're talking about the case."

"We're asking questions," she says carefully.

Doug shifts in his seat, clearly looking like he wants to say something.

"What is it?" she asks. "Spit it out."

"Well," he says, "I was just thinking that maybe I could help."

She laughs and immediately regrets it from the look of embarrassment that crosses his face. "Sorry," she says. "I'm not trying to make fun of you. It's just that I don't know what you'd help with. We're kind of flailing around."

"Your sister will tell you that I'm actually pretty well-connected around here," he says. "I never left town and I've got my ear to the ground."

"I'll keep that in mind," she says. "But we barely know what we're doing, so I doubt we'll need any help."

"Whatever," he says, irritated.

"Oh come on," she says. "Don't be like that."

Doug looks at her carefully. "Sam," he says, "can I ask you something? Why did you really come to see me?"

She finds herself, uncharacteristically, at a loss for words. She scrambles internally for an excuse—she's worried about Alice, or she doesn't want him to tell anyone about the note—but finally she settles for the truth.

"I wanted to know if you saw my dad."

She can tell by Doug's bewildered expression that he doesn't catch her meaning.

"When you snuck into his office," she explains. "That was his last day alive."

Doug's face softens with understanding. "Right. Well, I really only caught a glimpse of him. He was giving some kind of presentation to a bunch of other cops. I assume they were talking about the case."

Sam nods. She can picture him in that zone.

"Did he look happy?" she asks, and she's angry at herself for the break in her voice.

Doug smiles, and the expression is so kind and understanding that she can barely look at him. "Yeah," he says, and she can hear the compassion in his voice. "He looked like he was in his element."

"Can I see the note?" she asks.

"Sure."

He gets up and walks to the bookshelf on the other side of the room, returning with the notebook stuffed full of paper.

"The results of your investigation?" she asks.

"Something like that," he says. He opens to a page in the middle of the binder and slides it across to her, and Sam stares down at the page with a dim, aching horror.

A quarter century ago, her father, living and breathing, used his living, working hand to write these words. But what did they mean?

She stares for so long and so intently at the note that she doesn't even notice when her coat starts buzzing.

"Is that your phone?" asks Doug.

"Shit," she says, snapping from her trance and digging into her pocket. She doesn't recognize the number, but something tells her to answer it anyway.

"Hello?"

"Sam?" The voice on the other end of the line sounds weak and distant, and she doesn't recognize it at first. "It's Evan." He takes a sharp intake of breath, and Sam can tell instantly that something is wrong.

"What's going on, Evan?" she asks, standing up.

"I've been attacked, I think?" he says.

"What do you mean, you think? Was it bullies from school?" Sam is aware of Doug casting a quizzical look in her direction.

"No," he says. "I mean, I don't think so. I didn't see them. They kind of snuck up on me."

"Where are they now?" she asks. "Are you safe?"

"I think so," he says. "Whoever attacked me ran away." He pauses, and then he begins to cry softly. "I'm at Birch Crest Elementary."

Sam scrambles to process. "What the hell were—" She catches herself. "It doesn't matter. I'm going to call the cops right now."

"No!" Evan's voice is frantic. "Please, don't call the police."

"Evan, I have to," she says. "I'll call Chief Young; he's a friend. You won't get in trouble."

"It's not that," he says. "I don't . . . I don't want my parents to find out about this. Can you just come alone? Please?"

"I'm on my way," she says.

Doug insists on coming with her, and as she pulls into the parking lot she's happy he's tagged along. It's started to drizzle, and the abandoned building looms over them, casting even more shadow onto an already gray scene.

They find Evan sitting on the ground under the awning at the front door. Hunched over his bent knees, he looks even smaller than usual. As they approach, he looks up and Sam gasps. His face and hair are smeared with blood from a scratch on his forehead, and he has a fat lip.

"Jesus, Evan," she says, hurrying to crouch beside him. "Are you okay?"

"I'm okay now," he says. "But I was pretty scared."

She looks up at the school, suddenly nervous. "Are you sure whoever did this is gone?" she asks.

"They're gone," says Evan. "If they wanted to kill me, they would have. I think they were trying to send me a message."

Evan looks past her and she realizes he's looking suspiciously at Doug.

"This is my friend Doug," she says. "You can trust him, I promise." She crouches and puts a hand on his shoulder. "Tell us what happened."

Evan slumps over again and puts his head on his knees. "I decided I wanted to see if I could find something. A clue. Maybe something connected to Justin. Even if I came up empty, I thought it would make for some great footage."

Sam resists the urge to remind him he promised to stay away from this building. "How did you get in?"

"One of the side doors is open," he says. "It looks boarded over, but it was easy enough to move. People have obviously been breaking in for years. There's graffiti all through the building."

"What happened when you got in?" she asks.

He closes his eyes, remembering. "I had a flashlight, and I was trying to find my way through the building, to the—" He cuts himself off, and Sam finishes for him.

"The gymnasium," she says.

He nods miserably. "I wanted to see where everything happened," he says. "I thought maybe if someone *is* trying to imitate the Janitor, and if they've been using the school as some kind of home base . . . maybe the gym would be sort of a natural place for them to operate, you know?"

Sam doesn't see the logic, but clearly Evan is making excuses. She assumes he wanted to see where the action took place.

"I was looking around," he says, "taking my time in case I spotted something interesting or relevant. And then I heard a sound."

"What kind of sound?" asks Doug.

In response, Evan pulls his phone out of his pocket. The screen is cracked, but it appears to still be working. He pulls up a video and hands the phone to Sam.

The image is a bit unstable, since Evan is clearly holding a flashlight in one hand while trying to film with the other. The camera scans the space, revealing filthy floors and graffiti on the walls.

"That's the central hallway," says Doug. "The gym would have been at the end, around the corner."

"I didn't even get that far," says Evan, and even despite everything that's happened to him, he sounds frustrated. "Watch."

The camera continues to move forward slowly, scanning back and forth, following the flashlight's beam. The only sound seems to be the shuffling of Evan's feet along the floor and a faint, distant drip of water. Then the camera abruptly stops moving, and Evan stands still. Then a new sound, a faint but audible bang, happens off camera, and the image spins around. The flashlight peers to the end of the corridor, disappearing into the shadows.

"Hello?" asks Evan in the video. He sounds young and terrified, and Sam's heart clenches.

There's no response. He turns and continues walking, but a moment later he pauses again.

"Who's there?" he asks. He begins to run, the camera still rolling. The image is dark and disorienting with only brief flickers of light from the shaky flashlight. Offscreen, Sam can hear Evan's heavy, gasping breaths mixed with the hollow sound of footsteps echoing through the hallway.

Then Evan cries out in terror, and the phone twists through the air before landing on the floor with an audible crack. The screen is black now, presumably focused on the floor, but the sound is still audible. A frantic scuffling combined with a rough rustling noise that's difficult to identify, followed by a couple of large smacks. Finally, the sound of running footsteps, receding before disappearing entirely.

There's a long pause, the only sound a miserable whimpering sniffle, and then the camera lifts, briefly revealing Evan's bloody, tear-stained face, before he reaches in to shut it off.

"Holy shit," says Doug.

"Evan," says Sam, handing him back the phone and putting a hand on his knee. "You are very lucky to be alive."

"Maybe," he says, thoughtfully. "I was terrified, and when I got thrown on the ground I just curled in on myself and prepared to die. But I think they just wanted to scare me. They could have killed me but they didn't. They just slapped me around a bit and punched me in the side of the head, then they leaned down right next to my ear and whispered, 'Stay out of it.'"

"Did you recognize the voice?" asks Doug.

Evan shakes his head. "No. It was low and gravelly, kind of like a cartoon. They were obviously trying to disguise their voice. I think it was a man but I can't be sure."

"Did you see anything?" asks Sam. "A glimpse of their face or hair, or even what they were wearing?"

Evan shakes his head. "I was tackled from behind and I had my eyes closed for most of it. But there was this weird rustling, like fabric or something. Like they were wearing something weird."

Sam remembers the description Lizzie Carroll gave of her encounter in the woods. Her attacker was in a gray hazmat suit.

"Finally they left," Evan finishes. "I stayed on the floor until I was pretty sure they were gone, then I found my phone and went outside and called you."

They turn as a vehicle comes tearing into the parking lot. It's a police cruiser.

Evan gives Sam a hurt, indignant look. "You called the police."

"I had to," says Sam. "Chief Young is a friend of mine. We can't just pretend that this didn't happen."

Evan's eyes are frantic, and his voice is low and urgent. "Sam. He'll call my parents."

The cruiser parks and Nash Young gets out and walks over to them.

"Sorry it took me so long. I was caught up in something across town. What's going on?"

Evan stares at them miserably as Sam fills Nash in on the basics.

"I'm going to have to take him in for a statement," says Nash. "I'll call the parents and have them meet us at the station."

Evan looks stricken, and Sam takes Nash off to the side so they can speak out of earshot. Doug tags along behind them.

"Nash," she says. "I know this kid and I am convinced he's scared of his father. Is there some way to file a report without bringing his parents into the mix?"

Nash grimaces. "I can't bring a minor in for questioning and not involve the parents. That would land me in a ton of shit."

"What if you don't bring him in for questioning?" asks Sam. Nash opens his mouth to protest but she pushes on. "Just hear me out. If you make this official, Corvallis will take over and insist on doing the interview herself."

"That's her decision," says Nash. "She's in charge of the investigation."

Sam rolls her eyes. "And how's that going? From what I hear, she refuses to consider a connection between what happened back then and what's happening now."

Nash narrows his eyes. "You've spoken to Joey, haven't you? He told me he wasn't involved."

Sam throws up her hands. "We're all involved, Nash! Alice told you about Vicki's missing key. I told you about the secret path between the school and the clearing where Justin was killed. Has any of that made any difference?"

"No," he admits. "Because both of those examples can be passed off as coincidence. *I* don't think it's coincidence, but what I think doesn't matter. If I bring this kid in and Corvallis hears his story for herself, she won't be able to ignore it anymore."

Sam shakes her head. "I think you're making a mistake, Nash. If you hand this over to Corvallis, she's going to find some way to fuck it all up. I'm begging you, just keep this between you and the kid. Ask him some questions here, with us, but hold off on taking an official statement until you know for sure you need it."

"You're one of us, dude," says Doug, and they both turn to look at him as if they'd forgotten he was even here.

"What do you mean?" Nash asks.

"You were here back then," says Doug. "You know better than anyone what things were like, because you were right in the thick of it. You know the stakes, man. Does this Corvallis person know the stakes?"

"He's right, Nash," says Sam. "Don't let her sideline you. Handle it yourself. We can help."

Nash seems to waver, sucking in his upper lip and thinking silently for a long time. Then he turns and glances back to where Evan is still sitting on the ground, curled in on himself, and makes up his mind.

"I agree with you," he says. "Something is going on beneath the surface here that the official investigation is missing. But I can't afford to go rogue with this. He's just a kid. It would be unethical for me to ignore due process, and it could destroy a court case when we get to trial. I need to bring him in for an official statement."

Evan is clearly unhappy about this turn of events. As Nash ushers him into the cruiser, he drops his head miserably and slumps into the back seat. Nash shuts the door, then turns back to face them.

"You have to trust me," he says. "Once she hears his story, I'm going to insist we come back and carry out a thorough sweep of the school. There's no way she'll be able to turn down that suggestion after this. In the meantime, I'm sure I don't need to say this, but don't even think about going inside. Capisce?"

They nod, and as he drives away, Sam tries to catch Evan's eye, but he refuses to look at her.

"What do you think the chances are that the new killer was using that school as a home base?" asks Doug.

"Zilch," says Sam. She's already come to the same conclusion. "If that was the killer, Evan didn't track them down. *They* tracked *him* down."

Doug furrows his brow. "All because of his TikTok account?"

"He's been poking his nose in all over the place," she says. "Maybe someone is worried he's getting too close to learning something."

"But if it was the killer," Doug continues, "why didn't he just take the kid out when he had the chance? It would have been easy."

"If he's a copycat," she says, "this was his chance to imitate what happened to Lizzie Carroll. She got away."

Doug doesn't respond, but she knows what he's thinking. Twenty-five years ago, two murders and an attempted abduction were only the first phase of the terror that fell on Edgar Mills.

And if history really is repeating itself, the next act is about to be much messier.

CHAPTER SIXTEEN: JOEY

Joey pulls into the parking lot of a well-maintained apartment building. Around back, he can see an attractively landscaped garden full of senior citizens taking advantage of the nice weather. Inside, he tells the woman at the desk that he'd like to speak with Brenda Regent.

"Certainly," the woman says brightly. She clicks away at her keyboard for a moment. "Ms. Regent is in room 446, but I'd check the common room first. She spends a lot of time in there. Just around that corner and at the end of the hallway."

Joey is a bit surprised at how easy this is but thanks the woman and follows her directions. As he approaches the common area, which turns out to be a large sunlit room that looks out on the back gardens, he becomes aware of cheerful, tinkling piano music. In the corner of the room, a bunch of smiling seniors sit on chairs in a half circle around a very small and spry-looking woman at a piano. Between the show tunes she's cranking out and her bright red hair, he's pretty sure he's found who he's looking for.

She's halfway through "Hello, Dolly!" when she glances up and notices him watching from across the room. A couple of minutes later she wraps up the tune and closes the piano to a chorus of groans from her audience.

"Sorry, pals," she says, beginning to pull together her sheet music. "I'm feeling a bit worn out today. I'll throw in a couple of extra tunes tomorrow."

The crowd begins to disperse, and Joey approaches, raising a hand in greeting.

"Excuse me," he says. "Are you Ms. Regent?"

She nods, smiling pleasantly.

"I'm—"

"I know who you are, honey," she says, cutting him off.

Joey stares at her, surprised. "You do?"

"Of course," she says. "I'm old, I'm not stupid. I knew one of you would get here eventually. Just surprised it didn't happen sooner. Why don't we go up to my room, where we can speak in private."

Joey follows Brenda upstairs to her room, which is dynamically decorated, its low ceilings, fluorescent lighting, and institutional furniture camouflaged by the elderly woman's belongings. Eclectic blankets and quilts cover every surface, and colorful scarves are draped over the lamps. Plants thrive in the direct sunlight streaming through the window, and her walls are covered with photographs of various people from throughout the years, most of them posed with her.

"My students," she says. "I didn't have children of my own, but my students were my kids."

He's about to turn back to her when one photograph catches his attention, and he leans forward to get a closer look.

"Yep," she says as his eyes widen with recognition. "That's the Van Dyne twins."

Joey is surprised Brenda has their picture on display, considering that they seemed to think she didn't like them.

"They were resisting their mother," she says. "She wanted them to make it big. Typical stage mother stuff. If you've seen it once, you've seen it a million times. If you tell a kid that learning an instrument is a fun challenge guaranteed to provide a lifetime of joy, they might just stick with it. If you tell them the instrument is a means to a career in the entertainment industry, you're just sucking the fun out of it."

"So they didn't keep singing?" Joey asks.

"They kept it up for a few months," she says. "All because the mother pushed them. She would invite me for tea and cookies, buttering me up so I'd give her precious girls extra attention. I wasn't about to turn down some good cookies, so I'd come a half hour early every time, eat the cookies and gossip a bit. More importantly, I'd make all the right noises about how talented they were."

"Were they?" asks Joey.

"Oh, sure," she says, shrugging. "They could both carry a tune. But something else took over their attention."

"The detective stuff," Joey posits.

She nods. "Of course I heard about it just like everyone else. It was a fun story, the way the two of them stepped in to help their old man solve crimes. I didn't know him as well as I did Joanna. But I could tell that he was as proud of them as anything, and you know girls and their fathers: they both gravitated right to that approval. Singing wasn't on their radar anymore, and I don't blame them. They'd only been doing it for their mother, and so it was impossible for them to just quit. They made me do the dirty work instead."

"How so?" asks Joey.

"They became clear-cut little assholes," she says. "They didn't practice. They screwed up on purpose. They showed up late for rehearsal. I knew what was going on, of course, so after a few weeks of that I made my excuses to Joanna and stopped teaching them. I felt bad for her. She just wanted her girls to be successful. And of course they were—just not in the way she had hoped. Instead of pop stars, she got detectives. And we all know how that ended. That's why you're here to see me, of course."

Joey nods and she points at a chair. "Have a seat and ask me whatever you want. I'm an open book."

"Did you speak to Chief Van Dyne the day he was murdered?" Joey asks.

"I did," she says, without hesitation. "I called to tell him that Bruce Kershaw could not have killed Mary Ellen Spakalitis. He was with me, out of state, the day she died."

It turns out Brenda Regent is full of surprises.

"You were with him?" Joey repeats, after a long, flabbergasted pause.

Brenda nods. "I was teaching at the high school when Bruce started working there. He's always been associated with Birch Crest Elementary, for obvious reasons, but after it closed he worked at the high school. We struck up a friendship, one thing led to another, and we began dating."

Joey can hardly believe what he's hearing. In twenty-five years' worth of news stories and retrospectives, he has never heard a single thing about Bruce Philip Kershaw dating anyone.

Brenda can obviously tell what he's thinking. "We kept it very quiet," she explains. "We only met up in private after school hours.

Sometimes he came to my house, parking a couple of streets away and using the back entrance. A couple of times I went to his apartment, but it was harder to be discreet about that. There was always the chance I'd run into someone in the elevator."

She stops speaking as she remembers, and a look of genuine sadness shadows her face. Joey stays silent, waiting for her to continue.

"I don't know why I was so embarrassed," she says finally. "He was very sweet and kind and attentive. Interesting. He liked to talk about films and books he'd read. I know the media made him out to be a bit slow, but he wasn't. He was just different. I thought he was beginning to fall for me as well, but then, well . . ."

"The murders," he says.

She grins ruefully. "We could have had it all if it hadn't been for that pesky serial killer thing."

"When you say you were out of state with him, were you in Vermont?"

Brenda's eyes widen. "How did you know about that?"

"Some evidence has recently come to light," he says, keeping things vague.

"Well, it's true," she says. "We did go to Vermont, on the exact same weekend that Mary Ellen Spakalitis was supposed to have been killed, and I called and explained that to Bill Van Dyne directly."

In Joey's mind, the data point slots into place and confirms what he and the twins have speculated: that there's a direct line from "Goldfish" to "Kershaw didn't do it" on Chief Van Dyne's note. But there's something that still doesn't fit.

"Were you still dating Bruce Kershaw right up until the end?" he asks.

She nods. "To the very last day. He came to my apartment when he received that email from the twins."

"Are you serious?" Joey definitely didn't expect this.

"Oh yes," she says. "He was in an absolute state of panic. He was pacing around my living room, trying to figure out what to do. Thinking back, I guess maybe I should have been suspicious of his reaction, but at the time he just seemed . . . I don't know, freaked out and blindsided."

Joey thinks this over carefully. "Why on earth would he have told you about this? Isn't it the last thing he would have shared?"

Brenda turns up her palms. "Honey, you don't know how many times I've gone over this in my head. The best I can come up with is that he started to think he was going to get caught, and he was in some kind of spiral, and I just happened to be there. When I'm in my darkest thoughts, I imagine that maybe he came over that day to kill me and changed his mind at the last minute. He didn't stay for long, and it was the last time I ever saw or spoke to him. That's when I called the police station and asked to talk to Chief Van Dyne."

"Why didn't you come forward again after Van Dyne was murdered?" asks Joey.

She shakes her head, her lips pursed. "Well, the man had murdered a cop and all those other people," she says. "I wasn't inclined to help him off the hook. If he wanted my alibi, he could have sent them to talk to me. I would have told them the same thing that I told Bill Van Dyne—that he was with me when they thought Mary Ellen was killed—but beyond that I wasn't about to jump through hoops for him. But I'll tell you the truth: I felt relieved when nobody came asking questions. I never became associated with any of it, and I was happy not to have that cloud hanging over me for the rest of my life."

"When you called Chief Van Dyne," Joey asks, "do you remember what he said after you told him your story?"

"Of course I do," she says. "I introduced myself; he knew right away who I was when I mentioned the voice lessons. I told him that I was in sort of a relationship with Bruce Kershaw and that I knew he was a suspect but that I had spent the weekend with him when Mary Ellen Spakalitis had been killed and he couldn't have done it."

"What did he say?" Joey asks.

"He was very calm," she says. "That struck me, because I expected him to get cagey or angry that I was interfering with his investigation. I don't know. But in any event, he just asked me one follow-up question."

Joey leans forward. "What did he ask you?"

"He wanted to know what gave me the idea that Bruce was under investigation, and I told him that his daughters had emailed Bruce directly to confront him about it," she says. "That seemed to catch him off guard. He repeated it twice. 'My daughters? My daughters, the twins?' I told him yes, Bruce told me about the email himself."

"Did you tell him that they wanted Kershaw to meet them at the elementary school?" asks Joey.

"No," she says. "Bruce didn't tell me about that. I wish he had, because maybe it would have made a difference. I guess he was just figuring out how he was going to make it all go away."

She sighs, and for the first time she really does look old. "Over time I've come to believe—or maybe it's more as if I've convinced myself—that the person I spent that weekend with was wearing a mask the whole time. He was acting. He was a split personality. He had a secret, evil twin." She stares directly into Joey's eyes. "Because the man I was with all those months could never have killed a woman in cold blood."

Joey leaves the old folks' home reeling. Brenda Regent might be wacky, no question, but she doesn't seem delusional. If anything, she seems as sharp as a tack, with solid insights into the people she spoke about. Could she have really misjudged Kershaw so dramatically?

He thinks back to the guards at Bay State Penitentiary saying Kershaw was a model prisoner just minutes before he clearly bent over backwards to mess with their heads. Obviously, the man is a sociopath who pulled the wool over the eyes of everyone he ever encountered. Maybe he's just a master of shifting identities. Maybe that's necessary for a serial killer.

But Brenda is the only person he knows of who was genuinely *close* to the man. Something about her uncertainty about Kershaw's true nature leaves him unsettled.

Back at his car he texts the twins to let them know what he's learned. He drops his phone on the seat and starts the ignition and is just about to pull away when he receives a video call from Austin. He answers.

"Do you have a minute?" his husband asks, his eyes glittering with excitement.

"I do now," says Joey as he throws the car back into park.

"The agency called," Austin says. "They want to meet with us tomorrow!"

CHAPTER SEVENTEEN: ALICE

Perry Lemire and Bill Van Dyne were high school friends, and Alice remembers Perry around the house a lot when she and Sam were kids, stopping by to watch a game or just sitting on the front porch with Dad, drinking a beer on a hot summer afternoon. She didn't give much thought to Perry when she was a kid, but she remembers having the impression that her father felt bad for him, unmarried as he was and living with his widowed mother.

His mother has been dead for years, but he still lives in the same place, a depressing duplex a couple of blocks off Main Street. Beige and brown, shadowed by huge trees, the place has the vibe of a hollow under a tree. Alice rings the doorbell, and a moment later Perry opens the door. He does a double take, clearly surprised to see her.

"Alice," he says. "Is everything okay with your mother?"

"Mom?" she asks, surprised. "Yes. Of course. She's fine. Actually, I haven't spoken to her in a couple of days. That's not really why I'm here."

"What can I do for you?" he asks. He doesn't make any motion to invite her in, and she becomes aware of just how unprepared for her visit he is. He's wearing baggy sweatpants and a stained Boston

Bruins jersey, and she wonders if maybe she woke him from a nap. She doesn't think she's ever seen Perry without a necktie. He seems to read her mind.

"I don't have much reason to get dressed up anymore," he says. "Your mother was my final client."

"I'm sorry for the way Sam spoke to you," she says. "It was out of line."

He shakes his head. "If anyone was out of line it was me. Even all these years later, it's hard to let go of what happened back then. I let myself get too involved."

"Believe me," she says, "I understand. I'm sorry to just land like this, but I was hoping to speak with you about something. Can I come in?"

He hesitates, and then his face droops in resignation and he stands aside to let her in. "Be my guest. Fair warning, though, the place is a mess."

She smiles and steps past him. "I have a teenage son. I'm very comfortable with mess."

But she isn't quite prepared for just how disorderly Perry's house is. She follows him down a dim, unlit hallway, glancing into the grim little living room before they enter a kitchen at the back of the house that is at least partly lit from the large sliding glass doors that look out into a small back courtyard.

"Have a seat," he says, pointing to a table in the corner. "I'll make some tea."

Alice doesn't want to overstay, for his sake and hers, so as he moves around the kitchen she dives right in.

"I have a few questions," she says, "about what happened on the day my dad died."

His back is to her as he fills the kettle at the sink, but she is aware of him stiffening.

"Okay," he says. "What kind of questions?"

"Well, I'm just wondering if you remember speaking with him on the phone?"

Perry takes the kettle to the stove and pauses, thinking.

"I spoke with your dad a lot. It's hard to remember specifics so many years later."

He turns on the burner, then moves to sit across from her at the table. She looks into his eyes, but his face is blank and unreadable.

"So you don't remember anything from that day?" she presses.

He raises an eyebrow at her. "Alice," he says. "Come on. I remember that day more than probably any other in my career, if not my life. I remember your mother calling me in an absolute panic, and arriving to the chaos at your house, and coming inside and seeing—"

Alice finishes the sentence for him. "Seeing my father dead."

Perry nods, and she's surprised to see that his eyes have filled with tears. "I will never, as long as I live, forget the sight of Bill lying there on the floor and your mother crouched over him, covered in his blood."

A vague memory comes back to Alice of following Sam as she pushed her way through the phalanx of cops and through the front door of the house and seeing the exact same thing. Their father, lifeless on the floor. Their mother, hysterical and clinging to him. And hovering in the background, pale and speechless, Perry Lemire.

She can't let herself descend any further into that particular memory. She pulls herself back to the matter at hand and decides to approach it directly.

"Did my dad call you that day to tell you about Brenda Regent?"

Joey has given the twins a full recap of his visit with Brenda, and Alice really expects the name to register. Instead Perry looks genuinely confused. "I have no idea who that is."

"Okay," she says. "Did he call to tell you he'd received a tip that Kershaw couldn't have killed Mary Ellen Spakalitis?"

The kettle whistles and Perry stands and takes a few moments to find teabags and pour boiling water into two cups. As he sets them on the table he stares directly at her. "Alice, I don't know what this is about, but I had never heard the name Bruce Philip Kershaw until after he was arrested for your father's murder. As far as anyone knows, your father hadn't either."

Unless he's been taking acting lessons, Alice believes him, but she can't help but feel that he's holding something back from her. She decides to try one more thing.

"What about us?" she asks. "Me and Sam. Did he maybe call to tell you that he was worried we were caught up in something?"

This time something different flickers across Perry's face. But it's gone so quickly that Alice could almost be convinced she imagined it if she hadn't been looking so closely.

"Is that what this is about?" he asks.

"What do you mean?"

"Your father was immensely proud of both of you," he says. "All he wanted was for you and Sam and your mother to be safe and protected if anything ever happened to him." He leans forward. "Alice, I have to ask: What are you looking for?"

"Someone is killing people," she says. "In the same way that Kershaw supposedly killed his victims twenty-five years ago."

"I know," he says. "It's been an upsetting few days for all of us who were part of that awful experience. The fact that a copycat has decided to begin again is beyond words."

"What if it's not a copycat?" she asks.

"What do you mean?"

"What if Kershaw didn't commit those crimes?" she says. "At least, not all of them. And the actual murderer is back in action."

Perry pushes his chair back so suddenly that the table shakes, spilling some of Alice's tea over the side of her cup. He gets up and walks to the counter, turning away from her to look out the window.

"No," he says, firmly and decisively. "That man killed those people. He killed your father, Alice. I was the first person your mother called, even before the police. She was hysterical."

Alice pauses. She's said more than she intended to, but it's too late to turn back. She pulls her phone from her pocket and pulls up the photo of Doug's note, then hands it to him. He stares at the image for a long time.

"That's Dad's handwriting," she says.

Perry only nods, his attention still firmly fixed on the image. "Where did this come from?" he finally asks.

She runs through Doug's story in as few words as possible, then explains the meaning of "Goldfish." "The most important thing," she says, finishing, "is that this proves that Dad did know about Kershaw, thanks to Brenda Regent, and that Kershaw was innocent, at least in the case of Spakalitis."

Perry has been staring at the phone this entire time. He finally looks up as if breaking out of a trance and hands the phone back to her.

"When, exactly, did this happen?" he asks.

"The day he was killed. That's why I'm asking you if you remember a phone call with him that morning, because this note implies that calling you was a priority for some reason."

Perry closes his eyes and thinks for a long time before finally responding.

"I really don't remember speaking to your father that day," he says weakly, and there's a faint tremor in his voice. He opens his eyes and stares straight at her. "The truth is, it wouldn't have been unusual, because I spoke to him most days. But Alice, I can promise you with my hand on my heart that I never heard the names Brenda Regent or Bruce Philip Kershaw before your father was killed. Not from Bill, not from anyone. I swear to you."

Alice drives home the long way, on the river drive. Her visit with Perry came to a quick end, and she left feeling as if there was something significant that he hadn't told her. But what? If her dad wasn't calling to discuss Kershaw, what was it?

She comes to the four-way stop at Riverside Park and she's about to make the turn back to her neighborhood when something catches her eye and she steps on the brake, causing the car behind her to honk. She waves in apology and then pulls to the side of the road so she can get a better look in her rearview mirror.

On a park bench, two people are sitting together, eating ice cream. Their heads are close together, and it looks like they're engaged in an intense and intimate conversation. One of the people is her neighbor Drea Parker.

The other person on the bench is Levi.

CHAPTER EIGHTEEN: JOEY

Joey slides into the booth next to Austin, who gives him a tight *We'll talk about this later* smile, and reaches out to shake the hand of the woman sitting across from them.

"Joe," says Austin, "this is Sheila, from the adoption agency."

"I'm so sorry to be this late," says Joey. "I got caught up at work."

He's not about to mention that he just wrapped a two-hour meeting with Mike Bancroft. He's *definitely* not going to mention that despite his intentions going into the meeting—to turn down the Paris offer—he is pretty sure he left Mike with the opposite impression. He needs to talk to Austin as soon as possible, but this obviously isn't the moment.

Sheila waves away Joey's apology as if he isn't almost half an hour late.

"Austin has told me all about himself," she says. "Now I'd like to hear about you. He tells me you've been with the same company for almost twenty years."

Joey nods and slips into the smooth, well-practiced explanation of how he's been with Shoreline since the beginning of his career.

Sheila seems genuinely interested, and as she takes notes and asks follow-up questions, he can feel Austin relaxing beside him.

Once Sheila has finished asking him about Shoreline, she relaxes back into her seat and fixes Joey with a strange smile.

"I hope this isn't inappropriate," she says. "Are you still involved in, you know"—she leans forward and drops her voice to a whisper—"detective stuff?"

Joey forces himself to smile. "No," he says, hoping to shut the conversation down before it begins. "That's all water under the bridge."

She doesn't take the hint. "I'm sorry," she says with an awkward giggle. "I just had to ask. I had such a crush on you when I was twelve. My sister and I had a picture of you on the wall in our bedroom. Just something we cut out of the paper."

"Aww," says Austin. "So cute, right Joe?"

Joey's grin is hurting his face. "Yeah," he says. "Cute. I was never really a detective—not like the twins."

"Do you still spend any time in Edgar Mills?" she asks.

"Oh yeah," interjects Austin, reaching over to squeeze Joey's arm. "He's been there for the better part of a week, just hanging out with his mom. Joey has a big family, and they'll be an amazing support system when we have kids."

"That's wonderful," she says. She lowers her voice. "It's just awful what's been happening there. The new murders and all. Do you have any idea if the police have any leads?"

Joey shakes his head. "Nope."

Sheila waits for him to continue. When he doesn't, she clears her throat and taps a finger on the folder in front of her. "I have to say," she says, "we get a lot of solid applications, but few of them are this impressive. Financially, you're in excellent shape. You both have interesting careers, and you will clearly be able to comfortably provide for a child, or children."

Joey's heart rate picks up a bit at the mention of "children" but he smiles and nods.

"We're committed to giving our child a wonderful life," says Austin. "We can provide, no question. Joey has a wonderful, stable job walking distance from home. My graphic design business is doing really well, and it's flexible. I work from home and I have the ability to reduce my work load as needed." He reaches over and squeezes Joey's arm. "We can afford it. We have a nice house in a good school district, and we'll make sure education is a priority. And we'll be conscientious, but we won't be helicopter parents. It's not like we'll be monitoring texts and emails. Unless appropriate, of course."

Sheila laughs and puts up a hand. "We don't have to get that far ahead of things. Austin, you can relax: everything checks out, on paper at least. My job is to dig beneath the numbers and stats and to begin to get a sense of who you are as people. Why do you want children?"

Joey expects Austin to step in and answer, since he loves to talk about how much he's always wanted kids, so he is surprised when Austin reaches over to squeeze his shoulder.

"You go first," he says.

Joey knows he should be prepared for this, but something Austin just said has distracted him, and when he opens his mouth, nothing comes out.

The moment stretches out, and Joey senses Austin tensing next to him. Across the table, Sheila's expectant smile falters.

"There are no right or wrong answers," she says. "It can be a big decision for a couple."

"Right," says Joey. "Sure." He clears his throat. "Well, I guess the main thing is that I've known from early on in our relationship, from the very beginning, that Austin really wants kids. I think I've always expected that we'd get to that point."

"What about you?" she presses. "Have you considered what having children will mean for you?"

Joey nods, but again words escape him.

"We've been discussing this for literally years," says Austin. His voice is cheerful, but Joey knows him well enough to pick up on the undertone of panic. Austin wants this more than anything, and now that Joey is here, on the spot, he's blowing it.

Sheila closes the folder and puts her elbows on the table, leaning forward.

"I'll cut to the chase," she says. "I am going to have no problem approving this file. You're clearly healthy, well-adjusted guys, and from what I can tell your relationship is solid. Just as importantly, you're in excellent financial shape. As good as it gets. Like I said, everything tracks on paper. But at the end of the day, you're going to have to convince the mom that you're the kind of couple she wants to work with."

"The mom?" asks Austin.

Sheila smiles. "I have an expectant mother on file," she says. "I just met her last week, and she is very keen to find a good home for her child. She's interested in exploring an open adoption. Do you know what that means?"

Austin nods, and Joey looks at him blankly. "Babe, we've discussed this," says Austin. "That's where the birth mom is still involved in the child's life."

"Think of it as getting another family member as a bonus," says Sheila.

"You mean on top of the new baby family member?" says Joey.

"Exactly," says Sheila. "Is that something you guys are open to?"

Austin nods eagerly. "Yes, of course, for sure." He turns to Joey. "Right, babe?"

"Yeah," says Joey slowly. "I mean, we'll want to meet her first, right?"

"Of course," Sheila says. "Nothing becomes official until everyone meets and agrees that it's a good match. And she'll be able to tell if there isn't buy-in from both parents-to-be. That comes down to the two of you, okay?"

"Of course," says Austin. He reaches over to grab Joey's hand, gripping it more tightly than he needs to.

"We'll want to get the process started right away," says Sheila as she pulls over her phone and begins to tap away. "Biology doesn't wait for the stars to be aligned."

"How far along is she?" asks Austin.

Sheila holds a finger up as she finishes a text, then puts her phone back down on the table. "Almost five and a half months," she says.

Joey almost chokes. "So the baby would be ready in just over three months?"

"We'd better start painting the nursery right away," says Austin, clapping excitedly as Joey's vision briefly goes fuzzy. *Three months?*

Sheila's phone dings and she picks it back up. "Okay, she's keen to meet you and free tomorrow afternoon. That work for you guys?"

"Yes, totally," says Austin. "Joey, can you get off work?"

"Um, it's kind of short notice," says Joey, thinking of all the time he's taken off lately. But he clocks the pleading expression in Austin's eyes and smiles at Sheila. "We'll make it work."

Outside in the parking lot, Austin can hardly contain his enthusiasm. "I can't believe this is happening so quickly!" he says.

"I thought this was just a consult," says Joey, still spinning. He thought he'd have time to discuss France with Austin and that the two of them could weigh the options.

"I thought so too," says Austin gleefully. He stops and turns to look at Joey. "What's going on? Are you not feeling this?"

Joey scrambles to find his footing. "No," he says, forcing a smile. "That's not it. I just . . . It's a lot to take in so quickly."

"Okay," says Austin, and there's a light edge to his voice. "But *I've* been talking about kids since we met, which was *ten years* ago, so you've had plenty of time to wrap your head around the idea."

Joey knows this is the moment to tell Austin everything. He hates his job. He's terrified of becoming a father. They could move to Paris! He doesn't really want to move to Paris!

After spending his entire adult life on the right track, Joey is completely unmoored. He no longer has any idea who he is or where he's going or how to get there. The only thing he knows for sure is that he wants his future to include Austin, which is why it's so crucially important that the two of them sit down and have the conversation he's been avoiding for days.

But it will have to wait a bit longer, because his mind is stuck on what Austin said during the meeting: "It's not like we'll be monitoring texts and emails." It's given him an idea, and he can't afford to lose it right now.

"Do you know what we should do?" he asks. "We should go see my mother."

Austin squints, confused. "Your mother? You literally just got back from Edgar Mills last night."

"I know, but I think we should ask what she thinks. Get her take on things."

Austin considers this. "Well I do love me some Marion, but you know she's going to be on my side here."

"There is no side!" says Joey, and his husband laughs.

"Okay, whatever. Let's go to Edgar Mills and have your mom convince you that we need this baby."

Marion is predictably elated.

"Oh, your father would have been so happy."

"Nothing's happened yet, Ma," says Joey. "We're just meeting the woman."

"Oh, it'll happen," she says. "I've been praying to St. Brigid for you boys."

"Who's that?" asks Austin.

"The patron saint of babies," she says, clasping her hands in front of her heart.

"Brigid!" says Austin. "An icon!"

Joey watches them, bemused. "Double-check with Father Doucet. I'm pretty sure praying to the Catholic saints might be counterproductive in this case."

Marion ignores this. "We'll dig through the baby clothes in the basement. Do you know the sex yet?"

"We haven't even met the mom yet," says Joey. "Have you listened to anything we've said?"

"Doesn't matter," she says. "I have plenty for all sexes."

"Baby fashion show," says Austin. "Fun!"

Marion reaches out and puts a hand on his arm. "Promise me you won't let this baby grow up to be a detective. We've had enough of that for one family."

"I wouldn't worry," says Austin. "Joe hates to talk about it."

"I wasn't really a detective," says Joey. "Besides, it's in the past. There's no reason to dwell on it."

"I wish it were in the past," says Marion, "but it's happening all over again. It just doesn't feel fair. What kind of monster decides to put a nice little town like Edgar Mills through something like this for the second time?"

"What was it like back then?" asks Austin. "When the Janitor was killing all those people."

Joey's mother shakes her head. "It was awful," she says. "Just awful. Like living in a nightmare. And the whole time our Joey was upstairs trying to figure out how to stop it."

"It wasn't like that, Ma," he says.

"You did your part," she says. "We were all real proud of you for helping bring it to an end."

Under the table, Austin reaches over and squeezes his leg. Joey feels himself reddening.

"Why don't you two go dig around in those baby clothes?" he suggests.

They don't need much convincing, and when they disappear into the basement, he slips upstairs to his old bedroom.

Which is the real reason he wanted to come back home today.

CHAPTER NINETEEN: SAM

The Edgar Mills Community Cemetery is tucked into a quiet corner of town between the Catholic church and the river. Sam parks on the street near the entrance and sits in the car for a while, waiting for a procession of black-clad mourners to trail out through the exit.

Once the final cars have disappeared she gets out and crosses the street. She follows the central path, passing the older headstones, which sit closer to the church, and gradually comes to the newer and less worn stones as she enters the more recent corner of the graveyard.

It's been years since she visited her father's grave. She stares down at the simple granite stone trying to find the right words to describe how she feels.

"Dad," she says, finally, "everything is a mess, and I wish I could just talk to you one more time and get your advice."

She's quiet, waiting for something. Trying to remember the sound of his voice, which was so clear for so long and has recently begun to fade away.

Only the sound of birds and the distant river ring back to her.

"I know you figured something out back then," she says. "Something you didn't have the time to tell anyone. It feels like you wrote down *almost* everything you knew except for the one final piece of the puzzle. What did you pull together before you died?"

She begins to pace in front of the gravestone. "I know you would have told me to stay calm, analyze the scene, ask the right questions. But how am I supposed to do that twenty-five years later?"

She stops pacing and crouches beside the stone, staring head-on at the name and dates carved so crisply into the granite.

"I'm sorry," she says. "We never should have tried to confront Kershaw on our own. We should have gone straight to you instead." She looks away from the headstone as tears fill her eyes, and her next words come out as barely a whisper. "I should never have taken your gun."

She stops suddenly as something tickles at the back of her brain. She reaches out and runs her finger over the second date on the stone, *October 7, 2000*, trying to bring the flicker of insight into focus.

"If I hadn't taken the gun," she murmurs, this time to herself, and it comes to her. She stands and pulls her phone from her pocket. In just a couple of minutes, she's found what she's looking for. She stares, absorbing what she's learned, and then she turns back to the grave.

"I'll be back," she says. "I promise. There's something I need to ask someone."

It's dusk by the time she pulls up outside the little house on Bluebonnet Lane. At this time of day, the decay is hidden by shadows, and warm yellow light spills out of the downstairs windows, giving the house a more cheerful look than it deserves.

On the porch, she tries the door and finds it unlocked. She shakes her head as she pushes it open. Doesn't her mother know there's a murderer on the loose?

"Mom?" she calls out from the threshold. When there's no answer, she steps inside and glances up the darkened stairs before turning her attention to the kitchen door at the end of the hallway. Light slips under the crack beneath the door. "Joanna?"

Something is tickling at the back of her neck. She remembers what her father always said about intuition. There's only so far analysis can take you. Sometimes you need to follow your nose. Intuition was always Alice's strength, but Alice isn't here right now. She walks to the end of the hallway and stops at the door, suddenly wary of opening it.

"Mom?" she says again, her voice coming out in a croak. She reaches out, pushes the door open, and steps into the brightly lit kitchen.

At first she doesn't see anything out of place. The counters are covered with dirty dishes, but that's nothing new. The light over the stove is on, shining down on a half-eaten chicken pot pie. On the refrigerator door, a photo of Will smiles out at her. Everything is normal.

Then she turns, and time comes to a complete standstill before stretching back, back, back, dragging her through a winding wormhole of memory to the specific moment when Alice moved her flashlight over the gymnasium floor and their lives changed forever.

She snaps abruptly back to the present. Two chairs at the table in the corner have been knocked over and a bottle of whiskey has been tipped on its side, the contents puddling on the wooden surface. Just a few steps away, lying half in the kitchen, half in the porch, and haloed by a glistening pool of blood, is a body.

Sam stands frozen in shock, as her mother's words from just a few days ago echo in her ears.

I've lived the past quarter century in fear of that man finding his way here to finish the job he started.

She snaps out of her trance and pulls her phone from her jacket. She dials 911 and an operator answers right away.

"I'm at 15 Bluebonnet Lane in Edgar Mills," she says, keeping her voice calm and steady. "There appears to have been a violent home invasion. There's a lot of blood and at least one victim. His name is Perry Lemire and I'm pretty sure he's dead. Please hurry."

She's vaguely aware of the operator asking her to stay on the line, but Sam hangs up anyway. Blood is rushing in her head, and she has to take a few deep breaths to collect herself.

She takes a closer look at the scene. Perry is lying sideways on the floor behind the table. She moves closer, careful not to step in the blood, and sees that his neck has been slit. On the floor near her mother's toppled chair is a smashed tumbler, and when she crouches, she can see a second one that's rolled into the corner. Perry and Joanna were clearly sitting here, having a drink, when . . . *something* happened.

Moving cautiously, Sam walks around Perry's body and toward the door to the back porch. She sees immediately that the door is ajar, and, more chillingly, there are drag marks in the blood on the floor. Two sets of footprints, one clear and the other blurry, or swiped, as if someone was dragged out of the house against their will.

"Shit," says Sam under her breath. She knows that she can't go through that door without contaminating evidence, so she hurries back to the front door, and then sprints around the house to the backyard.

There are more bloody footprints leading down the porch steps into the overgrown yard. The tracks are visible in the high, unkempt grass, leading directly to the back fence that separates Joanna's house from the Stevens family's home.

Sam approaches with a feeling of dread churning in her gut. The wooden picket fence that her father built when they were kids and repainted every other year has long since rotted, and the back corner is detached entirely, sagging inward to form a large gap.

As she steps through the gap into the other backyard, she notices two things right away. The Stevenses' van is missing and the side door to the darkened house is hanging open. In the distance she hears sirens approaching, and she knows she should stop and wait for the police to arrive, but she doesn't. As if hypnotized, she crosses the driveway and steps up onto the porch and into the house.

The door opens directly into a darkened kitchen. A dim glow tells her there's a light on somewhere deeper in the house. Sam moves slowly through a dining room, where she notices the light is coming from a crack under a door.

"Hello?"

When there's no answer, she opens the door and steps into the living room. A television is flickering in the background, the sound turned down. On the floor, Isobel Stevens lies motionless and glassy-eyed in a pool of blood, a mirror image of Perry Lemire in the house next door.

There's no sign of Evan or his father.

Or her mother.

CHAPTER TWENTY: ALICE

Alice can't remember the last time she had anything to drink this early in the day—certainly nothing this hard—but she tips the glass back and lets a second shot of whiskey burn down the back of her throat.

"You want another one?" the bartender asks.

Alice considers this, then shakes her head. "I'll just have a light beer."

He grabs one from the refrigerator and cracks it, handing it over, and Alice spins around on her stool and takes stock of the room.

The windows are grimy enough to block the bright sunlight, and the place is almost empty. Just a few old men sit at the other end of the bar.

Alice slips off her stool and walks to the jukebox in the far corner. She slides through the music choices and selects a Lana Del Rey song, then moves to the dance floor and begins to sway in place.

The door opens with a jingle and a hot finger of daylight slips through and points across the room at her. She turns to see none other than Chief Nash Young, still in uniform. He walks to the bar and orders a beer, but she can tell one curious eye is on her.

Alice tips her beer back and keeps dancing in slow, languorous circles, fully aware of Nash standing against the bar, watching her. When the song ends, a couple of the old-timers hoot and clap and she shoots them the finger before leaving the dance floor and slipping into a booth. A moment later, Nash joins her.

"Well," he says, "I didn't expect to find you here."

"Oh, really," she says. "I thought you might have tracked me down to arrest me."

He laughs. "Arrest you for what?"

"For being a clueless asshole," she says.

"Oh, come on," he says. "You're too hard on yourself. Why do you feel clueless?"

Alice doesn't want to explain what she thinks she just saw between Levi and Drea. "We all feel clueless sometimes, don't we?"

Nash laughs ruefully. "You can say that again." He necks his beer and slams the bottle down on the table, then slides out of the booth and walks over to the bar, returning a few moments later with two fresh glistening bottles.

He hands her one and clinks his against it. "Did your sister tell you what happened at Birch Crest Elementary?"

Alice shakes her head, surprised. "No, I haven't spoken to her since yesterday." She intended to fill her in on the visit with Perry, but catching Levi with Drea kind of pushed that to the back burner.

He tells her about the attack on Evan Stevens.

"I took the kid to the station and called his parents so they could be there to witness his statement. Just to keep everything by the book, you know?"

Alice nods. "So what happened?"

"They showed up in about ten minutes," says Nash. "The father stormed in like a madman. The mom was a few steps behind, wringing her hands and just kind of hovering. I explained what had happened at the school, and when the father heard that I'd already got most of the story out of the kid, he lost it."

Alice is fully engaged, Levi and Drea relegated for the moment to the least important corner of her brain. "He got angry?"

"Blew his top!" says Nash. "He was railing about due process and pressing charges. All bullshit: it's totally legitimate to ask questions at the scene of a crime. But he wouldn't listen to reason, and frog-marched the kid out of there."

"Why would he do that?" asks Alice, genuinely puzzled. "That attack was more than likely connected to the killings."

Nash takes another swig from his bottle, shrugs. "Your sister tried to warn me, she said the kid was afraid of his father, and I believe it."

"You're still going to check out the school, though, right?" Alice asks.

"Yeah, of course." Nash shakes his head. "Well, *I'm* not. Corvallis sent some uniforms over there to look around. It's out of my jurisdiction now."

"What are you talking about?" Alice leans forward, suddenly registering the implications of the chief of police day-drinking in a dark pub while there's a major investigation going on.

Nash sighs. "She accused me of losing an important interview and told me the state is going to take over the investigation. That's been her goal since the beginning anyway; now she has a solid excuse. She told me to take a hike and she'll let me know if she needs anything."

"*What?*" Alice is outraged. "She can't do that, can she?"

Nash shrugs. "Apparently she can. I haven't been fired or anything; I've just been sidelined. Which is why I'm here, drinking my troubles away."

"But you know this town," says Alice. "You know the original case. You bring such an important perspective to things."

Nash shrugs. "Angela Corvallis isn't interested in my perspective. She wants to be the one to solve the case, and now that I'm out of the picture, she doesn't have anyone else to compete against. It is what it is."

Alice sips her beer, thinking.

"Nash," she asks finally, "do you think the murders are connected? I mean *all* of the murders."

He answers slowly. "I didn't think so at first, but now I'm not so sure. There are just so many odd details that don't add up. Corvallis is convinced they're all just coincidences, distracting us from a simple solution. I really thought she'd come around when she heard about the kid being attacked in the school, but she thinks it was just someone singling him out for a prank because of his videos."

"What if there were more evidence?" Alice asks. "Evidence that proves Kershaw couldn't have killed all the victims."

Nash pushes his beer to the side and leans forward. "What are you talking about?"

Alice wonders if she's making a mistake confiding in Nash, but she's already opened the barn door. Besides, she likes and trusts him, and she's pretty sure Sam and Joey would agree that now is a good time to bring him up to speed. She pulls Doug's note up on her phone and passes it to him.

"My dad wrote this on the day he died," she says.

He stares for a long time, not saying anything. Finally he lifts his head and stares at her, his expression impossible to read.

"Explain," he says.

She tells him everything, from Doug's note, to the receipt that Sam found in Kershaw's apartment, to what Joey learned about Justin Beagle becoming obsessed with the Janitor murders in the weeks before his death.

"You told us to let you know if we had a hunch," she says, once she's finished laying out what they've discovered.

"This is more than a hunch," he says. "This is some serious shit."

"Are you going to tell Corvallis?"

"I don't know. I probably should, but I don't trust her." He puts his face in his hands. "Every minute of this case, I've wished your father was here for me to talk to, but never more than right now."

"Nash." She reaches out and touches his wrist so he drops his hands and looks her in the eye. "I think Dad would have told you to trust your gut, to give yourself some time to think it through."

"Maybe you're right." He smiles sadly. "You guys must miss him so much."

Alice nods and tears sting at her eyes, but she smiles, pushing them away. "What was it like, working with him?"

He takes a sip of his beer and then smiles down at the table, remembering, before returning his eyes to hers.

"I was so green back then; didn't know my ass from my elbow. But your old man really helped me out. Put me on a couple of small but important cases. B and E's, that kind of thing. Worked them with me to help me figure out my way around a crime scene."

Alice smiles, remembering a similar dynamic between her and Sam and their dad.

"I was still fresh on the job, just a few months in, when the first body was discovered," he says. "I was pretty surprised that he put me on the case. Now I see that he really just needed every available cop to drop everything and work on it, but at the time it felt like a real vote of confidence."

"I'm sure it was," Alice says.

"You know I loved your dad, Alice," he says. "He was such a great guy. Such an amazing cop. He liked teaching us."

"He really did," she agrees. Suddenly, the weight of everything is too much. Her son is pulling away. Her sister might as well be estranged. Her mother is an absolute basket case. Now, to top everything off, people are being murdered once again, and the horrible, traumatic event she spent her entire life putting behind her has come back with a vengeance.

And, as if all that isn't enough, her husband is apparently having an affair with the "Real Housewife" neighbor who she thought was a friend.

"You okay?" asks Nash.

She lifts her head and smiles brightly. "Isn't there a part of you that wants to forget that any of this is even happening?" she asks.

"Why do you think I'm drinking by myself?" he asks.

"You're not drinking by yourself."

Alice is shocked at the suggestive tone of her own voice, at how brazenly she's pushed the words across the table, but she forces herself to hold Nash's gaze, and she feels a thrill of excitement when she sees his eyes light up with understanding.

"Is that such a good idea?" he asks.

Alice slides out of the bar and stands. "I think it's a great fucking idea," she says.

She doesn't wait for him as he slides out after her and heads to the bar to pay. She just walks through the room and pushes through the door into the blinding sunlight.

Nash's car is parked behind the building, away from the street.

"I didn't want to get spotted," he says sheepishly as he unlocks the doors and they climb inside.

"Where are we going to go?" she asks.

"We can head to my place," he replies. "Just prepare yourself for a grim divorced workaholic vibe."

"A glimpse into my future," she says.

"You're getting a divorce?"

She shrugs. "It looks like things are headed in that direction." Without warning or any real plan, she stretches across the center console, reaching for his neck, and pulls him into a kiss. He responds easily, falling into the actions smoothly, in a way that implies she isn't the first woman he's been intimate with since his divorce.

She doesn't have the benefit of the same experience; as she works her lips against his, lightly biting his lower lip, slipping a tongue into his mouth, all she can think is *This doesn't feel like Levi.* The thought lands on her like a bucket of cold water. She wanted to feel like she was sixteen again, but not like this.

Nash pulls away and she slumps back into her seat with a sad groan.

"You okay?" he asks.

"I don't think this is such a good idea," she says.

He smiles kindly. "I think you're right. I think we're both trying to find something that isn't available to us right now, no matter where we look for it."

Alice nods. She feels relieved, like she's passed a test of some kind, even if Levi is currently failing it. Her attention is already returning to the conversation they just had inside the bar.

"Isn't it kind of suspicious how insistent Evan's father was that he not give a statement?" she says.

"It was weird for sure," says Nash. "But parents these days are nuts. Everyone wants to protect their children against everything. Bad grades. Losing at sports. Hurt feelings."

"But that's just it. You'd think he would want to know who hurt his son."

Before Nash can answer, the radio on the dashboard crackles.

"Officers on duty: We have reports of an incident at 15 Bluebonnet Lane. All available personnel should report to the scene immediately."

Alice turns to stare at Nash.

"That's my mother's house."

CHAPTER TWENTY-ONE: JOEY

Joey sits in the small desk chair and is immediately transported back to the many late weekend nights he spent sitting in front of this monitor, exploring the internet and learning how to code.

It was on one of those nights when he broke his first case, tracking down the online scammer who had ripped off old Mrs. LaRiviere. Using only the email address she'd provided him, he'd followed breadcrumbs into a database of banking information belonging to mostly elderly women. He was fifteen, and the thrill of realizing he'd accomplished something the police couldn't had lit a flame inside him. He's always insisted he was never really a detective, but the truth is, he felt like one that night.

Joey would give anything to have that feeling back, a perfect combination of focus, enthusiasm, and youth.

He almost doesn't expect the computer to boot up, but it springs to life immediately, the resonant chime of Windows 95 announcing its resurrection. The interface is shockingly archaic compared to the powerful, gleaming mini-computers everyone now carries in their pocket, but Joey's old instincts are sharp, and it turns out returning to your first computer is like revisiting your childhood home: totally alien and entirely comfortable.

He clicks through folders inside folders, calling up bits of random digital detritus that he hasn't thought of once in the intervening years but that instantly unlock vivid memories: the ninth-grade geography assignment on the tectonic plates, complete with graphics he generated in MS Paint; a collection of still images from an old Abercrombie & Fitch ad campaign, hidden in a folder named "Math Problems."

Deep inside his download folder, he finds what he's looking for: the archived emails from the Van Dyne household. Like most homes at the time, including his own, the Van Dynes' had a family computer that everyone shared for homework, internet, and email purposes. Unlike in today's online cloud-based model, emails in the old days were saved on your hard drive, and it wasn't unusual for several family members to have individual email addresses that were actually linked and archived together in a parent folder.

It was his fateful, ethically questionable decision to tap into the twins' email addresses that led to his download of the entire Van Dyne archive. He reopens the archive now and, acting on instinct, navigates to the email cache for the twins' address, TwinTeen DetectiveAgency@webzone.com, and clicks on the subfolder for the day before the events occurred, looking for the email that kicked everything off. It isn't there, and for a moment he wonders if he's somehow deleted information, but then he remembers: of course, the twins *sent* Kershaw an email; they didn't receive one in return.

He clicks on the menu and navigates to Sent, and then it's sitting there right in front of him: the final email the Van Dyne twins ever sent from their detective account. The email he discovered after Levi's tip-off.

He opens it, remembering.

> Dear Bruce Kershaw -
>
> You may have heard of us - we are the Van Dyne Twins: Twin Detectives. It might surprise you to learn that we have certainly heard of you. We have discovered your cache of supplies and materials at the Birch Crest Elementary.
>
> We want to hear your side of the story. We want you to meet us there tonight at eight o'clock.

He could recite this email from memory, but he's not here looking to revisit things he already knows. He returns to the parent folder and skims the full cache. Sure enough, there's an additional address for Chief Van Dyne: BillVanDyne@webzone.com.

A burst of laughter comes up the stairs and he smiles, grateful that his mother and husband have become so close over the past few years. If it was up to Austin, they'd be in Edgar Mills every weekend.

He clicks to open the email archive for Bill Van Dyne, and his heart skips a beat as dozens of emails appear in a basic text database. He quickly adds date parameters to begin the day before the discovery of the first murder, Mary Ellen Spakalitis, and begins to skim. There's a lot of junk mail and a few personal messages, primarily from extended family planning holiday get-togethers, fantasy football leagues, and a group thread with some friends planning a fishing trip.

Finally, at the very end of the list, something catches his attention. It's an email Chief Van Dyne seems to have sent from his work account to his personal account, with the subject line CONTRACTOR CONTACTS: BASEMENT RENOVATION. Joey clicks on it and can see right away that it isn't a list of contractors. At the top of the page are two words in capital letters:

RELEVANT DATES

Joey continues reading, his pulse quickening as he scans a short list of names and dates that he recognizes immediately.

DJ Cartwright: 09/11/00 (Dept. annual softball tournament. Beer and wings at Scoobie's.)

Mary Ellen Spakalitis: 09/17/00 (B&E Southland Mall. Three businesses hit.)

Lizzie Carroll: 10/09/00 (Major collision, 6th St. and Bryant Ave. Four vehicles, multiple injuries.)

Then, after a few blank lines, a final sentence:

This adds up . . . the connections are clear.

It seems clear that Van Dyne was chasing a theory of some kind. Had he discovered some kind of connection between the murders? More to the point, did he have a suspect in mind?

But it's the date and time of the email that really sets alarm bells ringing: 3:45 p.m. 10/20/00.

Bill Van Dyne sent himself this email from work just a few hours before he died.

CHAPTER TWENTY-TWO:
SAM

Sam stands across the street and watches as police stream in and out of her mother's house behind a cordon of yellow tape. She pulls out her phone and steels herself, preparing to call Alice, but before she has the chance, a patrol car pulls up nearby and, to her surprise, Alice and Nash get out. Alice notices her right away and hurries over, Nash following close behind.

"Sam!" Alice's eyes are wide with fright. "What is going on?"

"Mom is missing," says Sam, "and Perry is dead."

Alice gasps. "*What?* What do you mean, "missing"?"

"Tell us what you know," says Nash.

"It was the neighbor, Parson Stevens." Sam describes what she discovered when she arrived at the house.

"No sign of the kid?" asks Nash.

Sam shakes her head. "He's gone too. Their van is missing."

"I can't believe this," says Nash. "We were so close to the bastard."

"What do you mean?" asks Sam.

He tells Sam about the scene at the police station. "He refused to let Evan give a statement about what happened at the school.

It seemed nuts to me at the time, but if he carried out the attack, everything suddenly makes sense."

"Why would he attack his own son?" asks Alice.

"Think about it," says Sam. "Parson believes he's gotten away with two murders. But then he discovers Evan has been poking around and asking questions, and begins to worry he's getting too close to the truth. He orchestrates the attack to scare him off the case."

Nash nods as the theory takes shape. "Only he doesn't anticipate the police getting involved, so when he gets a call from the station, he's caught off guard. He pulls Evan out of there before he says anything incriminating, but he knows it's only a matter of time before he finds himself under the microscope. Which leads us to whatever this is."

"But why did he target Justin and Vicki?" asks Alice. "Or Mom and Perry?"

"I'm going to see what I can find out," says Nash. "Hang tight and I'll report back." He reaches out and puts a hand on Alice's shoulder, squeezing gently before heading across the street.

The parting gesture doesn't go unnoticed by Sam, and she wants to ask Alice why she and Nash showed up together, but Alice is clearly too shocked by what's happened to focus on anything else.

"I just saw Perry this afternoon," she says in a daze.

Sam nods, her expression grim. "He must have come to see Mom right after that. What did he say to you?"

Alice shakes her head, trying to focus through a vague haze of alcohol. "He insisted he didn't remember calling Dad on the day he died," she says. "He was . . . I don't know; he was acting kind of vague, but when I showed him the note Doug found, I think it triggered him. It was hard to say, he didn't really give me much to work with."

"But why would he come see Mom?" Sam muses. They're interrupted by Corvallis striding across the lawn toward them, Nash following close behind.

"Can I have a few moments of your time?" she asks.

"Of course," says Alice as Sam nods. She has a feeling from the way Corvallis is looking at them that she's about to deliver bad news, and she doesn't disappoint.

"We're searching the Stevens residence for any clues that might lead us to where he's gone," says Corvallis. "There's no easy way to say this, but some disturbing evidence has come to light."

"What kind of evidence?" asks Alice, her voice urgent.

"We've gained access to the computer in Parson's office," she says. "We hoped to find an internet search or a cached map that might give some insights about where he was headed. So far, no luck in that regard, but we did find a great deal of archived information about Bruce Philip Kershaw, including details of his crimes, timelines, court transcripts, you name it. It appears he was obsessed with the Janitor, and with your family."

"Our family?" asks Sam.

Corvallis nods. "He had camera feeds coming from your mother's house."

Alice's mouth drops open. "*Camera feeds?*"

"He was using spy cams," says Nash. "You can buy them on Amazon for next to nothing."

"Have you gone through them?" asks Sam.

"I have techs working on it," says Corvallis, "but unfortunately everything from today has been deleted, and it appears that older footage has been encrypted and uploaded remotely. We've also managed to track down some contacts from their previous residence in a small town about an hour north of Albany, near the Vermont border. We spoke to his boss at his last job. He worked at a home security firm."

"Jesus Christ," says Sam, seeing where this is going.

"Yeah," says Nash. "He was there for several years, apparently without issue, and then the company started to get some odd complaints from customers. A few people independently claimed that their houses had been broken into. But in each case nothing was stolen. Things had just been moved around, so management basically ignored the complaints. But then a woman returned home to find her dog dead."

"Oh my God," says Alice.

"They took that one seriously," says Corvallis, "and did an internal audit. It turned out that Stevens had serviced all of the houses in question. He was confronted and confessed, offered his resignation on the spot, packed up his family, and left town."

"They moved into the house directly behind Mom's," says Sam. "That has to be more than a coincidence."

"That's right," says Corvallis. "We also have to consider the fact that one of his other victims lived next door to you, Alice. I think there's a strong likelihood that you were the intended target, and he mixed up your houses."

"How does Justin Beagle fit into this?" asks Sam.

Corvallis shakes her head. "We aren't aware yet of any connections between Parson Stevens and Justin Beagle. Perhaps it was just a test run. Whatever the case, we have to assume he's not done with either of you or your family."

As the implications of this sink in, the blood seems to drain from Alice's face. She pulls her phone out of her pocket and makes a call.

"Will," she says in a rush, "is your father there?"

Sam watches as Alice listens to the response from the other end of the line. Her sister's anxiety is gone, replaced by a firm, decisive attitude. She's entered full mom mode.

"You need to listen to me carefully," Alice says. "Make sure all the doors are locked, and then I want you to turn off all the lights and go into the basement and stay there until either your father or I get home."

Sam hears Will's raised voice on the other end of the line. She can't make out what he's saying, but he's clearly alarmed.

"Listen to me, Will," says Alice, "there's no reason to be scared. I need you to hold it together until I get home, okay? I'm on my way right now."

She hangs up and turns to Sam. "Can I take your rental?"

"Yeah, of course," says Sam, pulling the keys out of her jacket. "Do you want me to go with you?"

Alice shakes her head. "No. Stay here and keep me in the loop."

After Alice leaves, Corvallis turns to Nash. "I need you to coordinate a neighborhood sweep. See if any of the neighbors saw anything and get details on that van; we'll want to put out an APB right away."

Sam remembers something. "When I first met Evan, he mentioned that his father used to live in Edgar Mills, years ago. That could point to a connection between both sets of murders. How far back are you looking into his background?"

Corvallis regards her coolly. "I'm going to be blunt," she says, as if she hasn't been blunt every single time she's spoken to them. "Get out of my way."

"Excuse me?" says Sam, taken aback.

"Your plucky sleuth routine led to disaster twenty-five years ago," Corvallis continues, "and now you're back looking for a do-over. That's not going to happen on my watch."

"I have no idea what you—" Sam begins, but Corvallis cuts her off.

"Nash has brought me up to speed," she says. "You encouraged that kid to keep up his wild-goose chase. You even visited a crime scene with him instead of coming straight to me with any information. If you had, we might have been able to zero in on Stevens before things went sideways. Now we have another dead man in there and two people are missing, presumed kidnapped and in serious danger, quite possibly dead, all because you wanted to play detective again. I know it must be tempting to get drawn back into the excitement and the thrill, but this is the real deal, not some low-budget reality TV show. Have you even considered that you brought this on yourself?"

"Hang on, Angela," says Nash. "That's not entirely fair."

"Isn't it?" asks Corvallis, turning on him. "I should never have let you talk me into arranging the meeting with Kershaw. It opened a whole can of worms, and if it was up to me, you'd be handing out parking tickets. Unfortunately, I need you working with me on this, because it's an all-hands-on-deck scenario, but I'm sure as hell not going to have amateurs sticking their noses in, muddying up my investigation." She turns back to Sam. "Your mother is missing,

Ms. Van Dyne, and I intend to bring her home alive if possible. In the meantime, stay the hell out of my way."

She turns and strides away before Sam has a chance to respond. Nash smiles at her.

"You should see her before her coffee," he says.

"Nash," says Sam urgently, "we have to find out if he was here twenty-five years ago. He might have been the copycat."

"We will," he says. "You need to trust me, Sam. Alice told me what you guys have learned, and I promise we'll reopen the old case. But right now the only priority is finding your mother and Evan and bringing them home safe, okay?"

Sam nods. At least she knows Nash is on their side.

"I need to get on with things," he says, "but keep your phone close to you in case I need to get in touch about anything, okay?"

Sam watches as he returns to the house and merges with the action. Suddenly the adrenaline that's been powering her for the past hour seems to drain away, leaving her tired and despondent. Maybe Corvallis is right: maybe she did mess things up by humoring Evan. Now he and her mother are in danger, most likely dead, and there's literally nothing she can do to change that. If there's one thing Sam learned from the events of twenty-five years ago, it's that time only moves in one direction and regret tends to go the same way.

Her phone dings inside her pocket, and she pulls it out, expecting to find a text from Alice. But when she glances at the screen, her heart seems to stop, and a hollow ringing fills her ears.

The message is from Evan Stevens.

Help us

And with it, a geographic pin.

Sam stands on the sidewalk, staring down at the message. She knows she should turn around, go back, and hand over this new information. But she thinks back to the way Corvallis just spoke to her, and her feet remain planted.

She hears an engine approaching and looks up to see a beat-up hatchback pulling up along the curb beside her. The window rolls down and Doug Shiftley pokes his head out.

"You need a ride?"

CHAPTER TWENTY-THREE: ALICE

When Alice gets home, the doors are locked and the lights are off. When she steps into the house, it's eerily quiet.

"Will!" she yells down the basement stairs. "I'm home!"

There's no answer, and her heart plummets into her stomach. She drops her bag on the floor and hollers down the stairs again, a mounting panic filling her mind.

"He isn't here."

Alice follows the voice to the living room, where Levi is sitting in an armchair in the dark, holding a bottle of beer. She snaps on a light.

"Where is he?" she asks as her heart rate gradually comes back under control.

"I sent him to my folks' house in an Uber," he says. His voice is flat and affectless.

"Have you lost your mind?" she asks. Levi's parents live in a retirement community two towns away. "You sent him off with a stranger instead of taking him yourself?" Still, she can't help but feel relieved that Will is so far away from Edgar Mills.

Levi's eyes flare and he sits up in the chair, slamming the bottle of beer onto the table next to him. "I came home and found him hiding in the furnace room in the dark, scared shitless."

Alice falters. "I didn't tell him to hide in the furnace room," she says weakly.

"You might as well have. He didn't know what the hell was going on. He just said you sounded frantic and made him think he was in danger."

Alice approaches with her hands held out, trying to take the mood down. This is no time for a fight. "Levi, you need to understand a few things."

Levi isn't in the mood for her explanations. "Oh, I understand plenty. You think I don't know what's going on around here? You and Sam are playing detective again, bringing that bullshit back into our house. You think our lives aren't messed up enough?"

"Wait a minute," she says. She feels blindsided.

But he's just getting started. "I know you're desperate to get back your glory days, and I can kind of understand that, but did you think for ten seconds that maybe it's embarrassing for your kid or traumatizing for me?"

Alice walks over and sits on the couch near Levi's chair, perching on the edge and placing her hands on her lap. Her mind is spinning. First her mother, now this. It's too much, and she needs to get things under control.

"Levi, something's happened."

"Yeah, no shit," he snaps. "You've been sleeping with Dougie Dog Shit," he says, practically spitting the accusation at her.

She stares at him, her mouth hanging open. "I'm sorry, what?"

"You heard me," he said. "You've been running around with Doug Shiftley behind my back for God knows how long and you didn't think I was smart enough to figure it out."

"I am not *running around* with anyone!" Alice has crossed the line from bewildered to indignant. "I have never *slept with* Doug Shiftley. For your information, he's a good friend. Lately he's been my *best* friend."

Levi laughs, one harsh heavy note that drops to the floor with a thud. "If it's so innocent, why the hell have you kept that from me? Don't piss on my leg and tell me it's raining, Alice."

"I kept it a secret because I can't remember the last time you gave a shit about *anything* I do with my time," she snarls, matching the rage in his voice. "And I don't know if you remember how you treated Doug back in high school, but it wasn't nice. You gave him that nickname, for one thing. So forgive me for keeping our friendship a secret."

"I did not give him that nickname!" Levi is indignant.

"You certainly did," she fires back. "You were a bully and an asshole, Levi, whether you care to remember it or not, and lately I'm beginning to think you still are."

Levi is momentarily silenced, and a faint, shamed wince flickers across his face.

"Is that what you two do?" he asks, quietly. "Sit around and talk about how much of an asshole I am?"

"No," she says. "We don't. We talk about all the stuff that we can't talk about with anyone else. He's been a good friend to me."

He stares at her with a pained, closed-off expression that makes her feel like she is falling off a cliff, and suddenly she just wants to explain how much she misses the husband she used to have.

Doug would like that version of Levi, and vice versa. If that version of Levi was still around, maybe the two of them could be friends. Unfortunately, that version of Levi seems to have disappeared.

"Anyway," she says, "you're honestly one to talk, considering I saw you with Drea Parker *today*. You want to tell me there's nothing going on there?"

She's taken aback by his response, another harsh burst of laughter.

"Drea is the one who told me about Doug," he says. "She saw you sneaking into his apartment one day and she asked me to meet up with her so she could fill me in on everything."

"There is no 'everything'!" Alice's head feels like it's going to explode. "Levi, I am not cheating on you with Doug, no matter what Drea saw."

"You have to admit, it all seems pretty suspicious," he says, with an edge of sanctimony that makes her want to punch through a wall.

"Levi," she says, her voice cold and disengaged, "I don't even know how to begin taking this apart, but right now I have bigger things to worry about. Perry Lemire was murdered this afternoon at my mother's house, and now she's missing."

Now it's Levi's turn to look shocked. "What?" he asks. "Are you serious?"

"Dead serious," she says. "There's a homicidal maniac on the loose, and I think our family is being targeted. That's why I told Will to hide in the basement until I got home."

Levi looks stunned. "Is your mother— I mean, do they—"

"Nobody knows anything," she says. "But one thing is for sure: this house isn't safe and you should leave and go to your mother's house to be with Will. I'll be in touch."

"Wait a minute," he says. "I'm not leaving you here alone."

"I think we've moved past the point where either of us has much say in what the other one can or can't do," says Alice.

Levi looks like he wants to argue, but then he seems to make a decision. He stands and crosses the room to the entryway, grabbing his keys from the hook on the wall.

He turns back to look at her, and as the moment stretches out in front of them, Alice realizes that something between them has changed, probably forever.

"What are you going to do?" he asks.

She shakes her head. "I haven't figured that out yet."

"I hope your mom is okay," he says finally. "Let me know as soon as you hear anything."

"I will. Tell Will I'll be in touch soon."

"Alice," he says, and in the long pause that follows, a million things hang in the air between them. "Be careful," he says finally.

She nods and then he's gone.

She locks the door behind him and then wanders through the house, making sure the lights are all out and the windows are closed and locked. She finishes in the kitchen, staring through the window at the trees in the backyard. Did Parson Stevens stand there and watch Vicki's house when she was all alone? Did he watch *her* house?

She turns off the under-cabinet lights, dropping the kitchen into complete darkness. She's about to turn away when she glimpses something moving on the back deck of the house next door. She moves to the sliding door for a better look and sees that Joelle Williamson is standing outside, also staring out at the trees. Alice unlocks the door and slides it open, stepping out onto the deck.

"Joelle?"

The teenager turns to look at her, apparently unsurprised at her appearance. She's underdressed for the cold, barefoot in leggings and a hooded sweatshirt, her arms folded around herself. She's clearly been crying.

Alice moves to the railing. "What are you doing outside in the cold, sweetheart?"

"I just needed some fresh air," the girl answers. Her voice is thin and strained.

"Is your father . . ." Alice's question trails off without a clear ending, and Joelle picks it up.

"He's in bed. He's been in bed for most of the past few days." She hesitates. "I heard about your mom and Evan, Mrs. Brakes. Do you think they'll be okay?"

Alice sighs. If Joelle has heard, that means the story must already be spreading like wildfire. "I hope so. The police are doing everything they can to bring them back safe."

Joelle's eyes are wide and frightened. "Is it true what they're saying about Evan's dad? That he killed my mom and Justin?"

Alice chooses her words carefully. "Nobody knows anything for sure, but it looks that way."

Joelle's face widens in a cartoonish expression of shock, and then, to Alice's dismay, she begins to cry again, this time loud and abandoned. "It was my fault!" she wails.

Alice stares. "Joelle, what are you talking about? Nothing is your fault."

But the girl is inconsolable. "He never would have known about Mom or Justin if it wasn't for me."

Alice is at a loss, until suddenly she understands. "Joelle, I spoke to your mom a few days before she died and she told me she thought you were seeing someone. Was it Justin Beagle?"

Joelle nods, wiping at her face with the arm of her sweatshirt. "We really liked each other," she says miserably. "He was older than me. It wasn't anything creepy; I mean, he was eighteen and I'm sixteen, but I knew my parents would be pissed, so we kept it a secret."

Joelle trails off, and even across the gulf between their back decks, Alice can feel waves of profound sadness rolling off her.

"I know this is hard," she says, "but I need you to explain why you think you're responsible."

Joelle takes a deep breath. "A few weeks ago Evan and I were hanging out in the park, just sitting on a bench and talking. I like Evan: he's weird, but he's interesting. Quirky, you know? Anyway, this van pulled up and a man got out and started yelling at him. It was really sudden and crazy and it took me a minute to realize it was his father."

"What was he saying?" asks Alice.

"He said Evan had broken the rules, he wasn't supposed to leave the house without permission, stuff like that. It was nuts. Then he looked at me and it was like he had only just noticed me. He told me to stay away from his son. I was scared; he was acting insane. Evan was trying to drag him away from me. It was a scene. I was freaked out, and I was embarrassed for Evan. Then they got in the van and drove away."

Alice imagines it: wild and chaotic like the scene in her mother's kitchen. "Did you talk to Evan about it?"

Joelle nods miserably. "He called me that night and told me we had to be really careful not to be seen together again, because it wasn't safe. I knew Evan's parents were super protective and strict. He was homeschooled and he wasn't allowed to date girls. I think he was even physically abused, because sometimes he had these weird bruises and cuts. So when he said that, I thought he meant it wasn't safe for *him*. But now I think maybe he meant it wasn't safe for *me*, and maybe that means it wasn't safe for my family or my boyfriend."

Alice's brain is working overtime trying to keep up. "You said you and Justin kept things a secret."

Joelle shakes her head. "From adults. Evan and some of my other friends knew. Justin was kind of jealous when he learned I was friends with another guy, but I told him it wasn't like that, and showed him some of Evan's videos about the Janitor just so he could see he had nothing to worry about. But Justin thought it was really cool, so he asked me to introduce them. The three of us went for a walk on the river trail one day, and they basically talked about the Janitor the whole time. It was about a week after that when Evan's dad caught us in the park."

Alice tries to assemble this complicated series of clues. Joelle's story proves that Parson had a connection to Justin and Vicki. Did he target them because of his son's connection to Joelle? That seems like a thin motive, but she still feels in her gut like the picture is slowly coming into focus.

"Joelle," she says, "you need to wake up your father right now. You're going to tell him everything you just told me, and then we'll call the police, okay?"

Joelle nods, then begins to cry again. "I'll tell them everything, Mrs. Brakes. I'm worried he's going to kill Evan, and that will be my fault too!"

CHAPTER TWENTY-FOUR: SAM

Sam stares at the flashing beacon on her phone's map as Doug races his shit-box Mazda along a deserted stretch of unpaved road about ten miles outside of Edgar Mills.

"We're getting close," she says. "It's about a mile up ahead on the left."

The headlights of the car illuminate a poorly maintained road, bordered by thick trees on one side and by abandoned, overgrown farm fields on the other. A few miles back they passed a couple of ramshackle but apparently, judging from the lights and vehicles in their driveways, still inhabited houses, but since then it's been a deserted, forgotten stretch of terrain.

"I can't believe this is really happening," says Doug. "I can't believe I'm helping Samantha Van Dyne chase down a killer."

"Doug," she says, looking up from her phone, "this is dangerous shit we're dealing with. You know that, right?"

He nods eagerly. "The more dangerous the better, honestly. I think I've been waiting for this moment my whole life."

She examines him, suddenly wary. "Don't be a hero, Doug." They come around the corner, and suddenly a light appears in the darkness. "There it is," she says. "Shut off your headlights."

Doug does as she says and slows to a crawl as they approach a trailer set back from the road behind a chain-link fence. A few rusted-out vehicles sit on blocks out front, surrounded by piles of scrap. A dog on a chain barks furiously as they pull to a stop out front. There's a light on in the trailer's window, blinding them to whatever is hiding in the vast darkness behind it.

"Okay," says Sam. "Let's think this through."

The gate is pulled shut but it isn't padlocked. Doug climbs out of the car and pushes it open enough to let them pass, trying to ignore the snarling, bloodthirsty dog straining at the end of its chain. He climbs back into the car and pulls through, stopping near the door to the trailer. They sit for a moment, staring at the small structure, but nobody appears in the door.

"Maybe this is a bad ide—" Doug begins, but Sam is already opening her door and stepping out of the car. The dog lunges, snapping at its chain, and she turns to it and points.

"No!" she yells, and to Doug's amazement the dog immediately stops barking. It stares, surprised, and then lets out a small whimper and curls up on the ground.

Sam is already stepping up onto the trailer steps, and Doug scrambles out of the car to follow her.

"I don't know about this," he hisses, but she's already pushed the trailer door open and stepped inside. Reluctantly, Doug steps in behind her, preparing for an ambush.

The trailer, he realizes right away, isn't a home but some kind of office. There's an old, beat-up sofa under a window, but the rest of the space is dominated by some filing cabinets, a worktable with a few pieces of automotive parts clearly in the process of being tinkered with, and a large metal desk covered in paper.

There's no ambush, because the only other person in the room with them, a diminutive elderly man with a neckbeard and thick glasses, is clearly dead, lying in a pool of blood on the floor next to the desk.

"Holy shit," says Doug.

Sam doesn't respond. She goes to the man and carefully rolls him over on his side, revealing a pistol that he obviously didn't have time to use.

"He's been shot," she says. "But not with this gun."

"Why wouldn't Parson have taken this one with him?" asks Doug.

Sam carefully removes the gun from the man's loose grip. "He probably doesn't think he'll need it," she says. "He probably thinks by the time anyone shows up, they'll all be past the point of saving."

Doug swallows hard.

Sam steps to a switch plate on the wall and flips some switches. The trailer goes dark, and a moment later a floodlight snaps on outside.

Through the window over the sofa, a vast junkyard sprawls into the distance.

"They must be out there somewhere," Sam says. She slips the gun into her waistband. "I guess now we look for them."

She checks her phone again as she steps out of the trailer ahead of Doug. There's still nothing from Evan. She's texted him about a dozen times since they pulled away from the curb back in Edgar Mills, so his silence must mean one of a few things: his phone is dead, he can't reach his phone because it's out of reach, or . . .

"Fuck," she says, staring into the brown, shadowed expanse in front of them. Suddenly the situation doesn't seem as straightforward as it did a few minutes ago.

"That dude back there was shot," says Doug. "Which means that Parson has a gun."

"So do I," says Sam, cocking the trailer man's pistol.

Doug's eyes widen and he gulps.

"I'm going to call the cops," she says.

"Okay," says Doug, visibly relieved. "Good."

She pulls out her phone and finds Angela Corvallis's number. It rings twice before the other woman picks up.

"I told you to keep yourself scarce," she says.

"I thought you'd like to know that I've tracked them down to a junkyard about fifteen miles east of town," says Sam. "I'm going to send you a pin."

"Wait a minute," says Corvallis. "What are you talking about?"

"There's a dead man here," Sam continues. "I think he's probably the owner or some kind of employee. He was shot. I don't have a bead on the suspect or the victims, but I'm going into the lot to look for the van."

"You are not—"

Sam cuts the call before Corvallis has time to finish her sentence. She sends a pin and then turns to Doug, who is staring wide-eyed at her.

"Shouldn't we wait for the police to show up?" he asks.

Sam shakes her head. "If there's any chance they're still alive, we can't afford to wait. You don't have to come in with me. You can stay here with the car and wait for the police to arrive."

"No," says Doug. "I'm not letting you go in there by yourself."

"You're not *letting* me do anything," she says. "But if you're sure . . ."

She steps up to a pile of scrap metal and digs about, and a moment later she pulls out a long, rusted length of iron piping.

She hands it to Doug, who bounces it in his hand, weighing it. "So I guess I use it like a baseball bat?"

"Use it however you need to," she says. "Just stick with me, okay?"

She pulls the gun from her waistband and checks the clip; then, holding it in front of her, she leads the way into the junkyard.

They move past piles of scrap, rusted-out appliances, and a wild, random assortment of old vehicles, everything from speedboats to snowmobiles and what seems like every imaginable make and model of car in between. The fierce halogen glow of the floodlight blasts over them, turning all of it into a checkerboard of glare and shadows. The effect is disorienting and it's hard to know where to look.

"We should have turned that light off," Sam whispers as they step into an alley of decommissioned school buses.

"And do all of this in the dark?" asks Doug. "No fucking way."

They continue, Sam holding the gun in front of her and Doug brandishing the iron bar over his shoulder. Abruptly he stops in his tracks.

"Look," he says, pointing. On the ground a few feet away is a cell phone.

Sam crouches and picks it up. She recognizes the case right away.

"It's Evan's," she says. She glances at the screen and sees all the missed calls and messages she's sent him over the past couple of hours. "Either he threw it or someone else did."

"At least it proves we're on the right track," says Doug.

They turn a corner and they're standing in a large central lane that branches off into the distance.

"Should we yell?" asks Doug.

Sam shakes her head. "If he doesn't know we're here yet, we don't want to tip him off."

"He would have noticed the floodlight," says Doug. "Maybe you should shoot off the gun just to let him know we're here and we mean business."

"Doug," she says, "can you stop talking so I can think?"

"Sorry," he whispers.

During Sam's time on *Rebel House*, there were people almost everywhere and cameras almost everywhere else, but she did discover one place where she could actually hide. The bathroom was the one camera-free zone on the property. The thing was, she couldn't get away with hiding inside the bathroom for long, since one of the other four women she shared it with would inevitably come knocking. But there was a window that opened onto a narrow porch roof, and she discovered that if she slipped into the bathroom when nobody was paying attention to her, she could climb out onto it. Up there she could sit and look out over the valley, taking a few moments to herself to think and grieve.

"I have an idea," she says. Slipping the gun into her waistband, she moves to a nearby school bus and climbs onto the fender and then the hood.

"What are you doing?" asks Doug.

"Getting a better view." Keeping her steps as light as possible, Sam steps to the windshield and manages to hoist herself up onto the roof of the bus.

"Sam!" Doug whispers urgently from down below. "This is a bad idea: you'll be in full sight!"

Sam ignores him. From her new vantage she has a full view of the junkyard. From there she can see that it ends at a fence that borders a farmer's field. She scans carefully, her eyes skimming over debris and wreckage until finally she spots it, tucked into a corner behind a pile of old lawn mowers: a white panel van.

"The van is there!" she says, keeping her voice low but unable to hold back the excitement.

"Is there anyone with it?" Doug asks.

Sam squints but she doesn't see any motion near the vehicle. "I can't tell," she says.

She climbs down from the bus and they continue through the junkyard to where the van is parked. Sam pulls the gun out and holds it in front of her as they approach. As they come to the far corner of the junkyard, and the van comes into sight, Sam's excitement is replaced by a sense of mounting dread. They can't hold back now, but she needs to be prepared for what they might find.

The van is parked neatly in a bare spot near some abandoned lawn care equipment. The surface gleams in the glare of the floodlight and the doors are all closed.

"What do we do?" asks Doug. "What if he's waiting to ambush us?"

But Sam is done hiding from terrible men. Before Doug even has a chance to react, she's striding across the empty space to where the van is parked and with a closed fist she slams on the side.

"We've got you surrounded!" she yells, her heart pounding so loud that she can hardly hear herself.

For a long, fraught moment there's no sound at all, save for an empty hum emanating from the deepest parts of her mind. Just when she's given up entirely and she's resigned herself to the horrible truth—that Parson Stevens has killed Evan, her mother, and himself—she hears it.

"Sam?" comes the voice, thin and anxious.

It's Joanna.

"Mom?" Sam yells. *"Are you okay? Is he in there with you? Tell me if you're in danger!"*

There's another long pause, and then Joanna responds again, with a voice that's suddenly gained more strength. "We're okay," she says.

And to Sam's intense shock and relief, the back doors of the van are thrust open from inside.

The scene is so unexpected that it takes Sam a minute to understand what she's looking at. She's barely aware of Doug coming up behind her or the sirens approaching in the distance as she stares in horror into the van.

Joanna stares out at her daughter, her eyes wide with fear and her clothes covered in blood.

Sam flashes back to the night the Janitor killed her father and Levon Brakes. Somewhat unbelievably, she and Alice left Levi behind with his brother's body—to be fair, he refused to come with them—and went with Joey, who she remembers drove unbelievably fast, back to their house. But it was too late. Cops were in sight, and Kershaw was being pushed into the back of a police van. As the twins pushed their way into the house, their mother had looked up from where she knelt next to their father's lifeless body and locked eyes with her daughters.

The look in her eyes that night was blank, hollow, and disbelieving, and her expression didn't shift even as medical techs appeared in the front doorway, pulling their father's body out on a stretcher. It remained like that for days: through the funeral, through the investigation and the frenzy of media attention—even through her testimony at the trial—her expression, her emotional affect, her *personality*, stayed the same, distant and removed.

It wasn't until after the trial was over, and Kershaw was locked up for good, that she began to shift into something new. Bitter. Resigned. Broken. And Sam has always thought that a part of her stayed back in that night, caught up in the terror that defined her life.

But this is a different woman staring out at her from the van. She's fully in this moment, her eyes glittering and present, almost wild with a jittering, frenetic energy. Behind her, curled up into himself in the corner behind the passenger seat, Evan is shaking and crying softly, whispering to himself. Up front, slumped heavily over the steering wheel and drenched in blood, is Parson Stevens. He's clearly dead.

"I had to do it, Sam," says Joanna, and Sam notices for the first time the box cutter clutched tightly in her fist. "He was going to kill us."

CHAPTER TWENTY-FIVE: JOEY

Joey can't get Joanna Van Dyne out of his head. He doesn't think he's even met the woman, but the fact that she's going through this kind of nightmare for the second time in her life seems to undermine any sense of karmic justice. That is, if she's even still alive.

It didn't take long for news about what happened on Bluebonnet Lane to escape the boundaries of Edgar Mills and begin flying around the internet. There were dozens of neighbors and other witnesses on hand to begin a game of spread the rumor, so there are plenty of different stories circulating, but the accepted facts are that Joanna Van Dyne was attacked in her house by a neighbor, who killed the family lawyer, Perry Lemire, and then abducted Joanna and his own son.

Joey considered texting the twins to find out how they're doing, but he felt awkward about it and texted Doug instead. But it's been a couple of hours and he hasn't heard back.

He glances over at Austin, who has been uncharacteristically silent as he drives them to their appointment. He wonders if his husband is having the same kind of second thoughts that he's been having—when he has time to think them.

"You know," he says, "if this isn't a great fit, we are under no obligation to go through with anything. Remember what Sheila said: it's just an interview. Nothing about this is set in stone."

Austin turns to look at him, and Joey is surprised to see genuine anger flashing in his eyes. "You'd love that, wouldn't you?" he says, before turning his eyes back to the road.

"Love what?" asks Joey, genuinely confused.

"You'd love for me to be the one to back out of this so you don't have to grow some balls and do it yourself."

"Wait a minute," says Joey. "I don't know what you—"

"I ran into Mike yesterday," says Austin, interrupting him. "You remember Mike, right? Your boss?"

"Shit," says Joey.

"Yeah, shit. Do you know what he asked me?"

Joey shakes his head, although he could make a guess.

"He asked me what I thought about Paris," says Austin. "Which seemed random, but then he kept talking and I started to get the gist. Fortunately, I was able to smile and nod and imply that I knew what the hell he was talking about!"

"Listen," says Joey. "Give me a minute to explain."

"No," says Austin, "*you* listen. If you really aren't into the idea of kids, I get that, okay? What I don't get is planning a secret move to another country to avoid it."

"What?" says Joey. "No! That's not what is happening!"

Austin pulls up in front of a block of grim-looking town houses. He switches off the ignition and turns to look at Joey, crossing his arms as he does so. "Okay, so why don't you tell me what's happening."

Joey reaches up to rub his temples. "Okay, so lately I've been feeling as if, I don't know, maybe I wasted some part of my life on stuff that doesn't matter." Austin's eyes widen and Joey hastens to continue. "Not like that. I'm talking about work. Sometimes it seems as if I devoted all of my life's energy to getting this fancy degree and working in tech and making a lot of money, and now that I'm where I always thought I wanted to be, it feels kind of empty. Does that make sense to you?"

"I think so," says Austin, softening slightly.

"At some point I must have mentioned that to Mike, because out of nowhere he brought up this idea of me taking this job in France."

"When?" asks Austin.

"I don't know—a week ago?"

"A whole week, and you didn't mention it?" Austin is still irritated, but Joey is relieved that he doesn't still sound furious.

"I didn't have the chance because this whole adoption agency thing came up, and then all the stuff at home in Edgar Mills. It was just kind of overwhelming, you know?"

"Okay," says Austin, "fair enough. But I need to know what you want to do."

"I don't know," says Joey. "I wanted to talk to you about it, but things started moving super fast. This has always been about wanting to talk to you when I had a chance. What do you think?"

"Of course moving to Paris sounds incredible," says Austin. "But, Joey, I want a kid more than that. Like, a thousand times more than that, and I don't think we can do both."

"I know," says Joey. "Okay, well that settles it. The minute I'm back at the office, I'll tell Mike I am going to stay here, and now we'll go see a woman about a baby."

He moves to open the door, but Austin reaches out and puts a hand on his arm. "I don't think anything is totally settled yet," he says. "I mean, if you're really unhappy at work, we should be able to talk about it. We have options, you know. Everyone deserves to chase their purpose. If you could do anything with your life, what would it be?"

Before Joey has the chance to answer, there's a loud bang on his window and they both scream with surprise. A hand wipes away the rain, and then a face peers in at them.

A young green-haired woman, dressed in a bright yellow raincoat that does nothing to hide her obvious pregnancy, smiles widely and waves. "Hi! I'm Carla! I saw you guys out here and thought maybe you got lost! Come on in!"

It turns out that Carla has an apartment of sorts in the basement of one of the town houses.

"It's my aunt's," she explains as she brings them into a small but cozy living room. "She said I can stay here as long as I want but, honestly, this has always been temporary for me. I'm hoping to start school out of state next year."

"What are you going to study?" Joey asks.

"Architecture," she says. "I'm accepted to Pratt. I was actually supposed to start this year, but they gave me a deferral when, you know . . ." She pats her stomach cheerfully, then makes an odd face.

"This is going to sound weird," she says, "but I'm wondering if you guys would be okay if I put the TV on for ten minutes."

"Um, sure?" says Austin.

"I know," she says apologetically. "I don't know if you guys have heard about this murder-kidnapping thing that's been going on?"

"Oh, we've totally heard of it," says Austin, shooting a glance at Joey.

"It's bananas," she says. "Anyway, right before you guys came in, I read online that there's been a break in the case and there's going to be a press conference in a couple of minutes."

Joey sits forward in his chair. "I'd like to watch that."

Her face lights up. "Are you into true crime too? I'm obsessed."

"Not exactly," he says. "But I'm interested in this case."

"You have no idea," says Austin.

She points them to the sofa and drops heavily into an armchair. She flips on the TV and finds the local news just in time to see Angela Corvallis step up to a microphone to a flurry of flashbulbs.

"Early this morning," Corvallis begins, "two individuals connected to last night's double homicide and kidnapping in Edgar Mills were located alive. Our prime suspect in the case was also located, deceased."

Several questions are yelled out from the audience and Corvallis points into the crowd, isolating one.

"Is there any indication that this case is connected in any way to the murders of Justin Beagle or Vicki Williamson?"

Corvallis nods. "Yes, it's our strong belief that the deceased culprit in this case was also responsible for the earlier deaths. As such, law enforcement has determined that there is no further risk to the public at this time."

"She's a shitty actor," says Carla.

Joey turns to look at her, surprised. "What do you mean?"

"You get used to these things when you listen to as many true crime podcasts as I do. These top cops are always playing a part. Most of them want to get into politics or whatever, and this kind of thing is like an audition. They're putting on a performance for the powers that be."

The news conference ends and Carla turns off the TV.

"Thanks for humoring me. So, let's talk adoption. Do you guys have any questions for me?"

"Just a few," says Austin. "Sheila tells us you're interested in an open process."

She nods. "I'm not in any position to raise a kid, and to be totally honest I'm not interested in raising a kid. But I also don't want to cut ties entirely. I want to be a presence in their life. Not like a mom exactly, but more like a cool aunt." She looks at them seriously. "It's a deal-breaker for me. Will that be a problem with you?"

"We are totally on board," says Austin. He reaches over and grabs Joey's hand. "Aren't we, Joe?"

Joey smiles and nods. "Absolutely." He promised himself he would contribute to this process fully, and he leans in and prepares to engage.

But in the back of his mind he's wondering if Angela Corvallis is the only one who has been playing a part.

CHAPTER TWENTY-SIX: ALICE

Alice races down the corridor of Edgar Mills Consolidated Hospital, slowing only slightly at a nurses' station, where Nash is standing with a couple of other cops, talking quietly. When he spots her coming, he points around the corner.

"Room 415," he says. "Sam's in there with her."

"Thank you!" yells Alice, hurrying on.

She stops, breathless, in the hospital room doorway. Sam is sitting in the window, looking down at Joanna, who is smiling weakly up from her pillow. They both turn to look at her.

"She just woke up," says Sam.

"Hello, darling," says Joanna. She holds out a hand, and Alice rushes across the room to take it.

"Oh my God, Mom," she says, kneeling beside the bed. "Tell me you're okay."

Joanna releases a deep sigh. She nods. "Yes. I think I'm okay. I mean, I'm not hurt. I don't know what would have happened if Sam hadn't shown up."

"I had nothing to do with it, Mom," says Sam. "You saved yourself."

"It wasn't like that," says Joanna. Her voice is weak, and she looks smaller and frailer than Alice can remember her ever looking. She's hooked up to a series of IVs, and her heart rate is being monitored. But she's alive, and Alice is overcome by a wave of emotion as she clasps her mother's hand.

"Don't cry, Alice," says Joanna. She reaches up and gives her daughter's hand a light squeeze. "My worst fear came true, but I lived through it. We can only look forward from here."

"Mom," says Sam, her voice uncharacteristically gentle. "Can you tell us what happened?"

"You don't have to talk about it now," says Alice, shooting her sister an exasperated look. "Get some rest and we can talk more later."

"It's okay," says Joanna, releasing her hand and settling back into the bed. "I've already told the police everything. It helps to talk about it."

Sam pulls up a couple of chairs and they sit, waiting for their mother to tell her story.

"Perry came by," Joanna begins. "He said you'd been to see him, Alice."

Alice nods, suddenly feeling very guilty and wondering if she was responsible for all of this. "I needed to ask him some questions."

"He told me that the two of you were looking into Kershaw," says Joanna. "That you thought maybe he'd had help back then. That he hadn't done the things we know he did."

Alice looks away, embarrassed at how wrong they got everything, but Sam holds her mother's gaze.

"There was a killer on the loose, Mom," she says. "We had a responsibility to look into all options."

"Yes, well . . ." Joanna sniffs, unable to suppress her passive-aggressive tendencies even under these circumstances. "I think we can put that to bed now."

"Go on, Mom," Alice says gently.

"Perry was upset," her mother continues. "So I poured him a drink, and we talked about your father for a while. You know, there aren't many people around who knew your father as well as I did, but Perry was one of them, God bless his soul."

"So you were just catching up," says Sam.

Joanna nods. "I expect he would have left soon, but then there was a knock on the back door. We were sitting just a couple of feet away, and I was about to get up and open the door, see who was there, but I didn't have the chance. The door burst open and there he was."

She pauses again, and her face seems to go even paler as she remembers the horrible scene.

"It was that man," she says. "Parson, just standing there with this awful expression on his face. I can't even describe it, it was angry but vacant at the same time. I was unsettled, but I had this automatic urge to be a good hostess. I said, 'Hello, Mr. Stevens, come in.' Isn't that something? He'd just pushed into my house uninvited, and I was welcoming him in. And then . . ."

She goes silent again and closes her eyes.

"Go on, Mom," Sam prompts softly.

"Then he stepped up to the table, and I don't think I saw the knife until he was drawing it across Perry's throat. Perry crashed to the floor, blood just pouring out of him, and I must have recoiled, because I fell back in my chair and then I was on the floor. He reached down and grabbed me by the hair and pulled me out of the kitchen and through the backyard. His van was running, and he opened the back door and threw me inside."

"Was Evan inside already?" asks Alice.

Joanna nods. "He was in the back, tied up. Parson crawled in, and I was whimpering and crying, and he slapped duct tape on my mouth and he zip-tied my wrists with my arms behind me, and then he climbed into the driver's seat, and the next thing I knew, we were moving."

"Did he speak while he was driving?" Alice asks.

Joanna thinks about this. "No, he didn't. But I knew he was going to kill us both. Or at least me. We were on the road for a long time, and at some point I saw the boy trying to send me some kind of message with his eyes. And finally I understood: he was using his eyes to gesture at a piece of metal that was sticking out the side of the van wall. I slid up against it and managed to slip my hand ties over it, and then I had somehow untied myself."

"Where were you at this point?" asks Sam.

Joanna thinks about this. "We must have been on the road to the junkyard, because there was a lot of bumping and jostling. I considered jumping out of the back of the van, but I knew he'd just stop and hunt me down, so I decided to bide my time. It was only a little while after that when he stopped and got out of the van."

"The junkyard office," says Sam.

Joanna nods. "As soon as he was out of the van, I moved to the boy. He was gagged and tied up, and I intended to untie him, but he started making noises and gesturing with his head and I realized he was trying to tell me to look in the glove box. I scrambled up front and found the box cutter in there. As I was grabbing it,

I heard a shot, and I managed to scramble back and hide the box cutter behind me. A second later Parson was back, and we were driving again—lots of twists and hard turns as he pulled us deep into the junkyard. Then he stopped."

Joanna stops speaking, and the twins hold their breath. She makes them wait for a long, pregnant moment, until finally, in a clear, matter-of-fact voice, she finishes the story.

"I knew this was my chance," she says. "The moment he parked the van, I lunged forward with the knife. He wasn't expecting it, and so his head was only just beginning to turn when I ran the blade across his neck. And that was that."

She removes her hand from Alice's, and as the twins stare at her, trying to process what she's just told them, she pushes herself up on her arms. "Girls, will you move these pillows so I can sit up a bit?"

As the girls adjust their mother, they exchange a *What the fuck?* glance over the top of her head.

"Mom," says Sam. "Are you going to be okay?"

"Yes, of course," says Joanna.

"You killed someone," says Alice gently. "I'm not sure you're processing that. I think you're probably in shock."

Her mother's eyes flash. "I'm processing just fine. Believe me, I know shock and this isn't it. This isn't the first time I've come face-to-face with a monster, as you know. The only difference is this time I got the better of him. I did what had to be done, and it feels great." She slumps back into the pillows, suddenly exhausted, and closes her eyes. "Now I need some rest," she murmurs.

The sisters leave their mother to sleep and step into the hallway.

"This is messed up," says Sam.

"You're telling me," says Alice.

Nash is now alone in the hallway, looking over some paperwork. He looks up as they approach.

"How's your mom?" he asks.

"She's doing surprisingly well," says Alice, "considering what she's been through."

"That makes two of them," says Nash. "Evan is holding up better than I would have expected."

"Really?" asks Sam. "Both of his parents are dead."

"I can't even imagine," says Alice. "To watch your father kill your mother and then kidnap you. It's a nightmare."

"I expect he's in shock," says Nash. "Things are bound to sink in soon, but for the time being he's in good spirits. He's helped us out with the investigation quite a bit, to be honest, filled in a lot of details around the edges. He repeated what he told you, Sam, about Parson living here around the time of the original murders. I don't want to get ahead of myself, but that might resolve a few unanswered questions."

"It's unbelievable," says Sam.

"You can say that again. You're welcome to go see him." He points. "He's at the end of the hall. Just see yourselves in. I have to go make a few calls."

Evan is sitting up in bed, staring out the window. He looks terrible, drawn and pale, with bandages on one side of his face and some tape covering one of the lenses in his glasses. But he turns and smiles at them when they enter.

"I didn't know if I'd ever see the two of you guys together," he says. "How's your mom?"

"She's going to be okay, Evan," says Sam. "She just needs some time to rest and recover. You both do."

"She saved my life," he says.

"The way she tells it, you saved each other," says Alice.

He doesn't respond to this, just sinks back into his mattress and closes his eyes.

"I knew he was . . . bad," he says, in a voice just barely louder than a whisper. "But I guess I never let myself believe he was *that* bad."

"When I met you," says Sam, "you told me you heard about the Janitor, about us, from your father."

Evan nods. "He was obsessed. I didn't realize it until he got in trouble at work and decided we should move to Edgar Mills. Once we were here he started talking about it all the time. I don't think it was a coincidence we moved in behind your mother. He wanted me to get to know her, pushed me to help her out around the house and stuff. Then he'd always be asking questions about whether she had mentioned anything about Kershaw, or either of you and your dad. She didn't, of course, and I wasn't going to ask about it. That pissed him off, so he found a way to get into the house and plant those cameras."

Something occurs to Alice. "Evan, did you start your TikTok account because of your father? That can't have been a coincidence."

"It wasn't." He looks away, embarrassed. "I thought if I learned as much as possible about the case, maybe we'd have something to talk about. I thought there was a chance he'd be impressed with me. Proud, or whatever. It was stupid of me. The funny thing is that I never even showed him the videos. I was worried that he'd think they were stupid, or worse. I guess he figured it out on his own though, since it sounds like he was following me."

"You think he was following you?" asks Sam.

"Who else would have attacked me in the school like that?" he asks.

The look on his face could almost break Alice's heart. "Joelle told me about your father confronting the two of you in the park."

Evan's eyes shift and his face drops. "He didn't like me to have any friends. He kept Mom isolated too. I never understood it, but now it makes sense. He had a lot to hide."

"Do you think that's why he homeschooled you?" asks Alice.

Sam stares. "You were homeschooled?"

Evan nods miserably. "Yeah. I always wanted to go to school, but he wanted me close. When he saw me with Joelle that day, he was really angry and he made me tell him everything I knew about her. I didn't want to, but I didn't know how *not* to. I thought he was worried about me trying to be with her; he didn't want me to have a girlfriend. I told him about Joelle and Justin and how her mom didn't approve of her dating an older guy and that I was just trying to be a supportive friend. And I—" He breaks off and looks away, suddenly anxious about something.

"Go on, Evan," says Sam.

"I . . . kind of mentioned the connection to you, Alice. That you were neighbors with the Williamsons. He was so obsessed with your story that I thought maybe he'd find it kind of cool. I think what actually happened is that he pulled Joelle's family into his messed-up plan. Maybe if I hadn't said anything to him, Justin and Vicki would still be alive."

"Evan," says Alice, leaning forward and taking his hand. "You can't blame yourself for any of this. Your father was a bad man, and you're lucky that you got out of there alive."

"To tell you the truth, Evan," says Sam. "I think, without your investigative instincts, things would have ended up even worse. Cut yourself some slack, kid."

He nods. "I'll try," he whispers.

"Knock knock."

They all turn to find Nash standing in the doorway. "Good news," he says. "I spoke with your mother's sister. She'll be flying in from San Diego tomorrow afternoon."

Evan rolls his eyes. "Great. Aunt Janet is such an asshole." He stares pleadingly at the twins. "Tell me you'll visit again? I could use the company."

"We wouldn't leave you here on your own with Aunt Janet," says Sam. She reaches down and takes his hand. "You're part of the Former Teen Detectives Club now. We stick together."

CHAPTER TWENTY-SEVEN: JOEY

Joey can tell from the moment he sits down across from Kershaw that this isn't the same man he visited just over a week ago. He's freshly shaven, his hair neatly combed, and his jumpsuit clean and smoothed out. He sits upright in his chair and folds his hands in his lap as Joey takes a seat across from him, meeting his gaze dead-on. But it's the way he speaks that is most noticeably different. Gone is the erratic, confrontational affect of a deranged serial killer; it's been replaced by a soft, clear voice that one might expect from a teacher, or a pharmacist, the man who delivers your mail . . . or the janitor in a public school.

"I wondered which one of you would come back first," he says with a small smile. "I suppose you're here to discuss the latest developments in the case."

"So you've heard the news." Joey isn't surprised. It's been less than twenty-four hours since the dramatic events at the junkyard outside of town, but Angela Corvallis was quick to find a podium and make a statement lifting the curfew and assuring listeners that there's no more danger to the public.

Kershaw smiles. "They can keep us out of the world, but they can't keep the world out of here. Do you know anything about the killer?"

Joey nods. Parson Stevens's identity hasn't been made public yet, but he got the inside scoop from a breathlessly excited Doug, who somehow found himself at the scene of the crime. Joey knows he'll be rolling on that high for years.

"Does the name Parson Stevens mean anything to you?" he asks. He watches Kershaw's reaction closely, but the man just shakes his head.

"Who was he?"

"He was Joanna Van Dyne's neighbor. Apparently he was obsessed with your case and with the Van Dynes. You're sure the police won't find some sort of hidden connection between the two of you when they go looking?"

"I've never heard of him, and that's the truth," says Kershaw.

Joey is convinced. "The thing is," he says, "you don't seem surprised by any of this."

Kershaw shrugs. "I didn't know how any of this was going to shake out. I told you when you first visited me that I didn't know who killed those people back in 2000, so I had no way of knowing if it was the same person committing this newer batch of murders. But it was worth looking into, don't you think?"

"Only if your story is to be believed," says Joey. "That you weren't responsible for all of the murders back then."

"And what do you think?" asks Kershaw.

"That's actually why I'm here," Joey says, without answering the question. "I'm hoping you can answer a few questions for me."

"Of course," says Kershaw. "I'd be happy to help if I'm able."

Joey sits back in his chair and regards Kershaw with curiosity. "Why didn't you tell us you hadn't killed any of them."

Kershaw raises an eyebrow, but he clearly isn't surprised by the question. "I've admitted I killed," he says. "I've never denied it."

"You killed Chief Van Dyne, and only Chief Van Dyne," says Joey. "I don't think you intended to. I think things just got out of control."

The calm expression Kershaw has been wearing drops away. He looks haunted.

"Who's to say how I intended things to work out?" he says. "I came to the man's house carrying a gun. I pushed my way inside. I pulled the trigger."

"There's a big difference between manslaughter and premeditated murder," says Joey. "I think you were scared and you wanted someone to explain to you what was going on, and things went sideways. But what I want to know is why you pretended you'd killed any of the others, because I am pretty sure you didn't."

"If that's why you're here," says Kershaw, "you must have a different theory."

Joey thinks carefully about whether he should keep going. But right now Kershaw is the only person who might be able to give him some guidance. A week ago, maybe even a day ago, he never would have considered such a thing, but a week ago he thought the man across from him was a depraved serial killer.

"I am pretty convinced that Bill Van Dyne had a suspect in mind when he died," says Joey. "And it wasn't you."

Kershaw smiles. "Well that's a relief."

"The problem is, I'm not really sure where to go from here," says Joey. "I can't take this to the police right now; they're dealing with enough at the moment."

"What about the twins?" Kershaw asks.

Joey hesitates, and he notices Kershaw notice it. "They're wrapped up with some other stuff right now."

Kershaw raises an eyebrow. "You're really not going to tell me? I think we're past the point of keeping secrets, wouldn't you say?"

Joey sighs. "Parson Stevens kidnapped Joanna Van Dyne, along with his own son. There was a confrontation and she killed him."

Kershaw's eyes widen. "Wow."

"Yeah, so under the circumstances I feel like it isn't a great time to show up and dump this on their lap."

Kershaw nods. "So you brought it to me. Well, I wish I could help you, but I have no idea who Bill Van Dyne might have suspected. I'll think about it, but I didn't know that many people back then. I was kind of a loner, which has also been well documented."

"There's something I don't understand," says Joey. "Why didn't you put up more of a defense?"

"I was in shock after what happened that night," says Kershaw. "I'd shot and killed a man, and then all of this evidence surfaced in my apartment tying me to everything else. I tried to tell the investigators that I'd been set up, but of course everyone expected me to deny it all, so nobody paid me any mind. My sister paid for a lawyer, but he wasn't interested in my stories either. He stuck around till I'd burned through my appeals, and after that, I never saw or heard from them again—my lawyer *or* my sister. I never had any visitors or friends, nobody to take up my cause. I've made a few friends in here over the years, but if I've learned one thing about prison it's that nobody wants to hear your 'I didn't do it' story."

"So you came to us," says Joey.

Kershaw nods. "I hold a lot of guilt in my heart for what I did to Bill Van Dyne. I'll live with the shame of my actions forever, but I've come to believe I've paid my debt to society, and when I heard there were new murders happening in Edgar Mills, I saw an opportunity. I knew if I could just speak to the three of you, it would stir up enough curiosity to convince you to begin digging around. It seems I was right."

"You were," says Joey. "But I don't understand why you had to put on the act, playing up the deranged killer and implying that you'd killed some but not all of them. Why didn't you just tell us the truth?"

"I had one chance," says Kershaw, "so I had to manage it perfectly. If I'd acted like the normal old man that I am and said to the twins, "Oh yes, I *did* shoot your father but I didn't kill the rest of them," it would have been a nonstarter. They had plenty of reason to hate me, and they would have written me off right away as a slick operator, trying to take advantage of an awful situation. So I played it the other way."

"You leaned into the Janitor," says Joey.

He rolls his eyes. "Such a stupid name. But, yeah, I played up the character hoping to plant just enough doubt that you'd leave thinking someone else was involved. If that seed sprouted, I knew the three of you would do everything you could to figure out the truth. I wish I'd had more to give you—a hunch, a clue, a suggestion—but as you know, I've got nothing. But I know I didn't do it, and that had to be enough."

"You are so calm about all of this," says Joey.

"I've spent this long in here," says Kershaw. "I can stay awhile longer. If you want the truth, I felt optimism for the first time in twenty-five years the day the three of you came in here to see me. And it turns out I was right to be optimistic. You've made it this far. I have faith you'll figure out the rest."

"If this is true," says Joey, "it means someone framed you. Do you have any ideas or theories about who might have done that?"

Kershaw shakes his head slowly. "No. Believe me, I've run through this a million times over the years. I had no enemies at all. No friends either."

"Except Brenda."

Kershaw smiles sadly. "So you found her?"

"Yes, I met with her. She told me about your weekend in Vermont, and that she had a hard time believing you were capable of murder. She said she would have testified for you. Why didn't you ask her?"

Kershaw smiles sadly. "I didn't want to drag her into it. We kept our relationship a secret, such as it was. By the time I realized how quickly things were moving in the wrong direction for me, I felt like it would have been cruel to involve her."

Joey has one last question.

"Did you ever have any dealings with the police?" he asks. "Before all of this, I mean."

Kershaw thinks about this. "As a matter of fact, yes. The break-in."

"Break-in?"

"About a month before DJ Cartwright was killed, I came home from work and my door was unlocked. I *always* locked my door. I told my lawyer about it, but he implied that it would just sound like

I was making it up to give myself an alibi. Besides, nothing was taken. Nothing I noticed, anyway."

"And you called the police when it happened."

"Of course," says Kershaw. "They sent someone over and I gave a statement. But since nothing was stolen, there wasn't a whole lot to do about it."

Joey tries calling each of the twins on his way out of the prison, but neither of them answers.

He heads straight for the hospital.

CHAPTER TWENTY-EIGHT: SAM

Sam sits outside the hospital on a bench that gives her a clear view of a small pocket park across the street. She remembers playing in that park with Alice when they were just kids and her grandmother was lying inside, approaching death. She hasn't thought about that in decades, and the memory brings an intense feeling of déjà vu, as if all of this is just the same story echoing back through time.

Her phone buzzes with a notification and she pulls it out of her pocket. It's a text from Joey.

Sam can you please call me?

She knows he'll want to hear about everything that happened yesterday, but she doesn't have the energy to go into it right now. She'll call him later.

She feels a tickle on the back of her neck as if she's being watched, and sure enough, when she twists around in her seat she sees Nash Young approaching from the direction of the hospital. Her father might be gone, but solid, dependable Nash has stepped into his shoes and kept things running. She's never really noticed how sad he looks behind the rugged smile.

"Can I join you?" he asks.

She slides over to give him room and pats the bench. He sits and leans back, stretching his arms over his head and yawning deeply.

"Man," he says. "I need some sleep. I'll probably head home shortly, now that things are settling down a bit. How are you doing?"

"I was just thinking about how old I feel," she says.

"Age doesn't matter," says Nash. "Action matters."

She turns to look at him. "My dad used to say that."

He grins. "He sure did. It was one of the first things he said to me when I joined the force. I respected the hell out of that man."

"So did I," says Sam, sighing wistfully as she settles back against the bench. She pauses, then spits out a question that's been on her mind. "Is there something going on between you and Alice?"

"No," he says firmly. "We ended up in the same place at the same time in the same state of mind, and I think we looked at each other for about ten seconds and said, 'Hey, you'll do,' but we came to our senses just as quickly. I don't really know Alice all that well, but I think she's going through some stuff."

"Yeah," says Sam. "Alice was always the one who wore her heart on her sleeve. I was a lot more reserved, but she never had an emotion she wasn't willing to share with the world. But lately I can't really figure out what's going on with her."

"We all go through periods of transition," says Nash.

They sit in silence for a while, considering this, before Sam speaks up again. "Can I ask you something? What do you think pushed him over the edge?"

"You mean Parson?" asks Nash.

She nods. "We keep hearing how obsessed he was with us, but if that was the case, why did he drag it all out like this?"

"My best guess is that he was building toward something," says Nash. "I think he had some kind of big finale planned, but when I brought Evan into the station for questioning about what happened to him at the elementary school, he realized he was in real danger of getting found out. His hand was forced."

"Yeah," she says. "I guess that makes sense."

The unfortunate truth is, they'll never have the chance to understand what was going through that man's mind, but she doesn't intend to spend the next twenty-five years of her life wondering. Her mother is safe, the murders are finished, and all that really matters is what happens next. She's done living in the past.

Nash stands. "I'm going to stop into the station to finish some paperwork, then I'm going home to grab a few hours of shut-eye. You should consider doing the same thing."

"I will," she says, "but I'm just going to take over from Alice and spend a couple of hours with Mom first."

He shakes his head in disbelief. "That is one tough lady. I can see where you get it."

Joanna is snoring softly when Sam gets to her room, and Alice is sitting in the window, staring out at the river, lost in thought.

She looks up and smiles as Sam enters the room.

"You all good?" asks Sam, speaking quietly as she moves to join her sister by the window.

Alice nods. "Yeah. She had a snack about half an hour ago, and she's been asleep ever since."

"I'm going to take over," says Sam. "You should go home and get some sleep."

Alice stands and stretches. "I will go home, but I doubt I'll get much sleep. Levi and I need to talk."

Sam raises an eyebrow. "That sounds ominous."

Alice shakes her head. "More like overdue. I'm going to tell him I want to separate."

"Wow," says Sam. "Are you sure you don't want to wait until things calm down a little bit? There's kind of a lot going on right now."

"No," says Alice, and Sam can tell from the tone of her voice that her mind is made up. "We've been on edge for a very long time, and it's only now that the shit has hit the fan that I'm beginning to realize that life's too short to just keep grinding along the same path, hoping things will get better. They're not getting better, and I'm running out of time. We all are. It's time for me to find the thing that I've been missing all these years."

"What is that?" asks Sam.

Alice shrugs. "I'll let you know when I find it."

She steps forward and pulls Sam into a firm hug, then grabs her purse and leaves. Sam walks to the doorway and watches her sister walking down the hallway with a purposeful stride before disappearing around the corner. She wonders if maybe she needs to find what *she's* been missing.

"It's about time she grew a backbone."

She turns to see Joanna looking up at her from the bed.

"You heard all that?"

Her mother nods, then attempts to shift herself up to a sitting position. Sam helps her, then pulls a chair over to the bed and takes a seat.

"Alice and Levi should never have gotten together in the first place," says Joanna. "At the time I was just happy that somebody was around to take care of her. I was too lost in grief to even notice it back then, and you couldn't get out of here fast enough."

Sam sets her jaw, but Joanna waves away her frustration. "It's not a guilt trip. I didn't blame you for leaving. I would have loved to leave myself, but old habits die hard. You were young enough to get away."

"And now all I want is to come back," says Sam.

Joanna stares at her intently. "You don't really mean that, do you?"

"I'm not sure. But I'm considering it. I think we could all stand to do some healing, and maybe that would be easier if I was here, at home."

Joanna reaches out, and Sam is happy—eager even—to take her hand. The older woman's grip is surprisingly strong, and Sam finds herself willed closer by the pressure of her mother's thumb on her palm.

Joanna shakes her head slightly, her eyes dim with tears and weary with things that she seems to need to say.

"Your father was so proud of you, Samantha," she says. "He was proud of both of you girls, of course, but he had a special place in his heart for you. You were the one most like him. His fondest wish was that you become a police officer just like him."

"Really?" says Sam, genuinely surprised.

"Oh yes," says her mother. "He knew you had a gift. When the two of you began following in his footsteps he was beside himself. Proud as punch."

The drugs must be kicking in, because her words come out slow and syrupy, and her eyes begin to flutter and close.

"I was proud too, Sam," she murmurs. "I hope you know that. You were destined for big things. I never expected it all to end so terribly. You girls didn't deserve what happened."

Her grip on Sam's hand loosens, and soon she's fast asleep, snoring quietly.

Sam gently pulls away and moves to take the chair in the window. As she stares out at the rapidly deepening twilight, she thinks about what she just told her mother. Is she seriously considering moving home? Until she spoke it aloud, she didn't realize it was even an option, but now it feels as if there's some logic to it.

As much as she has always tried to tell herself that she was happier as someone else, as Sammy Vee, living her West Coast life, wasn't she really just atoning for her sins by remaining in exile? She's never really made any connections of note in Los Angeles. But she has family here. She tries to imagine herself living back in Edgar Mills and all she can conjure is an image of herself at seventeen, stepping through the front door of Cordova's with her sister and some friends, blissfully unaware of the future.

But isn't it true that she's just as unaware of the future now? And doesn't she have the right to live that future here, now? Maybe if she steps back into her own shoes, she'll be able to start atoning for things, forgiving herself, or at least cutting herself some slack.

It's like Nash said: *everyone goes through periods of transition.*

She stands, suddenly restless as she considers the crossroads in front of her. She decides to take a walk down to the cafeteria to grab a coffee.

As she waits for the elevator, she glances to the far end of the hallway and notices a woman standing outside Evan's door, speaking with a doctor. There's a suitcase sitting next to her, and Sam realizes this must be Aunt Janet from San Diego.

The elevator arrives and Sam is about to step inside when her own words return to her. *We wouldn't leave you alone with Aunt Janet.* Evan didn't seem excited to see his mother's sister, and after everything he's been through, she decides he might appreciate a buffer. The least she can do is introduce herself and offer to get the woman a coffee.

They look up as she approaches and she smiles. "Sorry to interrupt like this. Are you Evan's aunt Janet?"

"Who are you?" the woman asks without answering Sam's question.

"I'm Samantha Van Dyne," says Sam. "My mother was in the van with Evan."

"I see," says the woman. "Yes. Isobel was my sister."

"I'm so sorry for your loss," says Sam. "I'm just heading down to the cafeteria and thought I'd see if you'd like a coffee. Or maybe Evan wants something?" She glances at the closed door.

"Thank you," says Janet, "but no."

"Is he sleeping?" asks Sam, glancing at the closed door.

The doctor, who has been watching the awkward exchange with discomfort, steps in. "What she's saying is Evan checked out of the hospital just over an hour ago." He turns to Janet. "If you don't have any more questions, I have some other patients to attend to."

He leaves and Sam turns back to Janet. "I don't understand. A fourteen-year-old kid can't check out of a hospital on his own."

Janet gives her a funny look. "I'm afraid you're mistaken. Evan is eighteen. He'll be nineteen in a few months."

Sam stares, struggling to comprehend. "But he's just a kid. His parents are homeschooling him."

Janet laughs, although there's no humor in it. "I realize he probably seems like a junior high student. He was always small and immature in a lot of ways, but I can assure you Evan has not attended school in several years, home or otherwise. His parents removed him after some unfortunate incidents. Isobel did her best to pick up the slack for a while, but Evan marches to the beat of his own drum, to put it charitably."

"What do you mean by 'incidents?'"

"He had a habit of developing unhealthy fixations on some of his classmates," she says. "Some of the parents complained. I guess it was inevitable, living in that house with that man. I don't know what will happen to him now, but I can tell you he won't stay with me. I don't trust him: there's too much of his father in there. I'll help him sort through his parents' affairs and sell the house, and then he'll have to figure out his next steps on his own. Isobel and I inherited a comfortable sum of money when our parents died, so he'll be okay as long as he doesn't squander what she's left him."

Sam manages to choke out a goodbye, then turns and hurries down the hallway to where a couple of nurses are quietly chatting behind the counter.

"Is Nash Young here?" she asks, and they both look up, alarmed by the tone of her voice. "The chief," she explains. "Or any police officer?"

One of the nurses shakes her head. "The entire force has been called out," she says. "Something about a bomb threat. There are security guards if you—"

Sam is running for the exit before the woman has even finished speaking.

CHAPTER TWENTY-NINE: ALICE

Alice is halfway home when an incoming call announces itself on the Suburban's console. Levi.

"I'm on my way home," she says, without bothering to greet him. "I think it's time—"

"Alice," he says, cutting her off. "We need to talk. It's important."

"Yeah, I think that's a good idea. I'll be there in ten."

"I'm not at home," he says. His voice is tight. "I'm at Birch Crest."

"What?" she asks, her heart skipping a beat. "Why the hell—"

"Alice!" he says, his voice rising. "I just need you to meet me here, okay? It's important."

"Levi, what's going on?" She grips the steering wheel even tighter. "Where's Will?"

He pauses just for a second, but it's a long-enough time for every imaginable worst-case scenario to run through her mind. "Where is he?" she says, forcing herself to remain calm.

"He's with my parents," says Levi. "Alice, I you need to come here right now. It's important."

"I'm not going anywhere until you tell me what this is about."

"Please, Alice" he says. "I need to talk to you about that night. When—" His voice breaks, but he catches himself. "I need to tell you the truth about what happened, okay?"

"What are you talking about?" she asks. Has her husband been on the verge of a nervous breakdown and she didn't notice?

"I'll explain everything when you get here," he says. "Please, Alice."

Over the speaker, she hears him begin to cry, and deep inside her heart she feels a pause and a shift, and then something begins to reverse.

"I need you," he says. "Come alone."

Then he hangs up.

It boggles Alice's mind that the old school is still standing after all these years, even after everything that happened. She remembers hearing something about a conflict between the school board and the town council, a dispute over property ownership and unpaid taxes.

She finds Levi's truck is parked around back, out of sight of the road. She parks next to it, dialing his number as she climbs out. It rings through to voicemail.

"What the hell is going through your head, Levi?" she mutters. Ignoring the HAZARD and CONDEMNED AND DANGEROUS signs, she approaches the maintenance door on the side of the building. The sheet of plywood that had been covering it has been torn away and lies on the ground nearby, chipped and frayed after years of neglect and water damage.

"Mrs. Brakes!"

She jumps at the sound of the voice. When she turns she sees Evan Stevens, of all people, emerging from behind the school.

"Evan? What are you doing here? Why aren't you in the hospital?"

"I checked myself out," he says.

"How di—"

He cuts her off. "You have to listen to me," he says urgently. "I don't think your husband has been honest with you."

Alice stares at him. "What are you talking about?"

Evan speaks in a nervous rush. "I don't know all the details, but I think he knows more about what happened on that night your father died than he's ever told you."

"How could you possibly know anything about that?" she asks.

"Will told me," he says.

Alice's brain scrambles to untangle what he's saying. "Will? I don't understand."

Evan explains in a nervous rush. "When I moved to town and started researching the Janitor for my TikTok, I found out where you lived from your mother. I decided to try to become friends with Will, because I thought he might have some insider information I could use in my videos. I used Joelle to get close to him. I know it was sleazy of me, I'm sorry."

"That doesn't matter," she says, impatient. "Just spit it out."

"At first Will seemed happy to talk about the murders, but he didn't really know much. He said you refused to discuss it with him, so most of what he'd learned came from the internet. When he realized how much I knew about it all, he seemed really interested, but as soon as he learned I was making videos about the case, he pulled away and stopped hanging out with me and Joelle. But before that he said something that caught my attention. He said that his dad had once implied there was more to the story than anyone knew."

Alice stares at him. "What do you mean, 'more to the story'?"

"That's all he said," says Evan, "but it stuck with me. I've been doing a lot of thinking, and I wonder if maybe your husband knew my father back when he lived here in Edgar Mills."

Alice stares at him. "That's impossible," she says.

"Maybe," he says. "But don't you think it's a massive coincidence that my father lived here at the same time everything went down? What if Bruce Kershaw wasn't responsible for all those murders? What if my father was involved, and your husband knows something about it? I figured it was a longshot, but I had to know for sure, so I went to see him."

"You went to my house?" Alice asks.

He nods. "I stole a bike from the playground across the street from the hospital and went straight there. When he answered the door, I asked him directly if he knew my father back then, and he kind of freaked out."

"Freaked out?" The uneasy feeling she's been carrying since she arrived begins to grow. Why hasn't Levi come out of the school yet. "Evan, what did he say?"

"He didn't say anything, he just looked crazy. His eyes bulged out, and his mouth hung open, and then he pushed past me and ran to his truck and peeled out of there. I had a hunch that he'd come here, so I headed in this direction and sure enough . . ." Alice follows his gaze and they both stare at Levi's truck.

"Have you seen him?" she manages to ask, even though her mouth is suddenly as dry as dust.

Evan shakes his head. "I was trying to build up the nerve to go inside, and then you showed up."

"Okay," she says, thinking. "I'm going inside to find him. You stay here."

He nods, his face a mask of worry. "Do you think he's alright, Mrs. Brakes?"

Alice turns and stares at the school. "I hope so."

The door is propped open with a rock, and Alice pushes through and steps inside. She fires up the flashlight and shines it down the corridor. Piles of debris line the walls, many years' worth of paper industriously shredded and carried into various nooks and corners to create nests. Something quick and dark, the size of a small cat, slips out of the edge of the beam and disappears into the depths of the detritus. Alice shudders.

"Levi?" she calls out. The sound echoes through the building before dropping back to silence. She stands still, listening, but there's no reply.

Her phone rings, and she nearly jumps out of her skin. It's Sam. She debates answering, in case something is going on with their mother, but she needs to deal with Levi first. She ignores the call and switches the phone to silent, then points the flashlight out in front of her and begins to walk.

The school is eerily quiet. As she makes her way through the dark, abandoned corridors, her mind begins to move as well, heading straight in a direction she's been avoiding. Has everything she ever believed about the night that changed her life been a lie? If so, what *is* the truth, and how much does Levi know about it?

Is it possible that the man she's loved for her entire adult life has been keeping a terrible secret?

Has it all come down to this?

She stops when she arrives at the double doors that lead into the gymnasium. Her heart, she realizes, is racing so quickly that it might explode. She does not want to discover what is behind these doors.

"Levi?" she calls again.

When he doesn't respond, she steps forward and pushes into the gym, then abruptly stops as her brain works furiously to take in what she's seeing.

In the middle of the gym, brightly lit by a single spotlight set up on a stand in the corner, sits Levi. His legs are bound at the ankles, his wrists tied behind him, and he's lashed tightly to a chair. A few feet away from him sits Will, tied up in the same way. Both of them are gagged.

She tries to make sense of the scene in front of her, and wonders briefly if this is some kind of awful practical joke. Then she snaps out of it and hurries to them, pulling the gags from their mouths.

"Alice," says Levi, as soon as he's able to speak. "You need to get out of here now."

"So quick?"

When Alice turns, Evan is standing in the doorway. He's holding a gun.

"I'm sorry, Alice," says Levi miserably.

"Shut up, sad sack," says Evan.

As he approaches, he holds the gun in front of him in his right hand, casually aiming it at each of them in turn.

"Evan," says Alice, willing herself to sound calm. "Please don't hurt them. Just tell me what you want."

He points at some chairs sitting nearby, a few coils of rope beside them. "Bring a chair over to sit near your little family and grab some rope while you're at it."

She does as he asks, and he directs her to tie her legs to the chair. When he's satisfied she can't move, he shoves the gun into his waistband and takes over, quickly tying her hands together behind her and binding her more tightly to the chair.

She turns to look at Will. "Are you okay?"

"Yeah," says Will. "I'm sorry, Mom. This is my fault."

"It's not your fault," says Levi. "He ambushed us."

Alice's mind scrambles to reassemble what she thinks she understands. She turns to Evan. "You lied about everything."

Something about this strikes him as hilarious and he begins to laugh. "Wow," he says finally, once he has himself under control, "believe me, you don't know the first thing about it."

"Whatever he told you, he's full of shit, Mom," says Will. "He showed up at the house and I stupidly let him in. Then he pulled that gun and forced us into the truck, and we came here."

"I told you to keep your mouth shut," says Evan. "Now listen up. We're going to handle things the way I want them handled. You got that?"

"Evan," says Alice, "you can stop this right now. You're just a kid. Whatever you've done, you'll get off with a slap on the wrist."

He laughs again, and it's a much more adult sound than she was expecting. Now that she has a chance to examine him closely, his entire look seems to have changed. He's standing tall, and he isn't wearing glasses.

"Let's be real here, Alice," he says. "An eighteen-year-old with five murders under his belt is well past slap-on-the-wrist territory."

Alice stares at him, horrified. "You're eighteen?" she asks.

Evan slouches performatively, and the hard expression slips off his face, replaced by the earnest, wide-eyed, innocent boy she met in the Williamson's basement. "I'm a young eighteen," he says. "Most people think I'm fourteen at most. And if there's one thing I learned from the fabulous Van Dyne twins, it's that you should always work with what you've got."

"I don't understand," she says. "What have you done?"

He grins at her. "Don't worry, you'll get the whole story soon enough, but before we start spilling the tea, I think we're missing someone, aren't we?" He pulls a phone from his back pocket. "Let's see if dear sister can shuffle around her schedule a bit and join our sharing circle."

He places a call and then walks away, the cell phone held to the side of his head.

"What did he say to you?" Levi asks again as soon as Evan has stepped out of the gym into the hallway.

"He said Will had told him you were keeping some kind of secret," she says. "About what happened back then."

"What secret?" asks Will, indignant. "I never told that guy a thing. Not that he didn't ask a million questions."

"He's been playing us," says Alice. "There is no secret."

"That's not entirely true," says Levi. He drops his head. "It was my fault that Levon died."

Alice's eyes widen. "What are you talking about?"

"When you and Sam told us you'd learned Kershaw was the killer and asked us to help bring him down, Levon thought we should go straight to your father."

"That's not true," says Alice, confused. "Levon was eager to help."

"He wanted you to think that," says Levi, "but he told me he was going to see Chief Van Dyne before things had a chance to get out of hand. But I persuaded him to stick with the plan. Kershaw was just some pathetic little loser. Levon and I were big and strong, and with the two of you we were four against one, plus we had the element of surprise. I convinced my brother it would be a piece of cake." He looks at Alice pleadingly. "I thought it was exciting. I wanted to be part of it. Levon wanted both of us to be happy, so he agreed to stick to the plan."

"Levi, you can't blame yourself," says Alice. "I pushed for it as much as you did. More, even. It was my idea."

Levi shakes his head, his eyes glistening. "You don't understand," he says, choking up. "I persuaded him to go into the school early and wait for Kershaw so we could surprise him from two directions. It wasn't at all what we'd planned with you girls, but I convinced him to go off script, and then everything went to shit. It *is* my fault that he died."

Alice stares at her husband, speechless. The story he's always told is that *Levon* had the idea to go into the school and hide.

"I thought I'd managed to get over it," he continues—he speaks in a rush now as tears run down his face—"but everything started to slip a few months ago as we started to get closer to the anniversary." He turns to Will. "The older you got, the more I began to see my brother in you. That should have been a beautiful thing, but instead it just reopened this chasm of guilt inside me. And then people started to turn up dead again, and I just couldn't cope."

Alice can't remember the last time she felt this much tenderness toward her husband. "I'm sorry I didn't realize what you were going through. I wish you'd talked to me about it."

"I didn't think I could," he says, and his voice is thick with misery. "You had your own shit to deal with. I wanted to stay strong for you."

"Jesus Christ," says Will, "you're both so *stupid*."

They both turn to stare at him.

"You're both struggling with the *same* shit," he continues. "Pointless guilt. For as long as I can remember, I've known that this awful thing happened to you guys when you were in high school. But you both pretend it never happened."

"That's not true, Will," says Alice.

"It is true," says Will. "You never, ever talk about it. You guys didn't even want me to come to Joelle's house after her mom died, because you thought somehow it would rub off on me. I know it's heavy what happened to Vicki, but I'm fifteen years old. I can handle serious things."

"Of course you can," says Levi.

"We were just trying to protect you," says Alice.

"Exactly!" Will is practically yelling by this point. "I don't need to be protected from reality!" He turns to Alice. "You try to keep everything from me. I'm not a moron. You think I don't know that Aunt Sam came back to help you solve the murders?"

"That's not true," says Alice weakly.

"The fact that you used to be a detective is like the coolest thing about you, Mom," Will continues. "But you try to make me believe that part of your life never happened, even when you're back out there doing it again."

"I just wanted you to have a normal life," says Alice.

Will laughs. "Right, like this is normal?" He stops speaking and takes a breath to center himself. "I know how Granddad and Uncle Levon died was awful, but maybe it's time to deal with it and finally let them go. Do you guys seriously think that either of them would have wanted you to spend twenty-five years of your lives wallowing in self-pity? I think they'd want you to move on with your lives. And here's an idea: maybe you could try to help each other move on instead of heading to opposite corners."

Alice stares at her son, caught off guard by his outburst. Every single thing he's just said resonates with her, and when she turns to look at Levi she can see on his face that he feels the same way. But before either of them has a chance to respond, they're interrupted by the sound of Evan's return.

"As much as I'm loving this killer group therapy session, maybe you want to pause until Sam shows up. I just got off the phone with her and she's graciously agreed to rearrange her schedule. She should be here soon, and all will finally be revealed."

CHAPTER THIRTY:
JOEY

Joey grabs the first available parking spot and jumps out of his car. He's running to the hospital doors when he spots Sam standing a few feet away from the entrance, staring at her phone.

"Sam!" he yells. "I've been trying to reach you guys." She looks up and he stops in his tracks when he sees the expression on her face, a mixture of shock and horror. "What's the matter? Is it your mom?"

She pulls herself together. "Mom's fine. I just got a call from Evan Stevens."

"The kid from next door? Isn't he here at the hospital?"

"No," she says. "He's at Birch Crest."

"The school?" A quick, staccato burst of fragmented memories invades Joey's mind. A slice of his own younger face reflected in the window of the abandoned school's door. Hurrying through the darkened hallways behind Levi. The shimmer of a flashlight's beam in a thick puddle of blood. "I don't understand."

"I need to go there right now," says Sam. "I had everything wrong. It was him all along." She turns and begins to walk briskly through the parking lot.

Joey follows, hurrying to keep up. "Sam, I want to help you. It was *who* all along?"

She stops in her tracks and turns to look at him.

"Evan Stevens killed all of them," she says. "Justin. Vicki. Perry. His own parents. He isn't a kid; he's almost nineteen years old. He had us all fooled. Now he's got Alice and Levi and Will at the school, and he's threatening to kill them if I don't meet them there."

"I'm coming with you," he says.

She shakes her head. "He told me to come alone, and if I call or tell anyone, he'll shoot all three of them, no questions asked."

"We'll figure something out," says Joey, "but I'm coming."

Sam doesn't argue, and he follows her to her rental car. Before he even has a chance to fasten his seat belt, she's peeling out of the lot.

"You really think he killed all those people?" asks Joey. "His own parents?"

"Yeah, I do." Sam's face is grim and her grip on the steering wheel is tight.

"But your mother was there," he says. "Why wouldn't she have told the police what really happened?"

Sam shakes her head, as if trying to pull a hundred threads together. "He must have threatened her. But she'll only be drugged up and out of commission for so long, and he probably realizes it's just a matter of time before she cracks. He's trying to finish whatever it is he started."

"But what is that?"

"I don't know, Joey!" she yells, slamming her hand on the steering wheel. She takes in a deep breath, calming herself, then looks across as if she's just seeing him for the first time. "You said you were trying to reach us? What's going on?"

Joey hesitates. "I'm not sure if now is the right—"

"Just tell me!"

"I went back to see Kershaw today,"

"What? Why?" Sam clearly wasn't expecting this.

"I wanted to confront him, to tell him I don't think he killed anyone except your father."

"But that's not what he told us," says Sam. "He said he'd killed *some* of them, and a copycat killed the rest."

"That's what he wanted us to believe. He knew if he tried to convince us he was wrongfully incarcerated—that he was never the Janitor—we wouldn't have given his story a second thought. Think about it. Brenda Regent told me he was a lovely, considerate boyfriend. The prison guards all talked about him like he was a kindly uncle. For twenty-five years he's a model prisoner, until we show up and all of a sudden he's a psychopath? He was playing us, and it worked. All three of us left that meeting wondering if there was some truth in what he was saying."

They speed through Edgar Mills. On the sidewalk a few pedestrians hurry along, keeping their heads down against the wind. Through Cordova's front window Joey catches a glimpse of some regulars nursing coffee at the counter, and as Sam turns at the town square, he notices that the hands on the old clock tower are stuck at 3:17, holding on to a moment from some long-forgotten afternoon. The town feels like it has been frozen in time, waiting for a curse to finally be broken.

"Believe me," he continues, "I wanted nothing more than to leave the penitentiary, drive back to Cambridge, and never think about this again. Maybe I would have if Doug hadn't shown me that note. But then I saw that your father had written it all down himself, in black and white: 'Bruce Kershaw didn't kill Mary Ellen Spakalitis.' That seemed to confirm Kershaw was telling the truth, but it only told part of the story."

Sam considers this. "What did Kershaw say when you put this on the table?"

"He admitted it. He told me he had nothing to do with the murders of Cartwright or Spakalitis, that it wasn't him in the woods with Lizzie Carroll, and he didn't kill Levon. When you and Alice emailed to tell him you believed he was behind all the murders, he panicked and drove to your house, and that's when he shot your father. He said he didn't mean to, but things got out of hand."

"What about all the evidence found in his apartment?" she asks.

"He insists none of it was his," says Joey. "He thinks he was framed, but he has no idea by whom."

Sam absorbs this new information, chewing on her lower lip as she drives.

"If this is all true," she says, "why didn't any of it come out in his defense at the trial?"

"He tried to get someone to listen to him," Joey explains, "but there was so much evidence that nobody, not the police, not his lawyers, not even his sister, believed him. But there was never any question that he'd killed your father, and he felt so guilty about it that he took the punishment. But do you know the maximum sentence for second-degree murder in Massachusetts?"

"Twenty-five years?" Sam guesses.

Joey nods. "So just when he's starting to think that he's paid his debt to society, someone else turns up dead and he sees an opportunity to bring us together and hopefully start asking questions. What we didn't realize was that the real question wasn't 'Who was copying Kershaw?' The real question was 'Who framed Kershaw?'"

"So who was it?" asks Sam. "Parson Stevens? According to Evan he was living here in Edgar Mills at the time."

Joey shakes his head. "I think your father had another theory. I believe he thought it was a cop."

Sam barks out a laugh. "A cop? That's ridiculous."

"Don't dismiss it so quickly, Sam," Joey says urgently. He explains the email he found in her father's inbox. "I think your dad had narrowed in on someone who had the window and opportunity to carry out those crimes."

Sam looks skeptical. "That's a real stretch."

Joey persists. "You told me yourself that your father wrote everything down. He had notes all over the place. But in this one situation, he chose to send an email to his personal account rather than write it down on paper. I think he was covering his tracks, keeping his theory under wraps until he had more evidence."

"I guess that kind of makes sense," she concedes.

"That's not everything. Kershaw told me that, a month or so before the first murder, his apartment was broken into. He called the police and they sent a uniformed officer over to take a statement. The cop he described sounded a lot like Nash Young."

"Wait a minute," says Sam. "You're suggesting the mysterious serial killer cop was *Nash*?"

"Think this through," says Joey. "Everything hinges on the note your father left, right? 'BIRCH CREST ELEMENTARY.' If you and Alice hadn't found that note, you never would have found the backpack full of evidence and you never would have written that email to Kershaw. But nobody ever figured out why your father was thinking about Birch Crest Elementary. What if it was Nash?"

"I don't follow," says Sam.

"Hear me out," says Joey. "Back then Nash was new to the force. Maybe he always wanted to be a cop, but he had an ulterior motive: taking advantage of his uniform to kill people."

She frowns. "That's a bit far-fetched, don't you think?"

Joey shrugs. "What part of this *isn't* far-fetched? Just imagine for the sake of argument that Nash has an itch to kill, and he decides to find a patsy to take the fall. Maybe he even looks at it like a little game. He meets Kershaw when he goes to investigate a break-in in his building and realizes he's the perfect target. A quiet, lonely, arguably creepy man who lives by himself. He begins to follow him, learning his route, his rhythms. He knows that Kershaw stops at the Hollywood Nites video rental every Friday on his way home from work. He knows that he's friendly with the elderly woman who lives in the building across from him. He looks into Kershaw's background and learns he used to work at Birch Crest, and he probably has a key. At some point, maybe even on his very first visit, he steals an old credit card of Kershaw's that he can use when he needs it."

"Then he begins killing," Sam says, as she catches on to the story.

"Yes," says Joey, nodding. "He starts with DJ, gives the community just enough time to get anxious, then he goes for Mary Ellen. He tries for a third, but he slips up and Lizzie Carroll gets away. That spooks him, because he realizes how easily he could have been caught."

Sam continues to follow the thread. "So he puts the credit card in a backpack, along with some other evidence from the crime scenes, and plants it at the school."

"Yes. Then he goes to your father and drops a hint. "He says something like 'Hey, do you know where we should do some digging? Birch Crest Elementary School. It's abandoned. Worth a shot.'"

"Now it's on Dad's mind," says Sam, "and he goes home and scribbles it down on his newspaper."

"He intends to follow up," says Joey, "but before he has the chance, you and Alice find the note about Birch Crest. You search the school and find the backpack."

"And then we email Kershaw," says Sam, her voice growing grim as the plausibility of the theory sinks in. "He has no idea what we're talking about, and he freaks out. He tells Brenda Regent about our email, and she calls the police department and talks to Dad. She tells him Kershaw couldn't have killed Mary Ellen because he was out of town with her that night."

"Your father writes that down," Joey continues, "and gets to thinking: Why did Nash point him toward the school? On a hunch, he digs up Nash's schedule and realizes he had the opportunity to carry out the three crimes."

"But Nash sees Dad's note," says Sam. "He panics when he realizes that not only is Dad aware of Kershaw, but Kershaw has an alibi. He realizes his plan won't work, so he heads to the school, intending to grab the backpack. But he runs into Levon. And we know how that ended."

Sam slams on the brakes at a four-way stop and Joey is thrown into another memory, of his long-ago drive to warn the twins that their plan was collapsing. He stopped at this same intersection and watched as a police car raced off to the Van Dyne house, lights flashing and siren screaming. Just as Joey did on that night, Sam turns left and heads in the opposite direction.

"If this is all true," she says, "why would Nash push for us to come home and talk to Kershaw in the first place? Why wouldn't he just go along with Corvallis and let the whole thing lie?"

"Curiosity," says Joey. "Nash wanted to know what Kershaw was going to say. Whether he'd figured anything out over the years. But our meeting only proved Kershaw didn't know anything except that he'd been framed."

"That's quite a theory," says Sam as she turns onto a quiet service road and pulls over beside a thicket of trees, "but I feel like we're missing something. I wish we could run all of this by Alice."

"We'll just have to get her," says Joey.

She looks at him seriously. "Joey, you don't have to get involved in this. I will understand if you walk away right now."

"No," he says firmly. "We're in this together."

She nods. "Okay." She gestures at the trees. "If you push through this thicket, you'll get to the school. Keep to the edge of the trees and wait until you're sure I'm inside before you make a move."

Joey feels his insides go watery. "I've never done anything like this," he says. "You guys were always the detectives."

To his surprise, Sam laughs. "Joey O'Day, will you please give that shit a rest? You've been a detective from day one. If you hadn't hacked into our email and called the cops, our mother might be dead as well as our father. You went to Justin Beagle's funeral looking for clues. You put together this insane and complicated theory about Nash Young. Forgive me if I call bullshit, because you are one hell of a sleuth."

Joey smiles. "I appreciate the pep talk," he says.

She regards him carefully. "On the other hand, who the hell knows if you're physically capable of taking down a crazed serial killer less than half your age. But you're all that I've got. Now move."

Joey climbs out of the car. He leans down to look in at her.

"Good luck," he says.

"If we're going to fix this, we're going to need more than luck," says Sam. "Let's go kick his ass."

Joey ducks into the trees, heart pounding—not with fear, but with purpose. He moves forward, and the school soon comes into view through the thinning branches. He crouches, scanning the area. He spots Levi's truck and Alice's Suburban. Then Sam's rental pulls up.

She steps out and approaches the maintenance door. It swings open, revealing Evan Stevens—gun in hand.

Joey sinks lower, holding his breath. Evan scans the lot to confirm Sam is alone, then lets her step inside. The door closes.

Joey exhales, his grip tightening on the bark of a nearby tree. Whatever happens next is up to him.

CHAPTER THIRTY-ONE: SAM

As Sam steps into the school, her eyes are fixed on the gun Evan has trained on her. It's a Colt 1911.

"You recognize this?" he asks, following her gaze. "Of course you do. Your mother showed it to me during one of her endless, dreary monologues about how the Janitor ruined her life. I knew all about your particular relationship with this gun long before you ever got around to telling me about it. And when people see how I'm about to use it . . ." He makes a chef's kiss gesture. "Talk about poetic justice."

"What do you mean, 'when people see?' " Sam asks.

"Don't worry," he says. "We'll get there." He gestures impatiently, indicating that she should walk ahead of him, and Sam takes the hint. She leads the way to the gymnasium, hyperaware of the Colt's barrel pointed at her back.

As she pushes through the large double doors into the gym, her heart sinks to her feet when she sees Alice, Levi, and Will tied up in the middle of the room. She forces a wry smile.

"It's so hard to get everyone together these days," she says.

"You shouldn't have come, Sam," says Alice.

"What, and miss all the fun?"

Once Sam is tied to a chair near her sister, Evan stands back and regards them.

"Okay," he says, "here's how it's going to go. I'm going to tell you my story, then I'm going to kill you." He turns to Will. "Everyone except for you, that is. Somebody needs to stick around and shepherd your fucked-up family legacy into the future."

"Please," says Alice. "Let us just talk through this."

"That's the plan," says Evan. "I'm going to talk, you're going to listen, and then I'm going to shoot the three of you in the head and leave the youngster here to struggle with that image for the rest of his life."

It's obvious he's not bluffing. Sam can only hope that Joey O'Day is able to figure out some kind of plan, because he's the only thing standing between them and this maniac.

"You really think you'll get away with this and then just stroll into the sunset?" asks Levi. "The police will be onto you soon if they aren't already."

"I doubt it," says Evan. "I made sure they're all tied up with a bomb threat. In the meantime, I have a fake passport and a car I bought with cash a few months ago parked at the head of the trail. By the time the authorities figure out what's happening, I'll be in Boston hiding out and waiting for the heat to drop off a bit so I can catch a flight and disappear."

"You'll never get away with it," says Alice. "Your picture will be everywhere; you'll be reported and hauled in by the end of the day."

Evan grins at her. "It'll be a fun challenge, but I'm confident. You've got to admit, I'm a pretty good actor. A wig and a change of clothes and I'll be able to slip right into the crowd."

Sam can't deny that he's got some skills—the sinister young man standing in front of her is nothing like the anxious, earnest kid that she met just a few days ago in her mother's backyard—but she isn't about to give him credit.

"Keep telling yourself that," she says with an exaggerated eye roll. "I feel like I'm at a shitty summer camp for theater kids. You haven't got a chance."

But Evan is done humoring them. "Enough of this. We're wasting time."

He pulls out his phone and opens the camera, pointing it at himself and then moving back and forth until he's satisfied with the framing.

"Oh, come on," says Will. "You're filming this? You really are a loser, do you know that?"

"Don't antagonize him, Will," Levi warns.

"Of course I'm going to film it," says Evan. "You realize I've been filming everything, right? I have so much amazing footage. Hours and hours of material from the security cameras I hid in your mom's house. Some juicy bits and pieces of you two, running around playing Nancy Drew. And of course, Justin and Vicki's murders. Once I'm out of here, I will have an absolute crapload of content. When I have a minute to catch my breath, I'll start editing and uploading it to TikTok through some secure encrypted servers and wait for the world to go nuts."

"It'll get taken down immediately," says Sam.

"Of course it will," says Evan. "But someone will capture it first, and then it will live on forever, passed along through the dark web from one sick freak to the next. I like it that way. It feels kind of . . . nostalgic. You know what I mean? I'll become an urban legend with a platform."

As he speaks, Sam twists subtly in her seat to get a better look at the surroundings. Their chairs are set up in a half-moon created by the theatrical sets from that long-ago production of *Once Upon a Mattress,* mildewed facades depicting a fairytale castle. The garish spotlight, clearly set up by Evan for the benefit of his production, casts them in an unforgiving light, but it means the rest of the gym is a contrast of shadows and dark corners. Sam hopes the gloom provides Joey with an opportunity to sneak in without being spotted.

"Okay," says Evan. "Let's get this show on the road."

Holding the camera at arm's length, he begins to walk back and forth in front of them, launching into a monologue that Sam suspects he's practiced in front of the mirror more than once.

"I started reading about serial killers when I was about fourteen," he tells the camera, "and it wasn't long before I decided I wanted to become one. Bundy. Gacy. Dahmer. You name the psychopath, I read about him as obsessively as a kid watching video clips of his favorite athlete, trying to pick up skills. But the story I loved most of all was the one about the Janitor facing off against the teen detectives of Edgar Mills, Massachusetts. I wasn't even alive back then, but I felt a deep connection to that story. I wanted to become *part* of it, thanks to the Van Dyne family."

"Why us?" asks Alice.

"Usually people only remember the killer," he explains, "and the victims and their survivors are quickly forgotten. But that couldn't be father from the truth in this case, because Kershaw's story is undeniably intertwined with yours. Best of all"—here he pauses, fixing them with a devilish grin—"it's unfinished. What better way to cement my legend than to hitch my wagon to your star and become part of your story?"

"It's not a story," says Levi, his voice thick with emotion. "It's real life. People died."

Evan ignores this. "I knew if I was going to pull this off, I'd have to move to Edgar Mills."

"Obviously," says Will, drily. "How else could you possibly cement your legend?"

"Exactly," says Evan, not noticing the sarcasm. "But that was much easier said than done. There was no point in even suggesting it to my father. Let's just say he and I had a complicated relationship. But my mother was a different story. She would have gone anywhere if she thought it would help quell my demons."

"So she knew you were nuts," says Sam. It isn't a question.

"Unique," he corrects. "I started feeding her a line of bullshit about how inspired I was by the two of you." He adopts a childish voice. "'*They were only teenagers like me! They learned how to become detectives and solve crimes!*' I even started making videos about the case, to show her how dedicated I was to the story, and she was deluded enough to fall for it. Then I orchestrated a little scandal at my father's work, and when he was fired from his job, I was ready in the wings with the suggestion that we move to Edgar Mills and make a fresh start. As luck would have it, a house near your mother's had been sitting on the market for several months. It didn't take much persuading to convince her to buy it with some money she'd inherited from her parents."

"Did your father know you were behind his firing?" asks Levi.

"He figured it out," says Evan. "But what was he going to do, call the cops and turn me in? My mother would have never let that happen. She gave him an ultimatum: either we move to Edgar Mills as a family, or she and I would go without him. Obviously he tagged along. What else was he going to do? She had all the money. He was unemployed, outrunning a scandal, and trying his best to rein in a delinquent son who scared him. He was right to be scared, of course, because I intended to set him up."

Over Evan's shoulder, Sam catches a slight glimpse of movement, just a momentary flicker in the shadows along the back wall. Could it be Joey? Fortunately, Evan is wrapped up in his story and doesn't notice.

"I started dropping breadcrumbs even before we moved," he continues. "I made sure there were months of searches about the Janitor's crimes and the famous Van Dyne twins on his web browser. Once we moved in and I got to know your mother, I planted some spy cams in her house and begin storing hours of surveillance videos in a hidden folder on his hard drive. Then I started trying to get close to you and your family, Alice."

"That's why you became friends with Joelle," says Will, realization dawning on his face. "You were actually trying to get close to *me*, weren't you?"

Evan points a finger at the teenager. "Bingo. Only you didn't seem to like me all that much."

"Because you're a total creep," says Will.

"I'll choose to ignore that," says Evan. "Joelle was an easier mark. She was desperate for someone to confide in about her secret older boyfriend, and I was right there, nonthreatening and willing to listen. The problem was, she told Justin about me and he insisted on meeting me. I thought maybe he was jealous or something, but it turned out he was actually a really nice guy, and he just wanted to talk about the murders."

This surprises Sam. "The murders? Why?"

"It was my videos," says Evan. "They'd started to blow up by this point. I guess Joelle had shown him a few and he'd started to become obsessed. Not 'crazy obsessed,' more like 'true crime geek' obsessed. He told me a bunch of lame stories he heard from his uncle, and I got the impression he wanted to help me do research, maybe even appear onscreen with me. It was all a bit pathetic, to be honest, but mostly I was worried, because he also asked me a ton of questions."

"What kind of questions?" asks Sam. She has to admit, she's captivated by Evan's story, but she's also trying to buy time for Joey, who is so far nowhere to be seen.

"Oh, you name it," says Evan. "Why did we move to Edgar Mills? Why was I so interested in the killings? Did my parents know what I was up to? He was really nosy, and I didn't like it, so I told Joelle I didn't want to hang out with them again. But the alarm bells were already ringing, so I decided to kill him."

He says it so casually that an icy chill runs down Sam's back. If she had any doubt that he was willing to shoot them all here and now, it's gone.

"You killed that poor kid on a whim," says Alice, disgusted.

"It wasn't a whim," he says. "It was an adjustment. I still hadn't figured out how to deal with you guys. It occurred to me that if I arranged his murder to look like a copycat, it would freak your mom out and make things more exciting. What I didn't bank on was that the *actual* Janitor would get involved and even bring you out of hiding, Sam."

He points the camera at her and steps closer, bringing it close to her face to get her reaction.

"Thanks to those cameras I'd put in your mother's house, I had a front row seat to the big reunion when you arrived home. It was better than I could have imagined. Flying dishes! Tearful accusations! But imagine my surprise when I learned *why* you were back in town. The Janitor himself had summoned you. What a stroke of luck. I knew I had to take advantage of the opportunity, so the moment you stepped outside I introduced myself."

"As Evan Stevens, the Real True Crime Kid," says Sam.

"It was perfect," says Evan. "What would make a better second act than the two of you starting your own investigation? There was just one problem: you thought Kershaw was lying, and you were preparing to fly back to L.A. I needed to make a move. I needed another victim."

"Which is where Vicki came in," says Alice.

Evan nods. "Joelle was in a state of panic after Justin died, understandably. But when she told me her mother was beginning to suspect that she and Justin had been dating, I knew I had to act. If Vicki learned that Justin and Joelle had been an item, she would have gone straight to the cops and I would have ended up under the microscope. I convinced Joelle to keep her mouth shut, but I knew it was only a matter of time before she spilled the beans. So when she mentioned she was going to be out of town for the night with her father, I slipped into their house and killed Vicki. From then on, it was easy to keep Joelle in line."

"How did you do that?" asks Levi.

"I told her it was her fault," he says with a shrug. "If she hadn't been dating Justin, then Vicki would never have been on the killer's radar. I had her convinced she'd be blamed for the whole thing if the cops ever found out she'd withheld information about Justin. Joelle is a very malleable person. She's weak. I let her believe I was helping guide her through this experience, and she did as she was told, so I was able to turn my attention back to the two of you."

"You are a real piece of shit," Will says, his voice dripping with contempt. "She thought you were her friend."

"Once there was another body in the mix, things started to fall into place," he says. "Neither of you could resist the chance to tackle one last case, and you eagerly picked up every clue I dropped, like free candy. Kershaw's apartment. The secret path behind the river trail. I did everything I could to convince you that whoever was behind Justin's and Vicki's deaths was somehow connected to what happened all those years ago. It was perfect, and Kershaw had laid it up for me perfectly. I just had to give the puck a little nudge into the net."

"You faked your own attack," says Sam.

"Yeah," he says. "I had plenty of practice giving myself bruises, and the film was a fun little technical challenge. But it was a miscalculation. I didn't expect you to call your old buddy the police chief, and when he took me in to make a statement and called my parents, all bets were off. Parson was already suspicious of me by that point, but I think that finally convinced him that I'd killed Justin and Vicki. If my father had only told the police about his suspicions, that would have been the end of everything and he'd probably still be alive right now. Instead, he dragged me out by the collar and sealed his own fate."

Behind Evan, Sam sees a figure emerging from the shadows and her heart leaps. It's Joey, slowly moving from the other side of the gym. She knows Alice and Levi and Will must see him too, and she can only pray that they don't give him away with their expressions. He has to cover at least thirty yards, and if he happens to appear in the screen of Evan's camera, all bets are off.

Fortunately, Evan is so enthralled by his own story that he's oblivious to anything outside the tiny frame of his phone.

"Like I said, the original plan was to kill your family and frame my father for the murders," he continues. "I knew I had to act fast, but as I was about to make my move I glanced out of my bedroom window and saw someone walking up to your house."

"Perry," says Alice.

Evan nods. "I had no time to waste, but my curiosity got the better of me, so I logged into the camera feed and listened in to his conversation with your mother. And what a conversation. In a million years I wouldn't have expected to get that kind of incredible scoop. It meant I had to totally overhaul my plan, but when you get a plot twist this juicy, you run with it, am I right?"

"What are you talking about?" asks Alice. "What scoop?"

Evan smiles like the cat who swallowed the canary. "You still haven't figured it out, have you? Of course you haven't. We can only let our imaginations take us so far, right? Otherwise we'd all go crazy."

Sam is staring into the middle distance behind Evan, hypnotized by Joey's approach, the cogs inside her mind spinning in a million directions at once before coming quickly, precisely to a stop. And just like that an insight is unlocked:

Joey was wrong. Nash wasn't the Janitor.

Their mother was.

She tries to shove the revelation back where it came from, but the barn door is already open, and the pieces of the puzzle come flying out to slot perfectly into place. Joanna's obsession with having famous daughters. The note in her father's newspaper that would have been so easy for her to forge and plant. The email Joey discovered in their father's outbox tracking the whereabouts of a cop on the force.

And of course there's the simple fact that's been staring her in the face: her mother lied to the police about what happened in the van, and to Perry. Not because she was afraid of Evan, but because she was his alibi.

And what had her mother said to her in the hospital just a few hours ago?

I never expected it all to end so terribly.

It's as obvious as it is unimaginable, but she doesn't have time to deal with it right now, because there are more pressing things on the agenda.

"I have a question," she tells Evan.

"Fire away."

"You claim that you were obsessed with the Janitor case," she says. "So I understand why you were fixated on our family, but you never mention Joey O'Day. He was a big part of the story, but you barely skim over him in your videos. Why is that?"

Evan laughs, surprised. "Joey O'Day? Are you kidding me? He was a footnote at best, a glorified hacker who rode your coattails. You two were the real detectives. That's the story worth telling."

"No, she's right," says Alice. "It's kind of a glaring oversight. Joey is a big part of the story. Kershaw even invited him to the meeting at the prison, and he's been helping us out ever since. I'm surprised you didn't know that."

"I didn't," says Evan. "But even if I did I wouldn't care. Why should I?"

Sam smiles. "Because he's right behind you, you suspicious bitch."

Evan reacts quickly, spinning on his heel as he reaches for the gun in his waistband. But Joey is quicker, and moving swiftly and elegantly he pounces from the shadows and tackles Evan to the ground.

CHAPTER THIRTY-TWO: ALICE

Alice's mind rings as she watches the two men wrestle on the ground. Where did Joey come from? What did Evan mean by "scoop"?

Far away on the edge of her consciousness, she becomes aware of someone calling her name. She forces herself back into to the moment and sees Joey and Evan advancing across the floor in her direction in a tangled, writhing mass of arms and fists.

"Alice!" Levi is yelling. "Look next to your chair!"

She glances down and sees that the gun has come to a stop on the floor just a few feet away from her. Evan is small, but he's wiry and strong, not to mention a quarter of a century younger than Joey. It's only a matter of time before he gets the better of the older man.

Without thinking, Alice tips herself over and lands on her side. Grunting with exertion, she begins struggling against her bindings, trying to gain enough momentum to shift position and get closer to the gun. Her progress is slow, and she's aware of the two men getting closer, but finally she is lying face-to-face with the barrel of the gun.

Time seems to slow as she becomes aware in her peripheral vision of Evan finally breaking free from Joey's grasp and leaping into a run. With every ounce of strength and mobility she can muster, Alice pulls her head back and then rams it forward into the Colt.

It connects without much force, but it's enough. The gun spins lazily across the polished wooden floor and just as Evan makes a final, awkward lunge toward it, it slips through a crack beneath one of the set pieces and disappears into the shadows.

He briefly considers his options before jumping up and grabbing his phone from where it landed on the floor during the struggle.

He begins to back slowly toward the exit, keeping his gaze fixed on Joey, who's still on the floor, trying to catch his breath.

"You know this is still a great story," he says. "I'll just have to finish it later."

"You killed your own parents," says Alice. She feels a genuine rage swelling up from her core. All that pain and misery, and for what? A social media following? A chance to feel powerful? "You killed your own mother."

"That's true," says Evan. "But you know, all she ever wanted was for me to get out of my room and do something with my life. I bet she would have been really proud of me."

With that, he turns and disappears through the door without a backward glance.

Panting and out of breath, Joey finally pulls himself up off the floor. He moves as if he's going to follow Evan, but Sam speaks up.

"You'll never catch him, Joey," she says. "He's young and fast and dangerous. He's gone."

Later, after Joey has untied them and Levi has called 911, they stand outside, silently waiting for the police to arrive, and Alice tries to come to terms with the theory Sam has just laid out for them.

Joanna Van Dyne: the Janitor.

Alice's heart does its best to push back against the allegation, but her mind returns over and over again to one thought: as much as she wants Sam to be wrong, something about it feels true.

A whoop of sirens alerts them to Nash's arrival. He tears into the parking lot before jumping out of his car and running to them.

"Is everyone okay?" he asks, but he's looking at her. She holds his eyes for enough time to let something pass between them, a shared understanding, and then she reaches for Levi's hand and pulls Will into her with her other arm. "Yeah," she says, "we're okay."

"Highway patrol is looking for him," he tells them. "But if we don't know what kind of vehicle he's driving, it will be difficult to pick him up. We've instructed them to watch for erratic drivers and we've distributed his photo for visual ID."

"He's probably in a disguise," says Sam. "He said he was headed for Boston, but who knows?"

"We'll find him," says Nash.

"There's something else," says Sam. "It's a very long story, but you're going to want to talk to our mother."

Nash nods. "That's in the works. We need to know what really happened in that van, and why she covered for Evan."

"There's more to it than that." Sam hesitates, clearly struggling to put the awful truth into words. "We think she is responsible for the murders of Mary Ellen Spakalitis, DJ Cartwright, and . . ." Sam hesitates and then glances at Levi, who squeezes Alice's hand before nodding at Sam to go on. "And Levon Brakes."

Nash stares at them all, wide-eyed and speechless, before collecting himself. "Right," he says. "In that case, let me make a call."

He steps away, and Alice turns to look at her son in the face. "Are you going to be okay?" she asks.

He nods, but his face is stricken. "Did Grandma really . . ." He stops and swallows, unable to finish the question.

"We're going to find out," says Alice.

There will be much to work through in the coming days and weeks, but right now she needs to focus her energy on her family. Whatever questions she might have had about the direction of her life have disappeared along with Evan Stevens. Her priorities are standing right in front of her.

"We'll get through this together," says Levi, echoing her thoughts, and Alice is so relieved at how strong and capable he sounds that she almost forgets to breathe. He pulls the three of them into an embrace. "We're safe, and that's the only thing that matters."

Alice knows deep in her gut that this is the beginning of a new era for them, that they're prepared to pull themselves back together and face the future as a team. Maybe the story she's been telling herself for twenty-five years is finally coming to an end, and with that comes a chance for a fresh start.

Levi loosens an arm and gestures to Sam, who is standing off to the side.

"You want to join?" he asks.

She smiles and shakes her head. "Group hugs aren't really my thing," she says. "But I'm very happy to watch. Just imagine I'm embracing you all in spirit."

And despite everything they've been through and learned, and the intensity of what's about to unfold in front of them, Alice bursts out laughing for the first time in what seems likes weeks.

CHAPTER THIRTY-THREE:
JOEY
TWO WEEKS LATER

Joey steps out onto the sidewalk just as snow is beginning to fall. He expected to be more emotionally conflicted, but really he just feels as if a huge weight has been lifted from his shoulders. A few minutes ago, after almost two decades, he wrapped up his final day at Shoreline.

He doesn't want to sit in an office and write code anymore. Not even in Paris.

So this morning, just a couple of weeks after he tackled Evan Stevens to the floor in the abandoned gymnasium at Birch Crest Elementary School, he returned to Shoreline headquarters, walked into Mike's office, and quit. He isn't sure what he'll do next, but he and Austin will figure it out. He still has stock in the company, and Austin, who as always is fully supportive, has already made some calls and signed up more clients. That does mean Joey will have to really step up once the baby arrives, but that's okay. He's actually looking forward to it, and considering the other changes on the horizon, he'll have lots of help. Maybe more than he wants.

The honk of a car horn grabs his attention and Austin pulls up to the curb. Joey brushes the snow off his hair and jacket and climbs into the car.

"Sorry!" says Austin. "Traffic was nuts. Look at this snow! So pretty!"

"You're okay to drive?" asks Joey.

Austin waves it away. "It's just some flurries. Do you forget that I grew up in Illinois?"

It's hard to believe, but even with fresh unemployment and a kid on the way, there are other, more pressing things to deal with. Edgar Mills is their destination, but first they have another couple of stops to make.

The old folks' home is lit up with miles of colorful Christmas lights, and at first he thinks the figure standing by the front door is a decoration, a statue of a gaudy elf. Then she raises her hand to wave at them and he realizes it's Brenda Regent.

"There she is," he says.

"Wow," says Austin. "That's one festive outfit."

"She's that kind of gal," says Joey as he climbs out of the car to help her into the back seat.

"Road trip!" she exclaims cheerfully, after Joey has made introductions.

"You're ready for this?" he asks her.

Brenda laughs. "Are you kidding me? I can't wait. Life is short, and I can only imagine how short it feels for . . . well, it will be great. Now, tell me about this baby. Do you have schools picked out yet? I would expect there are long wait lists in Cambridge. Lots of anxious, uptight yuppies, present company excluded."

"Actually," says Austin, glancing over at Joey and smiling, "we're thinking the schools in Edgar Mills might be a better fit."

"No kidding?" She reaches forward and slaps Joey on the shoulder. "You're moving home?"

"It feels like the right time," he says. "We want to spend more time with my family, especially once the baby arrives."

"I love it," she says. "The return of the hometown hero."

Joey rolls his eyes. "Hardly."

Austin twists around to look at her. "He hates the attention. I'd be eating it up."

"You and me both, honey," she says. "So, do the police have any leads on the whereabouts of you know who?"

"Not yet," says Joey. "He seems to have slipped off the face of the earth, but we know he's out there somewhere, thanks to the videos."

True to his word, Evan has wasted no time in rolling out a series of videos, leading eager followers on an ever-shifting scavenger hunt to find his latest burner accounts and grab the footage before it's scrubbed. So far, the clips have been brief and tame, but the content—eerie shots of the empty kitchen at the Van Dyne house, the abandoned theatrical sets in the Birch Crest gymnasium, and the forest clearing where Justin Beagle's body was discovered—leaves little doubt that he'll soon begin dropping more explicit footage. Joey shudders to imagine what he has in store.

"It's all so gruesome," says Brenda, "but what I really can't get over is Joanna. I didn't know her all that well, but she always seemed to be so put together, so in control. I wouldn't have guessed in a million years that she was capable of such horrible things. She had everything to lose if she was caught: a wonderful husband, two beautiful children." She shakes her head. "It boggles the mind."

"Well, she's finally behind bars, thanks to Joey," says Austin proudly.

Joey rolls his eyes. "It was hardly thanks to me."

"You found that email," says Austin. "The one that pointed Sam in the right direction."

"Email?" Brenda leans between the front seats, eager for details.

Joey explains how he uncovered Bill Van Dyne's personal email account. "On the day he died, he sent himself an email tracking police whereabouts," he says. "At first I thought he must have suspected another cop, but he was actually establishing where *he'd* been during the murders."

"Because if he was out on a call, she would have had the opportunity," says Brenda.

"Exactly. Sam put that together with some other clues and realized there was a good chance her father was beginning to suspect Joanna when he was killed."

"I'm not saying you aren't geniuses," says Brenda, "but that's some pretty flimsy evidence considering how much time has passed."

"Yes," Joey agrees, "and she might have gotten away with everything, but when it was explained to her that Evan had footage of her final conversation with Perry Lemire stashed away somewhere, and it was only a matter of time before he released it into the wild, she made a full confession."

"Well, we can all be grateful for that," says Brenda.

* * *

The Bay State Penitentiary is not as festively decorated as the retirement home, although there is a sad little Christmas tree in the window of the guard station where they stop to check in.

Bruce is sitting in the reception area at the front of the building, patiently waiting with a small duffel bag at his side, as if he's preparing to board a train. He stands, smiling curiously, as they approach and then his eyes go wide with recognition.

"Brenda?"

"I asked Joey not to tell you I was coming," she says. "Was that a mistake? It was probably a mistake."

"No," he says. "No, it wasn't a mistake. This is a wonderful surprise."

"I thought you could use an old friend." She steps forward and they embrace, and Joey averts his gaze as they spend a few tearful moments in each other's arms.

"I should have come to see you," she says, once they've pulled apart and regained their composure.

Bruce shakes his head, emphatic. "No. You did the right thing to stay away. The world thought I was a cold-blooded killer, and you had no way of knowing any differently. You're here now, that's what counts."

He bends to pick up his bag.

"Well, I guess this is it. Next stop, Edgar Mills."

"Do you think you'll stay there?" asks Joey. "You could move somewhere else, start fresh."

Bruce shakes his head. "Where else would I go? I've been in touch with my sister, and she's going to let me move back into my old apartment. All the friends I have left in the world are here right now. If I'm going to start fresh, I'd like to do it in a place that feels like home."

As they step out into the wintry evening, he stops and turns his face up to the sky. He closes his eyes and breathes deeply for a few moments.

"Okay," he says finally. "Let's get out of here."

CHAPTER THIRTY-FOUR: SAM

Sam barely recognizes the woman who is escorted into the room across from her. Shackled and dressed in a bright orange jumpsuit, her hair cropped short and her makeup gone, Joanna looks like a version of herself from an alternate universe.

But as she takes a seat on the other side of the glass from her daughter, it's her eyes and expression that really speak to a change. Gone is the anxious, furtive, self-medicated person whom Sam has come to know over the years since her father died. This woman stares through the glass at her, waiting for her to make the first move.

"Hi, Mom," says Sam.

Joanna takes a moment to answer, methodically working at the gum she's chewing and crossing her arms in front of her as she warily regards her daughter.

"I'm surprised to see you here," she says. "I figured Alice would show up eventually, but I thought you'd be back on the West Coast by now."

"I don't think you should count on seeing Alice anytime soon," says Sam.

Joanna shrugs almost imperceptibly. "I'm sure she'll come around."

"I'm not sure she will, Mom. You got dad *killed*."

Joanna's eyes flash. "Nobody can make me feel worse about that than myself," she says. "I have spent every day for twenty-five years blaming myself for what happened to your father. If it wasn't for me, that monster never would have come to our house."

Sam stares in disbelief.

"You think of *Kershaw* as a monster?" she asks.

Joanna's eyes flash. "He killed your father. Of course he's a monster."

"And what about you?" asks Sam. "You killed three innocent people. You killed Alice's *boyfriend*."

Joanna rolls her eyes. "Come on, she had no intention of staying with Levon Brakes, so spare me the doomed-lovers bullshit. Besides, it all happened so quickly that it was practically an accident."

"An accident," Sam repeats. "You stabbed him in the side of the neck, Mom."

"What do you want me to say, Samantha?" asks Joanna, her eyes flashing. "Did I screw up? Yes, of course I did, but I got through it, and if that Stevens boy hadn't moved to town, we would have continued with our lives and nobody would have been any the wiser."

Sam stares through the glass at her mother with something approaching curiosity. Does she genuinely think of this as something *she* had to get through? Is this narcissistic fantasist really the woman who raised her? She realizes with sudden clarity that she never really knew her mother at all—not if this is the person she was all along.

Joanna leans forward, as close to the glass as she can manage, and her eyes glint as she stares into Sam's. "I did it for you girls, and you know it."

"Jesus Christ, Mom," says Sam. "You are completely disconnected from reality, aren't you?"

"Honestly, Samantha," says her mother with a sigh. "Did you just come here to lay another guilt trip on me?"

"No," says Sam, "I came because I have questions."

She knows most of it by now, thanks to Joanna's confession, but there are still a few outstanding details that she wants to hear straight from the horse's mouth.

"Fine," says Joanna. "Ask your questions. Get it out of your system."

"How could you do it?" asks Sam. "How could you kill all those people and *live* with it?"

"What you need to remember, Sam, is that I wasn't a serial killer." Joanna says this with brazen conviction. "I was *pretending* to be a serial killer."

"But why?" asks Sam, skating past the insane, irrational logic of the statement.

"When you girls were growing up, I devoted every ounce of energy to you. I put you in dance, in music, in gymnastics, in figure skating. I tried everything. I know you remember."

"Of course I remember," says Sam. "You were desperate for us to be famous."

Joanna scoffs at this. "I was your mother. It was natural for me to want you to be successful. You were attractive and naturally talented in so many ways, and if there was a way to give the two of you a head start, why shouldn't I? But nothing stuck. Until . . ."

"We helped Dad with that first case," says Sam.

Joanna nods. "It didn't take much imagination to see the potential. The press couldn't write stories quickly enough. You solved that mystery and then another, and things began to snowball. Suddenly you were more than just Sam and Alice Van Dyne; you were the 'Van Dyne Twins, Teen Detectives.' Your father and I didn't really know what to think at first, but it was impossible not to be pleased. It was exciting. But where he saw it as an interesting hobby, something that he could do with his girls, I saw it for what it was: an opportunity."

Sam already knows where this is going. She hoped that hearing her mother explain what happened in her own words would give it some plausibility, but as Joanna speaks, she paints a picture so surreal and twisted that it seems impossible that it could be real.

"I think I was the only one who realized it was going to taper off," her mother continues. "You were solving all these dinky little cases. Pot dealers. Stolen bikes. Puppy mills. You were hired by that old woman to prove that she wasn't being haunted."

"Iris Langley," says Sam. "Her dead sister's children were gaslighting her with hidden recordings, trying to get her to give up the house."

"You don't need to remind me," her mother says impatiently. "I remember every detail about every single investigation. The point is, you weren't evolving. The media was getting bored, and I knew the whole thing risked fizzling out. You were talking about colleges, and Alice was thinking about getting into modeling, or acting. Your father didn't care what you did, as long as you were happy."

"How awful," says Sam.

"He didn't get it," Joanna snaps. "I was the only one who understood how much bigger things could get if only you landed on the right case—the kind of case that would be written up on the front page of *The New York Times*."

"So you decided to create a serial killer," says Sam.

"I decided to create an event," Joanna counters. "A big, messy crime that would rocket the two of you to genuine fame."

"A crime that required a villain for us to capture," says Sam. "How did you settle on Kershaw?"

"To tell you the truth, I don't even remember. I assume someone mentioned him to me at some point. Maybe at school drop-off or some other situation like that. I knew he was quiet, antisocial, and lived alone. He was perfect. I broke into his apartment and stole a spare key and an old credit card, then I spent a few weeks following him to get a feel for his schedule. He stopped at the same video store every Friday and always stuck around to talk to the young guy who worked there."

"DJ Cartwright," says Sam. If her mother doesn't want to name her victims out loud, then she will. "You decided he'd be your first victim."

"It was easier than I expected. I came in, locked the door and flipped around the open sign, did my business, and slipped out the back. He didn't see it coming."

It's almost more than Sam can handle to listen to her mother talk about it so flippantly, but she needs to hear the rest.

"I waited a week, then I took care of the woman."

"Her name was Mary Ellen Spakalitis," says Sam.

"She was even easier than the first one," says Joanna. "I just knocked on her door and she let me in. Then I tried for one more, the teenager on the river trail. When she slipped away, it spooked me. I realized how easily I could have been caught, and I figured I'd risked enough, and so I set the rest of the plan in motion."

"You wrote the note on Dad's newspaper, didn't you?" asks Sam.

Joanna nods. "It was easy enough. I wrote 'Birch Crest Elementary' in the margin and made sure the two of you found it. I was sure you and your sister would run with that clue and I was right. I'd already planted a bag and some evidence at the school, and just as I'd planned, the two of you went straight there and found it."

"And that's when everything went to hell," says Sam.

"You girls were never supposed to confront him," says Joanna, her voice rising with frustration. "You were supposed to tell your father what you'd discovered and let him take care of it. That would have been more than enough to make you famous. Your father would have taken Kershaw into custody and been the hero of the hour, and he would have had you two by his side for the all the press and accolades. You would have been superstars. God, when I think of the mess you made."

She closes her eyes and sighs deeply, the eternal victim, and Sam has to force herself not to stand and leave. She needs to hear the rest of her mother's story. Finally, Joanna continues.

"I had always intended to go back for the bag so I could plant it in Kershaw's apartment, but I didn't count on Levon catching me red-handed. I had no choice. Before he even realized what was happening, I'd stabbed him."

"Then what?" asks Sam.

"Somehow I managed not to panic. I made sure to get some blood on the backpack, then I took everything to Kershaw's building and waited outside until I saw him leave. I snuck inside and hid it along with the other evidence I'd been hanging onto, then I high-tailed it home and slipped through the back door into the kitchen just as Kershaw arrived. By the time the police pushed their way into the house, I was on the floor, cradling your father. Nobody ever questioned the blood on my clothes. For twenty-five years, nobody questioned anything until that boy showed up and ruined everything."

Sam remembers how upset Joanna was in the aftermath of their visit to see Kershaw. It wasn't fear of being killed. It was fear of being caught.

"What did Perry tell you?" she asks.

Joanna sighs. "Poor Perry. After Alice told him about your father's note, he put a few things together. Your father had phoned him on the day he died and asked some cryptic questions about whether he would be compelled to represent our family if any of us ever got in trouble with the law. Perry hadn't given it much thought at the time, assuming Bill was speaking theoretically, and then of course with everything that happened next it completely slipped his mind. But when Alice showed him the note, it jogged his memory and he wondered if maybe there was more to the story. So he came to see me. I'd always had a feeling that your father had suspected me, but when Perry told me about the note and his final phone call with your dad, I was convinced. He wanted to know whether Perry would be compelled to defend me in court if I was arrested."

Sam leans forward. This is the point that has eluded her, and she's keen to hear what her mother says next.

"Why do you think he suspected you?"

"It was that stupid newspaper," says Joanna. "I forgot to toss out the old papers and he came across the note I'd forged. He showed it to me and asked if I knew anything about Birch Crest Elementary, because he knew he hadn't written that down. I acted surprised, told him he was so overwhelmed by the case that he must have forgotten about writing it down."

Sam nods slowly as the last pieces of the puzzle click into place. "When Brenda Regent phoned Dad, she told him that we had mentioned Birch Crest in our email to Kershaw, and he must have connected that back to the newspaper."

She imagines her father sitting in his office, forced to consider a terrible possibility. Could his own wife be responsible for such horrible crimes? Cross-checking his own schedule against the crimes on record had only confirmed that she'd had the opportunity. All three of the crimes had happened when her husband was tied up at work and wouldn't have known where she was. Not wanting to write the details down and risk a colleague coming across them, he must have emailed them to his personal account at home, where he would have had the chance to think things over in the privacy of his own home and figure out what to do next.

But he never got the chance.

"Why did you confess to Perry," Sam asks.

"After twenty-five years struggling with the secret, I needed to tell someone," says Joanna. "Perry was a good man, very loyal to your father, and he took it all in stride, believe it or not. He was my lawyer, after all. After I came clean I poured us some drinks and we were sitting there, discussing how to proceed, when Evan appeared at the back door. I didn't understand what was happening at first, but he quickly explained that he'd heard everything and in the next moment he pulled a knife from his pocket and slit Perry's throat. I was sure that he was going to kill me too, but instead he sat down and made a proposition."

"You helped him kill his parents," says Sam.

Joanna shakes her head. "No," she says emphatically. "He took care of the dirty work himself. I was his alibi. I have to say, he's a very clever boy. He killed his mother first, then used your father's gun to persuade Parson to get in the van and drive us to the middle of nowhere."

"You just went along for the ride," says Sam.

"I had no choice," says Joanna. "When we arrived at the junkyard, he had me guard Parson with a knife while he went into the office and killed the night watchman. Then we drove further into the yard and set the stage for you to find us. It should have been over then. It would have been, if Evan had stuck to the plan we'd discussed."

"You didn't realize he was going to come for us once the dust had settled?"

"I really didn't," says Joanna earnestly. "I thought that would be the end of it. Parson would take the blame for everything, and we'd all move on with our lives. You have to believe me, Samantha, I would never have gone through with any of this if I'd known what he had planned."

Sam pushes back her chair and stands. "I don't have to believe a word out of your mouth."

Joanna looks surprised. "Where are you going? I'm not finished."

"I am," says Sam. "I've heard everything I need to. I hope you're able to take care of yourself in here, Mom."

"I suppose you'll be heading back to Los Angeles now that you can put all of this behind you."

Sam almost laughs at this, the idea that she'll ever be able to put any of this behind her. She debates lying, telling her mother that she's on the way to the airport right now. But something compels her to tell the truth.

"As a matter of fact, I've decided to move back to Edgar Mills. At least for a while."

Joanna raises an eyebrow but doesn't say anything.

"Just to be very clear," says Sam, "I'm not moving to be close to you. I'm moving to be closer to Alice and her family."

"That seems like an awfully big move to make just to play amateur marriage counsellor for your sister."

Sam bites back the instinctive reaction. She's being baited.

"You know what, Mom? I stopped my life twenty-five years ago and started a new one. But I've started to remember just how much I liked my old life. I never really wanted to leave it, as much as I tried to convince myself otherwise. So I'm going to give starting over a shot."

Joanna sniffs. "Your generation is all about closure."

Sam shakes her head. "It's not about closure. It's about opening something back up."

She turns away, but stops when her mother calls after her.

"I need you to do one last favor for me. Please, Sam. Visit your father's grave and tell him I'm sorry I can't come myself."

Sam is jolted by a sudden memory. A question that occurred to her when she last visited her father's gravesite, a question she was on her way to ask when she discovered Perry dead and Joanna missing. In the chaos that followed, and everything that's come to light since, it completely slipped her mind, but now it's returned and she needs to know the truth. She turns back.

"When Alice and I visited you the day we went to see Kershaw in prison, we asked you to tell us about the night Dad died."

Joanna raises an eyebrow. "Yes. Why?"

"You said Dad yelled out to you from the front door, where he was arguing with Kershaw. You said it all happened in a matter of moments. But I found the court transcripts online, and you testified that you heard an argument at the front door, but then you heard Dad yelling to you from the dining room. You speculated he'd gone to grab his gun from the china cabinet, but it was gone because I'd taken it, so he was forced to return to the foyer unarmed, and *then* Kershaw shot him. But if it really did take place in just moments, it couldn't have played out that way. Dad wouldn't have had time to go for the gun."

"It was twenty-five years ago," says Joanna. "I can't possibly remember everything precisely."

"You've told us a million times that that evening is etched on your brain, Mom," says Sam. She steps back across the room and stands at the window, staring down at her mother, unblinking. "Which one was the truth?"

Joanna pauses for a moment, then sighs. "Your father didn't have a chance to look for the gun. I realized it was missing after the fact, because you told me so as soon as you arrived at the house that night. You were inconsolable."

Sam's blood goes cold. "How could you let me believe that I was responsible for Dad's death?"

Joanna is unapologetic. "If I'd told the real story, there was a good chance he'd have gotten off on manslaughter. But if the jury thought he'd gone looking for a way to defend himself and Kershaw had come into the house after him, it felt like a more solid case for the prosecution. So it turns out you did everyone a favor by taking that gun. Sam? Sam?"

I was wrong, Sam thinks as she walks away. *This is closure after all.*

Sam arrives at Alice's house and climbs out of her car just as Will is leaving through the front door.

"Hi, Sam," he says as he lets her pull him into a hug. She thinks this is the first time he's addressed her without 'Aunt,' and it causes a small pang of sadness. The kid is growing up.

"Where are you headed?" she asks.

"I'm just going over to hang out with Joelle for a little while, but I'll be back for supper."

"How's she doing, anyway?" Sam asks. She's heard from Alice that Will and Joelle have been hanging out a lot since the events of the past few weeks. Considering what the two of them have been through, it makes sense that they would turn to each other.

"She's doing better, I think. She and her dad are taking therapy together, and I think it's helping."

"Therapy works," says Sam. "Maybe we should all try that out together as a family thing."

He makes a face. "I think I've already had my fill of Mom and Dad talking about their feelings. There's a been a lot of sharing going on lately."

She makes a face. "Gross."

He laughs, and then his expression grows serious. "Joelle has had a few nightmares about Evan," he says. "I wonder if . . . I mean, do you think there's any chance that he'd come back to Edgar Mills?"

"No," says Sam immediately. "I don't. Evan Stevens would be out of his mind to come back here after what happened. He values his freedom more than anything, and I guarantee you he has moved as far away from here as possible."

She wishes she felt as sure about that as she's letting on.

"Okay, cool," he says, visibly relieved. "Can I tell Joelle you said that?"

"Of course."

He turns to leave but then stops. "I'm really glad you're moving back here, Aunt Sam."

She smiles. "Me too, buddy."

As she enters the house, she hears laughter and follows it to the kitchen, where she finds Austin and Joey at the island, drinking wine and talking to Levi, who's busy preparing a salad at the counter.

"Hello hello," she says, crossing to the counter to pour herself a glass.

"Hello yourself, you suspicious bitch," says Austin.

She comes over and puts an arm over his shoulder. "Austin, if we're going to be friends, you'll have to retire that from your vocabulary immediately."

Austin throws up his hands in surrender. "I got to do it once, I'm good."

"Excellent," she says. "Where's my sister?"

"She'll be down in a minute," says Levi. "She's just getting changed." The doorbell rings and he moves to answer it, but Sam puts up a hand to stop him.

"Don't worry, I'll grab it."

She opens the door to find Doug on the front step, holding up a bottle of red wine. "I'm not sure if I have the right address," he says. "Is this the home of my terrifying childhood bully?"

Sam laughs and gestures for him to come inside. "Glad you could make it."

"Are you kidding? I wouldn't miss this for the world. They say it's cathartic to confront your most horrible memories directly. By the way, I wanted to say I had a great time chasing a crazed killer into an abandoned junkyard together."

"It was quite the evening," she says. "You make for good backup, Doug. I mean it."

He smiles. "This might be a bit out of the blue, but I was wondering if you might want to get a drink with me sometime."

She stares at him, taken aback. "Oh. I . . . don't know."

He shrugs cheerfully. "Can't blame a guy for trying."

Sam closes her eyes and takes a deep breath. "Actually, Doug, do you know what? I would love to get a drink with you."

"Are you two going to join us or just flirt in the hallway?" They turn to see Alice descending the stairs. She hugs them both, then leans in to whisper to Doug. "Levi is very nervous about seeing you."

"I'm not surprised," says Doug. "I'm an intimidating guy. Don't worry, I'll take it easy on him."

They head to the kitchen, and Alice beckons to Joey. "Can I steal you and Sam away for a few minutes?"

In the den she closes the door and gestures for them to take a seat on the sofa but remains standing, staring intently at them. "So what's our plan?"

Sam looks at Joey and can tell he's just as confused as she is. "What do you mean?"

Alice throws her hands in the air and begins to pace. "Is this really how we're going to leave things? The maniac who tried to kill us, who *did* kill several innocent people, is on the loose and we're just going to let that slide?"

Sam leans forward in her seat. "Alice, where is this coming from?"

"I don't know, Sam." Alice speaks forcefully and with purpose. "Maybe it's because I spent my entire adult life wondering whether I took a wrong turn at some point. Or maybe it's because everything we believed to be true was a lie, and we were screwed over and manipulated by the person we should have been able to trust the most. But mostly, it's because Evan Stevens is still out there somewhere and I will never have another proper night of sleep until he's rounded up and thrown behind bars and I know my family is safe."

"Shouldn't we wait to see what the police are able to come up with?" asks Joey.

"The police will do what they do," she says, "but it's been two weeks, and every day that goes by I get less optimistic that they'll find him. So what's stopping us from taking a crack at it?"

Joey opens his mouth to speak, but nothing comes out, and he snaps it shut again.

"Isn't this obvious?" Alice drops into a chair across from them and leans forward, her eyes glittering with a snapping, frenetic energy. "We're all here in Edgar Mills at the same time, and each of us is at a crossroads. Evan said it himself, the story isn't over, and he was right. But it isn't his story, it's ours, and I'll be damned if I'm going leave him space to finish it."

As Sam stares at her sister, she becomes aware of a shift, a ripple beneath the surface of her mind. It's an old, familiar feeling, and as much as she wants to pretend she's moved past this kind of impulse, she knows what she really wants is to lean right into it.

"How would we even begin?" she asks.

Alice smiles and shrugs. "We'll figure it out. That's the fun part, isn't it?"

Sam turns to look at Joey and sees the corner of his mouth is twitching. She realizes she's smiling too.

"Well," she says, "I guess the case isn't closed after all."

EPILOGUE:

TikTok Transcript:

@RealTrueCrimeKid

NEW SERIES! NOTES FROM THE ROAD

PART 1 - MISS ME YET?

[Video opens on @RealTrueCrimeKid standing in front of an endless stretch of ocean. The horizon is hazy, the lighting soft and impossible to place—dusk or dawn. His hoodie is loose. His hair, longer since we last saw him, is tousled by the wind. He looks straight into the camera with a bright smile.]

@RealTrueCrimeKid: "Hi all! It's been a while. Big apologies for the hiatus. I've been moving around a lot and dealing with some pretty massive changes in my life, but I'm finally back, live and in person!"

[He glances over his shoulder at the water, as if considering something, then turns back.]

@RealTrueCrimeKid: "I've been on the move and it's liberating. I'm loving life. Seeing the world. Meeting so many great people. It's been amazing."

[A pause. The waves crash behind him. He exhales, almost content.]

@RealTrueCrimeKid: "In the meantime, I want to thank you all for the amazing responses I've been getting to my latest videos. I didn't know how they'd be received since they're all old footage, but honestly guys, you have blown my mind with your support and enthusiasm. The powers that be keep doing their best to pull them down, but thanks to my incredible followers I know I can count on my content living forever. I still have a ton of great stuff to roll out from the vault, but you'll be happy to hear I've also been working on some new material. Plans are still in the development stage, but I'm really excited to show you all what I've been cooking up. So stay tuned. I might even be able to convince some familiar faces to make an appearance. Anyway, that's all for now, friends."

[He moves toward the camera and his face fills the screen. He smiles broadly.]

@RealTrueCrimeKid: "I'll see you soon."

[Video cuts to black.]

THE END

ACKNOWLEDGMENTS

Every book is a collective effort, and I am so grateful to the many people who helped bring this one into the world.

To my editors—Joe Brosnan at Atlantic Crime and Adrienne Kerr at Simon & Schuster Canada—thank you for your insight, clarity, and enthusiasm for this book, and for everything you've done to help me become a better storyteller. We work beautifully together, and I'm so excited about what comes next!

To my incredible publishing teams: at my American publisher Grove Atlantic/Atlantic Crime, including, but certainly not limited to, Morgan Entrekin, John Mark Boling, Deb Seager, Natalie Church, Rachael Richardson, and Gretchen Mergenthaler; and my Canadian publisher Simon & Schuster Canada, and again this just scratches the surface, Nicole Winstanley, Mackenzie Croft, Cayley Brightside, and Emily Rothwell. Thank you all for championing me and my books at every stage. Your dedication behind the scenes is helpful beyond measure. Thank you also to Dan Rembert and Alan Jones at Station 87 Design, two brilliant designers who designed two brilliant covers, one for each side of the border.

To my wonderful agents, Samantha Haywood and Amy Tompkins, and the rest of the gang at Transatlantic Literary Agency—thank you for your guidance, your advocacy, and your steady hand through every twist and turn of this journey. I couldn't have asked for better champions. Thanks also to my fantastic film agent, Kim Yau at Echo Lake.

Thank you to my friend Zoe Broad, who took the time to talk to me about her experience interviewing a serial killer, and shared details that really helped me craft two important scenes in the book. Thanks also to my brother Liam Ryan, who helped me nail down some technical details when I was at a loss trying to figure out how to write about guns.

To the readers who have connected with my stories and shared them with others, to the booksellers who put my books into readers' hands, and to the librarians who make space for them on their shelves—thank you for your enthusiasm, your word-of-mouth endorsements, and the priceless work you do to promote and amplify our voices.

To the bloggers, podcasters, reviewers, bookstagrammers, booktokers, and influencers who help spread the word: I see you, and I'm deeply grateful.

To my parents, family, and friends—thank you for your patience, your encouragement, and your ability to listen to me talk about these characters as if they were real people, and for cheering me on at every opportunity. A special shout out to my hometown of Inverness, Nova Scotia. I often say that for a mystery writer, it's like hitting the jackpot to have been born and raised in a small town full of deep roots, complicated connections and fascinating characters. The web of connection back home is as strong as it gets!

Finally, I save the biggest thanks as always for my husband Andrew, who convinced me fifteen years ago to take a crack at chasing my dream, and has supported me and that dream in a million different ways ever since. Thank you for everything. I love you.